I THOUGHT OF
DAISY

I THOUGHT OF DAISY

BY
EDMUND WILSON

NEW YORK
CHARLES SCRIBNER'S SONS
1929

I

1 THOUGHT OF DAISY

IT was a low red-brick house with a white door, a brass knob and brass name-plates, and new green-and-white awnings and green window-boxes: the sort of place which, in those days, downtown, seemed particularly smart. We rang, and, after a moment, the electric clicking began—with its quick and ready profusion, plucking distinctly the string of excitement which was still capable of vibrating in my breast at the prospect of meeting new people in Greenwich Village.

They were Hugo Bamman's friends: I had never met them. Rita Cavanagh, the poet, was to be there—and other persons reputed to possess genius or to whom I vaguely attributed romance. The stairs were soft-carpeted in green. The host, tall and smiling, in a dinner-jacket, met us at the door. The rooms were very bright and well kept: I saw lettuce-green cocktail glasses, a bruised-mulberry batik behind a divan and, on the wall, a set of framed designs for the costumes of some ballet, vivid tinselly golds, blues and purples. And there were girls, like the colored sketches, in the brightest make-ups and clothes, with red silk roses of Cuban shawls, and silver turbans, and red hair, and black arching Russian eyebrows, beautifully pencilled on.

The host waylaid the hostess, who had a cock-tail glass in each hand and appeared preoccupied. I thought her adorable—she was quite short and

3

had very small gold slippers and Buster Brown blond bobbed hair. "Oh, how do you do!" she said, stopping. "How about putting down the glasses and shaking hands?" said Ray Coleman. "Here, you take this, then," she said, making him hold one of the glasses: I thought he looked a little severe as he stood with the cocktail in his hand. "There's so much traffic," she remarked, "that it's hard to receive people right." She smiled charmingly with a little mauve-rouged, moist and lovely American mouth. Her hand, which she gave me now, was fragile and small, and, with her thin round bare arm, seemed like some soft little tentacle. "What a nice apartment!" I said. "It's the apple of our eye," she replied. That wasn't quite right either, but, as it evidently was the apple of Coleman's, he smiled with satisfaction as he demurred that they were "a little cramped for space."

A bulky woman in green—the one with the silver turban—blazed upon my vision. She recognized me and we shook hands. She was one of those plain elderly ladies who do something or other and whom we meet at parties, but whose names we have difficulty in remembering. I had a drink which Mrs. Coleman had given me and I asked the lady with the silver turban whether I couldn't get her one. She said: "A little of that Scotch—straight," and we sat down, at her suggestion, on a large ottoman in front of the fireplace. She had the hearty manners and broad speech of an old *vivandière*—an old *vivandière* of the social revolution, I thought, and approached her with a special respect.

"What we have in America," she declared—
we had arrived, through Prohibition, at politics
—"is government by headlines! What's the actual explanation of these booms for Cox and
Wood? Neither one has the brains of a rabbit.
But their names are one-syllable words. They're
one-syllable words! I'm a newspaper woman and
I know!" "So is Debs," I suggested. "Yes," she
replied, "but he's out." I felt that I had said
something stupid. I had let her see that I was
only an outsider.

My whole point of view at this period was still
largely taken over from my old school-friend,
Hugo Bamman: he had come, after the War, to
live in Greenwich Village, and I had been brought
there by his example. It was Hugo who had
taken me around and who had told me what to
think of what I saw; and I had seen through
Hugo's eyes. The people whom Hugo thought important seemed important to me, too: he and they,
I believed, were leaders, leaders of the true social
idealism which cut under capitalistic politics. To
them the social revolution seemed as real as their
love affairs; and I had often a guilty consciousness that it was not quite real enough to me. This
plain-spoken woman, for example, to whom I
presumed to talk of politics, might, for all I knew,
have just returned from Russia—might have
fought on the barricades. Her bad language and
her great bare chest might represent the heroic
braveries of some heart-breaking campaign—the
devotion to some anarchist lover, deported or put
in prison; the shouldering of some burden of poverty; or perhaps some point-blank vindication of

basic human rights in the teeth of the mounted police and the mob.

In that company I had always felt humble: beyond publishing a few satiric verses in a radical magazine, I had never myself struck any blow in the war for humanity (Hugo Bamman was a freelance and a communist, whereas I professed no political faith and had a tame and respectable job in a publisher's office); but, like Hugo, I had served in the other war, and had served as an enlisted man, and after seeing all the nations of the West temporarily scrambled together and the social order turned upside down, I had come away with a new conviction of the necessity of human solidarity. "Ten Days That Shook the World" —they had given me pause when I had read about them one morning, among the inanities of the Paris *Herald*, after a night spent sleeping in a puddle. In college, I had read of the Russia of the Czars as one reads about the Middle Ages; but now I had been forced to recognize, even among Americans, and as one of the strongest instincts of society, that horrifying contempt of a dominating class for the lives of those they dominate. So that, by the time I had got out of the Army, I had acquired a scorn for the pursuit of money, position or rank: the people who cared for such things seemed now to me sinister or childish. It appeared impossible ever again to accept conventional values complacently, to acquiesce in the prosperous inertia and the provincial ignorance of America. One could never go back again now to living indifferently or trivially; one was afraid of lending oneself to some offense against that unhappy humanity which one shared with other men.

"Yes, of course," I replied, "he's out.—And Wood is such a gentlemanly fellow!—he hasn't any of the Regular Army mannerisms—he's surprising in that way. You think he's going to be awful, and then he turns out to be quite a relief after listening to the regular West Point line. You can perfectly see why Roosevelt got on with him. Neither one was an ordinary ruffian. Yet both, at bottom, were stupid men. Roosevelt was only just civilized enough to know and remember more facts than his neighbors. But all his imagination was good for was habitually to make a melodrama out of the most serious affairs of the world—a melodrama with himself as hero."

Her eye had strayed, she hailed a young man with a slit-eyed impassive gaze, who, his hands in his trousers-pockets, had stationed himself near us. I felt abashed—what I had said had betrayed me as a young bourgeois trying to play up to her: it had given me away as never having been at the barricades!—"Oh, Bobby!" she exclaimed, "your ballet was marvellous! Those divine Chinese whites!" The young man accepted the compliment, with no attempt to turn it off or to pretend embarrassment. He seemed serious and complacent: I wondered whether he were Jewish—he was blond, but had a hooked nose. He replied without change of expression and bending over with his hands in his pockets: "It's the first time, so far as I know, that Chinese white has been used in the theatre. I have two different kinds of white contrasted." "How did you ever do it?" said Sue

Borglum (that, it turned out, was my companion's name). "I was experimenting for two years," he replied. I could tell from his accent that he was Scotch: besides, his eyes remained narrow and solemn, and a Jew, no matter how serious, no matter how relentlessly preoccupied with the importance of his own activities, would have veiled with some irony of politeness his human and earth-bound ambitions in this Valley of the Shadow under the eye of a Jealous God. "I don't see," she protested, emphatically, "how people ever have the patience to go on experimenting for effects they may never be able to get! In the newspaper game, it's different: we never experiment: we know how to get our effects and we get them right off, the same day.—And they're forgotten the same day!" He answered, without smiling: "There's going to be a photograph of my set in Bradley Foster's book on the ballet." He looked around as some one grasped his arm.

Daisy Coleman was talking in a corner with an anomalous slight little man; they were drinking the cocktails she had been carrying. She seemed appetizing in her lobster-bisque dress, her paler flesh-colored stockings and her little gold slippers. She was talking over the back of a chair, with one knee on the seat and with both hands clasping the top, like a little girl at school, chatting between classes: the conversation was accompanied with sympathetic movements of the elevated foot. As I watched her, I saw Ray Coleman, smiling in a curious fixed way at nobody in particular, go over, interrupt the conversation, detach Daisy from the little tadpole and launch her again on the com-

pany at large. She came forward rather blankly and, it seemed to me, a little sullenly.

Ray Coleman had left Hugo Bamman standing huddled against the mantelpiece and staring out through his thick myopic lenses; and it occurred to me at once that he could talk better than I to Sue Borglum. He would be sure to have the right tone—and besides, he never seemed to care whether women were young or old, attractive or plain. "Ah, there he is!" I cried—I disloyally used to kid him—"Bamman: The People's Friend!" He looked about, smiling vaguely, then, locating us, craned forward, and bubbled and beamed over Sue.—I got up and intercepted Daisy.

She began by making an earnest effort to discharge her obligations as a hostess, but I could see that her heart wasn't in it. "Don't you want another cocktail?" she suggested. "I'm afraid the one you got was all water. Ray has just made some new ones."

"You were in *Patsy,* weren't you?" I asked: I knew that she had been a chorus-girl. "I think that that was about the best musical show that I ever saw—I went to see it four times!" "Well, we couldn't complain," she said (it had had a phenomenal run). "Which one were you? I don't recognize you." "Oh, I was just in the chorus," she said. "And then I was one of the pages that came down the steps with the candles in the *Honeymoon Moon* number." "Oh, were you one of those pages?" I exclaimed. "You were awfully cute! I remember you well!—and that set with the lavender drop and the orange moon was marvellous!—Do you ever miss the stage?" "I'm be-

ginning to now. Of course, it's an awful lot of
work—so you don't get very much fun out of it."
With the intention of documenting myself—in
those days I shared Hugo's enthusiasm for soci-
ological documentation—I questioned her about
the theatre. I was delighted by her candor. "By
the time the show opens," she told me, "everybody
is groggy. When we were rehearsing for *Patsy,*
I drank so much to keep myself going that I finally got some kind of d.t.'s: I saw a horse sitting beside my bed." I expressed interest. "It
was sitting by my bed with its hoofs on its knees
—this way: like hands—its hoofs were painted
blue. It was sitting there leering at me." "Were
you able to go on?" "Yes, the doctor gave me a
great big drink of something bitter and I went to
sleep and slept it off." "It must be a terrific thing
to rehearse one of those shows!" "It's a lot of
work to be beautiful—especially when you aren't,"
she added. "Oh, come!" I replied, "I was just
thinking that you were one of the very few actresses I had seen who were as pretty on the stage
as off!" She made a gesture of burlesque de-
mureness, putting a finger to her mouth. I inquired about the hardships of the stage. "Once,
at the Winter Garden," she told me, "I was in one
of those living curtains: they left us up there for
an hour and we nearly got roasted with the lights.
When they let us down again, half the girls
fainted.—Oh, yes; us girls," she concluded, parodying us girls, "us girls has our trials!" I found
her interesting, attractive, amusing, and profoundly sympathetic. "What a lovely color your
hair is!" I told her. "Just the color of honey!"

"Mm-Mm!" said Daisy. "More! I eat that stuff up!"

Ray Coleman, smiling, came up behind her and put his arms about her, with his hands over her breasts. "Don't you think he looks like Ned Grover?" Daisy inquired of her husband. "No: not a bit," replied Coleman. He explained to me humorously: "She always has these insane ideas about people looking like each other—and there's never the faintest resemblance!" I seemed to make out that Ned Grover raised an issue.

"Won't you let me fill your glass?" he suggested. "I've got some real bonded rye over here that I've only just opened. I thought at first I wouldn't open it to-night, because when you have a lot of people like this, anything special is lost on them—you might just as well give them plain bootlegger's stuff." "I thought your cocktails were splendid!" "Well, I know you'll appreciate this rye: it's the real Old Overholt, bottled in bond."

"Is Rita Cavanagh here?" I asked over the glass-topped drinking-caddy. "Yes: she's here somewhere"—it gave him pleasure to feel himself master of a company among whom distinguished names might be casually mislaid. "Haven't you seen her?" "I've never met her." "I'll introduce you to her." He lifted his tall amber glass with an air: I saw that his dark eyebrows, which he was always raising in conversation with the air of a man of the world, nearly met above his nose.

He led me over to the divan. Rita Cavanagh was a sharp-nosed little thing with mousey bobbed hair; she wore a shabby black dress. She was so small that I hadn't noticed her. But, as I shook hands with her, she gave me from eyes of a greenish uncertain color, a curious alert intent look, as of a fox peering out from covert. She was curled up in the middle of the divan and evidently the centre of its company. I told her how much I had liked her poems.

Ray Coleman, with smiling politeness, requested her to recite. "Did you know I'd been asked to read in public?" she said. She spoke in rather a dry staccato voice, and with something like an English accent, which seemed to me artificial.— "Where is that?" inquired Ray Coleman. "At the Poets' League."—"Well, you're going to do it, aren't you?" said a young man who looked like a baseball player. "Well, would you? Do you think it's the thing to do?" She took a brief puff at her cigarette—staccato and precise. "Do they offer you money?" asked the man. "Yes." "Then do it!" "But they come up and talk to you afterwards, and you're supposed to answer their questions. What would you *say* to them?" "Say to them?" said the young man. "What did Shakespeare say to the horses? *Whoa! Get over there! Back up!*" She laughed, puckering her eyes, and again raised the cigarette.

This young man, I felt, was a good fellow— his hulking frame, his jutting brow and his prognathous jaw seemed to mask some gentleness and modesty—but I had the impression that he was jealously straining toward Rita with a maximum of nervous effort, was almost, in fact, on the point of seizing her; and I felt that all the three other men about her were bent in the same direction;

and that I myself, though I had only just met her, was about to become involved in the competition. And, since I had told her that I liked her poems and since she had turned to me, acknowledging my compliments, as if they had gratified her especially, I began to find myself resenting the other men almost as rivals.

She laughed—on distinct, impish, economized notes: "I might take an apple with me," she said, "or a lump of sugar." "Couldn't you rehearse a little for us?" Ray Coleman suggested, inclining and smiling again. "You'll find us an appreciative audience!"—"This is one that I wrote to-day," she said, taking a last puff at her cigarette—"This very day!" And, sitting back against the wall behind the couch, straightening her neck and throwing up her head, she began to recite.

The effect was, at first, to embarrass me: it was a little as if a Shakespearian actor were suddenly, off the stage, to begin expressing private emotions with the intonations of the play. The only girl I had ever known who had been able to write respectable poetry had been in the habit of reading aloud—when she read aloud at all—as if her poems had been compositions which she had never seen before, poems written by some other person and by some one of whom she disapproved. But in the gradual silence of the room, amid the respect with which all seemed to turn toward her, those deep sonorities of sorrow and wonder began to move me as much as a play. I had admired, in reading her lyrics, the uncounterfeitable force of sincerity which, in dealing with classic themes— themes in other hands commonplace—the longing for home, the shortness of life, the passing of love—with an effect both of boldness and austerity, had not hesitated to clothe them in an imagery drawn directly from ordinary life. But I had not known, till I heard her recite, to what music these things had been tuned: all her art was in her ear; her words had little color for the eye. Now, in the poem which she had told us she had just written, she described a bonfire built on the beach, which shut out for those around it the empty weight of the waters and the desolate litter of the shore, where a poor disfeatured corpse lay, worried by unresting waves, among the seaweed, bleached boards and dead dogfish—as the joy which we know to be doomed may seem yet to overflow the moment. And in a second poem, the sight of two children—one blotted from birth in face and mind, the other creeping on wry spider legs—yet dressed and fed and sent out every morning by the mothers of wretched streets to play with the other children, was made to shake us with that despair—the dammed anguish of our own frustration—which, in the presence of some pitiful human failure may overcome us with the sudden conviction that no satisfactions can be real beside the humiliations of life. And on her lips, the barrenness of the shore, the dingy images of the streets, were a kind of song.

In the pause after the second poem, dramatically tense and distinct as every syllable she had spoken, a smooth-faced and girlish boy whom, if my attitude toward all the company had not been so much one of respect, I should certainly have considered a fool, said, "That *does* something to me—that last one!" The baseball player shook his head and said: "Gosh! that's a knockout! Rita said, "Yes: I've written that one since I've seen you! You haven't heard that one! Im *so glad* that you like it!"

Somebody suddenly turned on the phonograph, which began jigging a popular fox-trot. Ray Coleman went over and stopped it, and I saw him engaged with his wife in what looked like a restrained altercation. Then he returned to us, bringing Daisy. "I'm sorry," he explained, smiling—his smile was beginning to get on my nerves. "Daisy has the phonograph habit: it's like a drug —she can't keep away from it! It was unpardonable to jar on those lovely poems!"

"Yes," said Daisy, "I hope you'll forgive me, but I thought you were all through." "We had hoped that you weren't," insisted Ray. "I wish you'd let us hear some more!" Rita replied, puckering up her eyes, "Oh, I think that's quite enough of me for one evening!"

"How sweet she looks in pink!" said Sue Borglum: Daisy had been standing by like a bad little child reproved. "She looks like one of those big pink bonbons on the top of a box of candy." "Melt in your mouth," said Daisy, with her frank and charming grin.—"Speaking of clothes," said Rita, "has anybody seen Myra Busch since she got back from Paris?" "*Have* I?" returned Sue Borglum. "She says she bought it all with what she got from writing for *McMoony's,* but if she did, *McMoony's* must pay her a damn sight more than they ever paid me. She's so wide-eyed about it, too! I asked her if she hadn't been able to find a night to go with that lace nightgown." "Oh,

Myra Busch is a push-over!" said Daisy, a little snappishly. "She's got round heels!"

Sue Borglum's pleasantry had been in the vein of the Village; Daisy's was in the taste of Broadway—I do not know which, at that period, enchanted me the more. Since I had come back to America from France, I had been noticing with a new attention the way the Americans talked: I had read, with astonished gratification, the first books of those American writers who seemed making a new kind of literature out of that sprawling square-syllabled speech where the words had been like colorless frame-houses on the outskirts of an American town, a language fit only, it had seemed, for the uses of a prosaic trade or of a plebeian extravagance and irony. And I noted American slang with an interest self-conscious and pedantic.

I felt, however, that Daisy's husband disapproved of her coarseness and sharpness, and I resented his failure to appreciate her.

"I understand you caught a thief," said Sue Borglum, addressing Ray. "Yes," said Ray, with satisfaction. "Caught him, convicted him, and sent him where he'll do no more thieving." "Burglar or sneak-thief?" asked Sue Borglum. "All kinds of a thief!" replied Ray. "He got into the house in broad daylight. Somebody rang the bell last Sunday afternoon, and I pressed the button to open the door, but nobody came up. Now, I always make it a rule, whenever that happens, to go down and find out what's up!"

I had often in my own apartment responded to these false alarms, but checking up on them, I reflected, was like Crainquebille's prison stool chained to the leg of the bed—an idea which would never have occurred to me.

"I went down," Ray Coleman continued, following Daisy with his eyes, as she quietly detached herself from the group and went back in the direction of the phonograph, "but there was nobody in the hall—and nobody on the floor below. Then I went to all the other apartments and asked whether anybody had just come in, and they all said that nobody had. Then I went back and got a gun and a flashlight, and I went down into the basement. I held the flashlight out to one side, so that if he fired he wouldn't hit me. And lo and behold! there was Mr. Thief hiding in the coalbin! I covered him with the gun and asked him what he was up to, and he began telling me a long sob-story about how he hadn't any place to sleep and had just come in to spend the night." Smiling steadily, he gazed at Daisy, who had gone back to the corner again to talk to the anomalous little man with the dark amusing eyes, the natty blue suit and the belling sailor's trousers. "I said, 'Well, you just wait here awhile till we find out a little more about that story,' and I locked him in the basement and telephoned the police. When we searched him we found all the jewelry hidden away in his shoes!—two stick-pins, a ring and a wrist-watch, and five dollars in bills and change. He'd stolen them from a man in Eleventh Street!" "Oh, they weren't your things, then!" said Rita, who had been listening with that odd tension which she seemed to apply to everything, whether of absorbing interest or not.

"Oh, no," Ray heartily reassured her. "He didn't get anything of ours. He didn't get the chance! I've got some etchings and some valuable firsts—so I can't afford to take risks. And Daisy has an ostrich-feather evening wrap that's worth three hundred dollars. The fellow on Eleventh Street had missed a lot of other things, too; but they couldn't get the little bastard to tell them what had become of them. They beat him up at the station, but they couldn't get him to tell—he was just sullen. A West Indian boy. We ought to have some way of keeping such scum out of the country. If they'd only do with all the criminals" —he spoke with a sort of exaltation and his eyes were rapt away to Daisy—"if they'd only do with all the criminals what they do with the regular gunmen! They're not supposed to beat a man up more than just so much, you know—but the way that they get around that in the case of the big thugs is to send them around from one police station to the other. As soon as they get done with them in one place, they just send them along to another—so that the men in any one station can always say they haven't beaten 'em up more than just so much, and yet they can give 'em all they want. If they'd been able to do that with my West Indian friend, we might have found out about the silk bath-robe that he'd stolen from the man on Eleventh Street."

"Yes," said Hugo, whose eyes, behind his spectacles, I had felt beginning to glow with antagonism. "They might even have made him confess to stealing the towers of Notre Dame!" "What do you mean?" asked Ray. "I mean, if you torture anybody long enough, you can make them confess to anything. That was what the Inquisition did, wasn't it?"

I perceived that, although Ray Coleman enjoyed entertaining poets and radical journalists, he was far from sharing the humanitarian feeling which at that epoch pervaded the Village. I had thought, when I first came in, that his dinner-jacket struck for the Village an unfamiliar and incongruous note; and I was growing more and more sympathetic with Daisy. I began to concoct an ironic short story, something rather in the vein of *Crainquebille* or of Maupassant's *Boule de Suif,* in which a vulgar but charming little wife was to be patronized and bullied by her husband —who would be editor of a popular newspaper: one day when the husband had gone out, the wife was to find in the basement a poor starving tailor's boy, who would tell her of the petty tyrannies of the presser for whom he had worked. And, remembering her life on the stage—the cruelties of the living curtain; remembering the harshness of her husband—all that money-grubbing anti-human world in which she had always found her own life so harassed—she would listen to the boy with sympathy, and would be just on the point of offering him some clothes and something to eat, when the husband would return with the police; the boy would turn out to be a thief whom the husband had caught and locked up!—There would have to be something more to it, though—I would think about it later.

In the meantime, Hugo's skirmish with Ray had ended in an emphatically disguised evasion on the latter's part as he had become aware that his attitude toward criminals might be considered intellectual bad form. I inquired of Hugo, aside, where Daisy Coleman came from. "From Pittsburgh, I think," he replied—then still chafing with repressed resentment over his argument with Ray, he added: "You never seem to be able to take people for granted!—you always want to know where they come from!" I answered that those things interested me.

And I brooded a little on Pittsburgh—I had been there as a boy—my mother had had a school-friend who had married and gone to live there, and we had visited them once. They had lived in a massive and formidable house, with dingy Ionic pillars, and with blue and green stained-glass windows which, far from adorning the interior, had seemed to me at the time merely sombre, forbidding and blind—there had been a boy about my age called Junior, and he had had a great many expensive toys; an Indian costume and a military costume (which I had thought a good deal of a bore) and the most elaborate toy railroad that I had ever seen outside a toy-store—a labyrinth of signals, switches, turntables and tunnels; it had covered the floors of several rooms and rendered them uninhabitable. This boy had also had fencing foils; a real rifle; a thing that he told you to look through but which squirted water into your eye; and a device of rubber tubes and bulbs, which made plates jump up and down on the table. These luxuries had strongly impressed me and they now presented themselves to my mind—as well as Junior's egoism and arrogance, the arrogance of an over-indulged child, which had kept me from quite getting on with him. Now, as I remembered it for the first time in years, I found that I detested that household. There had been a Pennsylvania Dutch father, who had made money in the coke business and whose domineering silences had oppressed the dining-table; and there had been a mother who had been always playing the piano, and singing, with inexhaustible vivacity, the scores of old musical comedies—from the *Sultan of Sulu* to *Forty-five Minutes from Broadday*—which she had heard in New York. I had, at the time I came to live in the Village, developed something of that inverted snobbishness which, in Hugo's case, had impelled him to go to all the garment-workers' balls at the same time that he would grimly decline a dinner where he knew he would be expected to dress; and I had at that moment the kind of emotions which I thought Hugo would probably have in connection with a large heavy house inhabited by a Pittsburgh capitalist. Thank heaven! I said to myself, spurred no doubt by Hugo's rebuke, if I ever go to Pittsburgh again, I shan't have to be visiting there! Here, in Daisy, is the real vital Pittsburgh: frank, vulgar, humorous, human!

"She married some fellow from Pittsburgh, I think, before she married Ray Coleman," added Hugo, after a moment during which he had gulped his drink, self-consciously and hurriedly—he was excessively sensitive and so haunted by the fear of hurting people's feelings that his sharpness was invariably followed by a spasm of special affability. "They made a honeymoon trip on a motor-cycle from Pittsburgh to Atlantic City. They had all kinds of fantastic accidents. She told me about it once. It must have been awfully fine!" I, too, thought that it must have been fine. That was the real, the live America—where our bravery and freedom lay! I drank my highball up. I saw them, skidding breathtakingly in the ditches— skinned, bruised and mud-beplastered! Dodging motors and trucks, shaking off towns and cities, like twigs that had been caught in their wheels and had scraped the mud-guard a little, and had then been whipped away!—masters of that new and American and almost super-human sense— the sense of motor traffic! Till, at last, after boiling hot baths, they had lain clean in Atlantic City, in their clean-sheeted hotel bed, with the ice-water in the pitcher and the room as warm as a hot-house. In the morning, they would have breakfast in bed!

Hugo had turned away to bubble, giggle, and gasp to a radical journalist with a harsh western accent and extraordinary personal charm: I rose to talk to the theatrical designer, who, with deep-lodged slit-eyed self-satisfaction, stood near me, his arms folded, unmoved by what went on about him. "Are you doing any shows," I asked, "this spring?" "Just the ballet in the *Merry-Go-Round*," he answered. "Next year," he went on to explain, "I want to stage the Iliad and the Odyssey." "The Iliad and the Odyssey?" I repeated a little blankly. "I want to do them in a cycle," he said—"something like Wagner's Ring." "How long would it take?" I inquired. "Not more than a week," he replied. "I shan't try to have every-

thing, of course. I'll have to leave out a good
many incidents—though I believe that, when the
public have been interested, I'll be able to put it
on in an outdoor stadium and do it on a bigger
scale—there would be a week for each. My pro-
duction next fall would be an experiment with
that in view." "That would be awfully interesting," I said: the air then, especially in the theatre,
was so full of high novelty and striving that no
project seemed impossible. "What sort of text are
you going to use?" "Fritz Fishbein is making an
adaptation of Butcher and Lang—it's in a sort
of free verse, that will be chanted to music. Bou-
lomé is working out the old Greek modes, so that
we'll have music that will be really Greek." "That
sounds extremely interesting," I repeated.—
"Come in here," he said, "and I'll show you the
drawings."

He led me into a little study with a desk, a
window-seat and some bookcases, and opened on
the desk a large portfolio—I don't know how he
happened to have it there. "How," I asked, "are
you going to do the clangor of Apollo's silver
bow?" "I'm not going to do it," he said, "that
is, I'm not going to make the attempt to reproduce the sound. I'm not going to do anything
realistically. There'll be no sound at all. You'll just
see Apollo off on a hill—just a little silhouette,
perfectly black, but awful, you know—with a bow
in his hands. And then every one will cover their
ears and sink down to the ground, and the stage
will turn green-black, and then everything will be
black." I turned over the water-color drawings,
so beautifully and lovingly covered with large

clinging sheets of tissue-paper. "What's this one?" I asked. "That's the slaying of the suitors in the Odyssey." "They look a little like white rats," I commented. "Yes: I meant to give that suggestion—those are masks that they're to wear throughout the play." I had never heard before of using masks.

Rita Cavanagh had come up behind us, and I made room for her to look at the drawings. I had been aware of her voice in the next room saying: "Oh, Bobby McIlvaine's showing his Homer designs!—I want to see them!"

"Oh, what a beautiful Pallas Athena!" she cried, as she stood over the portfolio beside me. I noticed again how shabby her black dress was: she must be very poor, I thought. "Almost like a man!" she continued. It was a figure all in silver-gray, spare, upstanding and clean, like some male heroic woman of the Village—with a helmet that shaded its eyes and with an owl perched on its shoulder—rather an odd-looking owl, I thought: thin and long, like Athena herself, but like her, austere and impressive. And I found myself delighted—especially now that Rita Cavanagh was admiring them—with McIlvaine's designs for Homer. I seemed to see that, for all their eccentricity, they were closer to the spirit of the poems than the sobriety and smoothness of conventional representations: they had something of the unclassical stiffness of archaic Greek sculpture. Rita Cavanagh smiled, and I smiled, at Venus caught in the net with Mars, her little rose-dotted breasts a charming pink behind the gold meshes.

Hugo suddenly blundered into the room in his purblind big-booted way and took down his old felt hat from the bookcase—where he had carefully put it, I realized, in order to get at it quickly and without searching among the other hats. I wondered how he could bring himself to leave so enchanting a party so soon. He signalled to me a friendly, but detached and remote, farewell—stooping, stuttered and bubbled good-nights over Rita and Bobby McIlvaine—and abruptly was gone. I heard him ask in the next room: "Where's Daisy?" and the host reply, as if with humorous frankness: "I don't know where she is!"

"Oh, what *lovely* browns and grays!" breathed Rita, before the autumnal smock of Eumæus. "I never saw such lovely browns!" Her italicized "lovely" was not gushing, but had a sort of disinterested and passionate conviction. That was the sort of thing that impressed me about her. She seemed to feast upon the color, eating it with her eyes. I should myself have stopped at something brighter, and I felt guiltily that I should have been wrong. But she lingered over Eumæus: "Like the leaves in October!" she went on. "Like the leaves in the autumn mud! Such delicacy and such color standing out against something neutral —and common!"

The baseball player, or whatever he was, whom I had noticed on the divan, was now standing in the doorway, with his hat in his hand. "I'm going along, Rita," he said, "take you over if you're ready to go!" I saw that he was unsure and self-conscious. "I'm not going for a long time yet," she replied—her voice had the tautness, the distinctness and the metallic quality of wire—though of a wire which twanged with the vibrations of some strong and superior temper; yet she tried at the same time to smile at him with a definite effect of good-will, at once elfin and sharply registered, as she added for his consolation: "I don't want to be taken home to-night, anyway. I came alone, and I want to go home alone! I'm an independent woman, I am!" "Well, go ahead and have your old single standard!" he met her, putting humorously his best face on it, and disappeared from the doorway.

She turned over to a group of nymphs, the wild girls of some northern loch. "Some people think they're not graceful enough for nymphs," said McIlvaine, without expression. "People who say they're not graceful," said Rita, "don't know anything about grace!" She spoke with a passionate vehemence which seemed to me rather excessive —yet I felt something of the awe of the infidel who overhears the prayer of the believer. "They think that grace has something to do with round bodies and Greek dancing! These nymphs of yours *are* beautiful!—they have the natural beauty of country girls—they're graceful even when they're gawky and awkward!"

The pretty boy—the one who had asserted that Rita's poem had "done something" to him—glided behind her in a sinuous newtish way and slid one arm about her waist. His hair was glossy and parted in the middle and he was scarcely taller than she: his tapering and shapely hand, which I saw—and saw with distaste—lying against her black dress, would have seemed too small for a man's, if her own hands had not been so tiny—not with the American thinness of Daisy's, but with a miniature complete beauty, at once childlike and mature, as of some muse or magic being. He did not speak at once, but looked with her.—The next picture represented Penelope, who had an unexpected proud angularity.

"Won't Ulysses get hell," said the boy, "when he comes back home from his trip!" "No," said Rita, "she's noble!" "Yes," the boy acquiesced at once, "she's beautifully done! Great austerity! Great restraint!"

She had come to the blank cover at the back and slowly turned it over, almost as if with reverence. "I think they're *beautiful!*" she said, *"beautiful!"* I had heard people say that the flowers were beautiful, or that the front room was beautiful, or even that the view of the Hudson or the painting of Renoir was beautiful—but I had never before heard it said with such authority and such simple intensity. Though still shy of her unconvincing accent and suspicious of a pose, I was, in regions just beneath the surface, excited by this authority and intensity—I found myself heated, too, by the fire which the drawings had seemed so to kindle in her. Bobby McIlvaine accepted her tribute in silence distended by pride and tied up the strings of the portfolio. I said: "I must go to see your ballet!" "It's not much," he replied, "but the white is something to see."

"Well, Princess," said Rita's friend, the boy with the insinuating hands, "are you ready to sail away?" I realized that her rôle of princess was

a part of some romance which they had spun together, and I divined, in another moment, that
it was a romance of which she was tired. "No,"
she said, "I want to stay a little longer," and
added, with her elfin smile: "Send the boatman
back at twelve!"—He swept low an invisible
plumed hat.—"Leave the outside bolts open: I can
push the door myself!"—He bowed again and
backed away, and, as he retreated, she became
more amusing, entering more willingly into the
spirit of the legend which they had evidently elab-
orated, which they had perhaps lived, together.—
"But shut the watchdogs in their kennels, so that
they won't bay at me when I come. Tell the old
woman who makes the fires that she shall have
her snuff on Thursday, and that I shan't wake her
from sleep to-night, when she's dreaming of the
little stony river of her girlhood in the North.—
Tell her to mind the fire, though," she added, giving good measure to her friend, who now impressed me rather disconcertingly as perhaps not
a boy at all, but a man of mature years whose
coquetry was wearing stale.—"Though sleep is
sweet, the sparks are always flying, even after the
faggot is dead!"

Some originality I felt in her having so entered
into the old woman, who seemed to have nothing
to do with the plumed hat which her partner was
pretending to doff, interested me and made me
like her, just when I was beginning to be rather
sickened by this business about the Princess and
the boatman.

I could hear the voice of her admirer, as he
left, just outside the study door, saying good-

night to Ray Coleman and asking him where
Daisy was, and Coleman's voice replying, as if in
frank humorous confession, disclaiming all responsibility: "I don't know! I haven't the slight-
est idea!"—Bobby McIlvaine, who had put away
his drawings, and, having finished his own per-
formance, was not disposed to be interested in the
comedy which Rita and her friend were acting,
had also gone out of the room.

"That river your old woman dreams about," I
began, hoping to keep Rita there, "sounds like
something in up-state New York." She looked
up at me in her unaccountable, quick, nervous,
searching way: "Do you come from there?" she
asked. "No," I said, "but I've been there a good
deal." She had a way of scrupulously following,
of checking up with a special exactitude which
suggested anxious conscious effort, all the moves
of social intercourse, at the same time that she
seemed always preoccupied with something different and more absorbing; she now nodded and
lifted a moment a brief interested stare.

"Let's sit down here, shall we?" she proposed,
moving toward the window-seat. She curled up
in one of the corners. "Do turn away that light
—it's so bright!" I turned aside the adjustable
desk-light which was the only illumination in the
room so that it lit only the farther wall: then I
sat down on the window-seat, leaning up against
the opposite corner.

Below the window lay Washington Square: it
was still smooth and gleaming with wet. When I
had come home before dinner to dress, idle, happy,
and vaguely expectant, breathing in the rainy side-

walks of the last day of May, I had seen the sky,
above the bulk of office buildings, high-piled with
white banks of solid light, and in the Square, had
found the pavements swimming with milky pal-
lors and freshened by tenderest green. When I
had gone to meet Hugo at the Brevoort, I had
seen a pale peach-silver sun dissolving the light
tree-fringes at the corner of the Avenue. Now
these wonders had sprung from that delight—so
long and so varied the days were! It was dark
—there were the lamps and the taxis with their
impudent brisk honking—spinning away through
rainy May in the wet relieved fresh freedom.

Rita was looking out the window with her same
strange trancèd seriousness. I asked: "Don't you
like the city just after it's been raining? Hear
how happy the taxis sound!" She smiled and said
simply, "Yes." I wondered whether she were still
thinking of the drawings, of which I was almost
becoming jealous. "Don't you feel a little,
though," I ventured, "that it robs Homer of his
own kind of subtlety to deliberately make him exotic by translating him into terms of the Russian
ballet?" "Why—I hadn't thought of that," she
said. "I hadn't thought of the Russian ballet. I
thought those drawings were beautiful in themselves—quite apart from Homer perhaps." Then
she added, after a pause: "That figure of Pallas
Athena—so slender—so strong—so grave—so
lightly built—as strong and yet as light as her
spear! No *man* could ever combine that power
and that lightness!" "Yes," I said, "that's true,
isn't it?" "And then they talk," she went on,
"about women never having done anything really

important! When the Greeks made the goddess of wisdom a woman! And just as important a woman goddess as the goddess of love!" I tried to assure her that I understood: "Yes, I know," I replied, "men are always expecting the wrong things of women, aren't they?"—while before my mind there aligned themselves, in the guise of long slender javelins, the long slender sentences of John Stuart Mill on the Subjection of Women. "It's so *false* of them," she went on. "You know, some people who pretend to admire independence in women really want to prevent them from doing things! They think that a woman's work is something she can put aside, as if she were laying down her knitting—or her embroidery! Whatever they may say, they can't really believe in their hearts that her work is the thing she lives for, that she puts above everything and everybody!"

I assented briefly, but with earnest emphasis: the generous flow of my feeling had been perhaps a moment impeded by the "above everything and everybody": my mounting moral exaltation lapsed for a space into a brooding happiness which hovered outside the window over the rain-freshened square—those romantic lamps that burned all night, while all night the speeding taxis, plying in happy privacy to a thousand dark addresses, took people, took lovers, home. To that part of my mind, however—the part which had been talking to Rita—from which my attention had been withdrawn, there presented itself a stupid remark: "I have read John Stuart Mill on the Subjection of Women!"

But it was Rita who, after a silence, went on

with the conversation: "I'm so *tired* of people,"
—she spoke with violence—"who pretend to understand what women feel about things!—and
then behave like any stupid stock-broker, who
keeps a wife just as he keeps a car!—The stock-
broker would really be more sensible, because
he'd expect to give his wife certain things in return for what she gave him—she'd at least be
paid in comfort and money for what she lost in
independence!" The figure of the baseball player
rose in my imagination: a good fellow, no doubt,
but dull and boorish, with no subtlety and no high
honor in his relations with women; quite un-
worthy of Rita! I was all on Rita's side now:
how I could share her fierceness against fools!—
"I don't believe *any* man can understand!" But
this seemed to shut me out again, and again I
gazed out into the Square.

I was, however, after a moment, on the point
of attempting to convince her that she might find
that *I* understood, when of a sudden, so peremptory and clear that we looked at each other startled,
we heard from the next room, which we now became aware had been silent, the voice of Ray Coleman demanding: "Well, what have you got to
say?"—and then Daisy Coleman, replying in a
voice which sounded constrained, "Where's all the
party gone to?" "You can see for yourself they've
all gone home: I suppose they saw that the hostess
had left and decided that they didn't want to stay!"
"We weren't gone so long, were we?" said Daisy.
"I just went around the corner with Pete to get a
glass of beer." "You've been gone for an hour
and a half!—And you!" he went on vehemently,

evidently addressing Daisy's late companion—the little man with the large eyes, I imagined. "You weren't invited here to-night and you can leave right away!" "I invited him," said Daisy. "Well, I asked you not to invite him!—Now, get out of here right away!—No: your things are not in there!—There's your coat in the fireplace!—and there's your stick in pieces over there!—and I threw your hat out the window! Maybe you can find it in the street!—Now, don't stand there staring at me like that, but get out!" We heard him slam the door.

Rita and I got up quickly from the window-seat, but the tirade which followed checked us. "You humiliate me in my house!"—now that Ray Coleman had Daisy alone, he opened upon her his fiercest fire. "You drive my friends away! You send C. O. D. packages home!" "I had to have some stockings for to-night!" "Well, why didn't you ask me for them? I won't have you running up bills!" "Well, I can't see what's the idea of this big third act!" "I told you not to bring that little rat here!" "Well, you have all *your* friends —I don't see why I shouldn't have mine!" "You sat in there on the window-seat and let him see your legs!" "We were just telling jokes in there —Gus Dunbar was in there, too." "I don't mind having Gus see your legs—he's a friend of the family, but—" "Well, will you just let me have a list of all the family friends that you're willing to have see my legs?" "Don't be vulgar!" he replied.

Rita determinedly and swiftly broke into the lighted room, and I followed her. "I must really go," she said. "It's been such a marvellous party!

—I've been having such a marvellous time that
I've stayed much too late!" I made my apologies,
also, and got Rita's coat out of the bedroom and
helped her on with it. "Why, it's not late at all,"
said Ray Coleman. "I'm afraid it's we who hav-
en't been very entertaining!" When we said good-
by to Daisy, she merely met us with a pale drunken
gaze, and remarked: "Well, I opened cold!"

Outside, I caught a taxi and asked Rita where
she lived. "Oh, dear," she demurred, "I don't
think I want to go home. I think I'll go to somebody's house—let's see, whose house shall I go
to?" I asked her if she wouldn't come to my
house. "But you want to go to bed, don't you?"
I assured her that I didn't, for hours.

"Pretty painful scene that was!" I remarked
when we had started in the taxi. "I shouldn't think
she'd stay with him." "No," said Rita, but assent-
ing, it struck me, from some different point of
view than mine. "She's such a dear, isn't she?"
I went on. "Yes," she said. "She's so beautifully made, isn't she?—her ankles and wrists."
I thought of Daisy under the guise of Bobby
McIlvaine's little blond Venus caught in the net
with Mars. "What do you make of him?" I
asked. "He's pretty poisonous, isn't he?" She
looked up at me with a little appreciative smile,
as if my saying that Coleman was poisonous had
been an original deliberate joke, instead of a familiar cliché. Then, "He's very jealous of her,"
she said; and then: "Yes, he is *poisonous!*" Her
way of agreeing that he was poisonous made it
neither a cliché nor a joke, but something convinced and bitter. "All jealousy is poisonous: it
poisons the woman as well as the man—it makes

both of them suspicious of all that has ever been
between them—and even when they want to be
nice, they sound hateful to each other!" I remembered some novel of Wells in which the hero
had overcome jealousy along with a number of
other ignoble and anti-social emotions: I reflected
that it was very foolish and very base to be
jealous. However: "I suppose," I said, "that
working for the *Telegram-Dispatch* makes him
hate himself, and so makes him awfully irritable.
How can people who are really sensitive and intelligent—as I have no doubt he is—but who are
obliged to spend all their working hours feeding
the public libels and lies—how can they possibly
be amiable at home?" "Yes," she said, "such lies
they print!—such cowardly lies! And even if the
facts are true, they cheapen the emotions behind
them—and to cheapen human passion, human suffering, is to lie! Like poor Lina Lemberg's letters."
(Lina Lemberg was a young Polish girl, who had
recently murdered her husband, and been much on
the front page.) "They may have been illiterate
and clumsy, but they meant something real.—To
tear people's hearts to pieces for all the grinning
crowd to see—and pick up a bit of it and finger
it, and perhaps wish they had one, too, and hate
the people who have—and then throw it back in
the gutter again!" Her passion had not ceased
to surprise me. She still seemed a little theatrical,
but I had never heard a woman speak so elo-
quently. "Yes: that's just what happens," I said
—it was all that I could say: I felt that I could
never express myself so well nor feel what I said
so intensely.

I lived in Bank Street then, and the taxi had

stopped at my door. Rita waited for me on the sidewalk while I was paying the driver: her little face seemed narrow and thin—almost nunlike.

When we had climbed to my apartment, and I had turned on the light, I was ashamed of the prospect disclosed. There were a large and comfortable couch, sets of books in glass-doored bookcases, Whistler's "Battersea Bridge," and a drawing by Leonardo, which I had brought up with me from college, a small mahogany desk, a green carpet and a French clock. Besides, the maid had been there that morning and everything was swept and neat. I was afraid that she would see at once —if she had not already guessed—that I was really not one of them, that I had never paid their price. The luxurious couch seemed vulgar; the sets in the bookcases pedantic; the pictures unbearably banal; and the little mahogany desk appropriate kindling-wood for the social revolution. I attempted to call attention to the only feature of the place which might be considered Bohemian and raffish: "That's not the right time," I pointed out. "That clock hasn't gone for years!"

"Oh, isn't this nice!" she exclaimed, looking quickly and interestedly about her. There was a little alcove off the sitting-room which I used as a study, and she stood looking into it, as if entranced. "Do you work in there?" she exclaimed. "What a *wonderful* place to work!" She came back and sat down on the couch: "Oh, it's so *nice* here!—so *nice!*" she smiled in an ecstatic childlike way.

I felt, at any rate, that she meant it, and that I possessed an unexpected advantage. None the less, I was a little diffident about producing a bottle of peach brandy, as I had seen her drinking whiskey straight at the Colemans' party: I brought out both liqueur and Scotch, and deprecatingly remarked that I didn't suppose she'd care for the former. "I'd love some!" she said.—"What a lovely label! It looks like lace, doesn't it?—like lace made out of wire!"

"You know," she went on, "I have no place of my own to work in now—and I miss it so! I'm living with my mother and sister, and the apartment is so small! I have to write with the sewing-machine going in the next room." "Oh, what a pity!" I said, "I should think it would drive you crazy. I know how nervous it makes you to have something going on to a different kind of rhythm from the one you're writing to!" "Do you write?" she asked. "I try to write poetry—but I'm not any good." "I'd like to hear your poems," she said, looking up with an intent gaze which seemed to pierce the politeness of her remark. "No," I replied. "After hearing yours to-night, I wouldn't have the nerve to show you mine.—I don't suppose you'd recite again the ones that you recited at the party." "I'm so glad that you liked them," she said, again with that incongruous intensity which gave sincerity and significance to even her formulas of courtesy. "I just wrote them, and I like them myself," she smiled with her funny grin, which left her as serious and as strangely pressing as before. She sat back against the couch, dropped her cigarette to her lap and recited the poems again —more beautifully, it seemed to me, than the first time: her voice, in the silent room, sounded lonely, and I was stirred and awed to be alone with this living voice of poetry.

All to me was a wonder then—her old dress, her mother's sewing-machine, her wide gamine's grin, her formidable dignity and her feverish pre-occupation with some unexplained disturbing reality which I was coming more and more to feel underlay everything she did. It was, I came to see, as she recited, the same thing—a kind of moral agony, unremitting and exalted—which made it possible for her, in her poetry, to deal with commonplace ideas—as she worked often with the tritest figures, the old debased currency of verse, which poets had then begun to pride themselves on ceasing to try to pass—making them carry whatever passion and whatever strangeness she chose.

Her cheeks were fiery now—all her face was suffused with fierce pink, and I saw that there was red in her hair. I saw now for the first time that she was beautiful. Her brow was very high and wide, and the resonant voice with which she recited—so different from her quick dry speech, a mere pizzicato of those strings—seemed the full-toned and proper music of what I saw now also for the first time was a long and lovely throat of a solidity and complexity of symmetry, like some harmoniously swollen musical instrument, almost incongruous with her tiny body—and through which now the lonely beach, beyond the meagre moment of fire, and the futile devotion of the mother to the blemished and dim-witted child, sounded the chords of some mode of feeling more profound than our human sadness, some ground-tone where human emotion becomes merely the process of life, of life in its labor through the universe. I knew, what I had never really felt in my intercourse with friends who had written, that literature could be reality—as natural as conversation, yet as deep as life itself.

For I have not, in speaking of these poems, in any adequate way described them: they were poems about love, and in them what was true of love was true not of love only. And even now, in this part of what I write, which deals with feelings and thoughts most remote from me, least real to the mind that writes—at the memory of that music, I halt and lose my way.

In another poem, which I had never seen, and which she had also recently written, she had some image of a swift up-country river lacerated by rapids, where a smooth and lovely flock of stones forever tumbled and crashed into splinters the black-silver mirror of its deeps, dismissing it, fiercer at first, then thin, querulous and shredded, divided in the threads of feebler streams that drip at last over slimy mossy banks among the last orange drops of the jewel-weed, and lose themselves in the fields. I have turned it all into ordinary literature, over-animating the water, describing the jewel-weed too exactly (it is I who supply the drops: she had only named the flower). I have used too many adjectives: she had only the barest verbs and nouns; but she woke through them the resonant ache of the throaty sound of the river, so noble in its dwindled fall. And I, knowing enough of literature to enjoy the consummate art, but not yet enough of life, to assent with my heart to the terror, the terror mastered by the mind, and clutched and wrenched into beauty, which I could only half divine, but which troubled me and made me solemn, could only tell her how wonderful I thought it, as if it had been merely a dress she had been wearing or a garden she had grown. And I sounded even sillier and lamer when I added: "I've seen those up-state rivers: I know exactly what you mean!" "Yes, I knew you did," she replied, "when you said that something I said this evening sounded like a New York State river. I come from up there, you know, and I've been getting homesick lately. That was why I was talking about rivers—and why I wrote that poem."

I was silent, and she looked beyond the lamp, through the little dark study, to where the moon seemed imbedded in the pane like a flaw of pearl in dark blue glass. "How lovely the moon is!" she exclaimed in her nervous, alert way. I looked out and answered: "Yes: it looks like a bubble in the glass." She noted the accuracy of this, checking it up: "Yes, it does exactly!"—so emphatically that I felt pleased at having said something clever. We stared at the moon without speaking —I thinking, a little dazedly, of the perfect felicity of the moment, full of brightness and freedom and peace—of the beauty of stony rivers, of the pearly moon in the pane, of intoxicating coldness and poetry—of stones, of lovely globes of a lunar fluidity of yolks, lodged unbroken below the translucence of a limpid vitreous stream.

Then I recalled my wandering senses and suggested another drink. "Oh, if I have another drink, I'll be drunk!" she said, screwing herself down in her corner and with a sudden rictus of her grin which transmogrified her grossly in a strange tense glee.

But I could talk to her only of poetry—of those terrific images of the commonplace by which the greatest poets can move us and which her own poems had brought to my mind—the Roman street-corners of Catullus, the prison-window of Verlaine, the race for the green flag at Verona which Dante remembers in Hell. She had read extraordinarily widely for a woman, and she talked about the poets as only a master can talk of the masters of his craft and with the fierceness with which only a woman, when woman's narrow concentration has been displaced from its ordinary objects, can concern itself with art—isolating in familiar poems phrases I had never thought of: some armor-joint of a preposition which rang with a solid sound or some unobtrusive adjective which troubled the whole line.

It was cold: she put on her cloak and I wrapped her legs in a blanket—but still we talked, and drank the peach brandy sip by sip. At last, as I was gazing toward the window, I became aware of an indigo deepness which deeply delighted me, like some full and triumphant staining of emotion and thought. It was the blue of dawning June, through which presently, as brooding I watched it, green and red began darkly to deepen. The blue brightened and now was translucent, now limpid, now dissolved. And, still talking of poetry, still quoting, still eager and glowing with the images of that life of literature which rejects or suppresses nothing that goes to make our common life, but where all is passionate, noble and rich, I saw, as it were with incredulity, that the brightening green and red were the rain-revived trees

and brick walls of my own backyards in Bank
Street. Now even the poor soiled yellows of the
downtown tenement houses, the leaves of the flaccid ailanthus swaying their fingery clusters in the
stir of morning air, through that first distinct
light of day were seen washed with libations of
light—till it seemed to me that I had waked—or
rather that, without sleeping, I had passed—to the
happier, more living hues of a different world. And
I knew, and knew with amazement, that we had
talked the night through, and only sunk deeper in
spring.

"Good gracious! it's morning!" she cried.—
"Oh, no: it's not so late,' I assured her. "The
nights are getting shorter." She laughed and put
out a cigarette. "I must go home!" she said,
springing up.

We found a taxi in Greenwich Avenue. She
gave the directions to the driver in her precise
and compelling fashion. I invited her, in the
taxi, to come with me to see McIlvaine's ballet.
"I'd love to!" she replied. We made an engagement for Tuesday (it was Sunday morning).
Then, with hesitation, I explained that I was
never at home in the daytime, and that if she
needed a place to work, I should be glad to have
her use my apartment. She demurred, but I
thought not unpersuadably.

I left her at an incredible address beyond the
Ninth Avenue Elevated—on Twelfth Street, almost at the docks—one of two or three red-brick
houses among warehouses and sordid saloons.
We parted, she quite tired and pale, but with a
queer tense final vibration even as I left her in the

doorway, just before, quickly closing the door, she seemed to disappear in a flash.

It was day. I walked home through a little open square—Abingdon Square, I saw with surprise: I had never heard of it before, though it lay almost around the corner from where I lived. I gazed vaguely at a statue of a man in a little triangular park and wondered who it was—some legislator or some patriot, perhaps—some patriot in the old style, like Garibaldi in Washington Square—some great man I had never heard of in that region I had never discovered. Farther on, I became aware of a kind of monumental stone pergola—it seemed to me then to be in marble— which I didn't understand—and which in my weariness, my happy weariness, I didn't try to. Some downtown equivalent of Grant's Tomb— but who was buried in it? It was almost like a temple. I was still moving in that strange daytime world into which, by staying up all night, I seemed to have been translated. Now the Village was at last revealed to me; it had that day come alive about me, and I felt myself part of its life. I, like them, had turned my back on all that world of mediocre aims and prosaic compromises; and at that price—what brave spirit would not pay it? —I had been set free to follow poetry!

In Bank Street, as I passed a presser's shop, it occurred to me that it would be, after all, a difficulty about the story which I had had the idea of writing when I had heard about Ray Coleman's thief, that the presser's boy would probably have escaped as soon as the wife opened the door.

When I came back to my rooms again, they

seemed no longer, through the drowsy eyes of
day, my own familiar husk: there was the couch
where she had sat—there was the ash-tray full of
ashes—there were the glasses from which we had
drunk. I poured out the last sweet dregs of peach
brandy.

It was Sunday—I did not have to work. I
dumped the Sunday paper on the couch. I pulled
down the shades in my bedroom—the sun made
them glow dull orange. I pulled Dante out and
read the lines about the green flag at Verona—and
the scene with Beatrice that began, *"Dante, perchè
Virgilio se ne vada—grieve not, thou needst must
grieve for another wound!"*—but scarcely paying
attention to the words, I pushed the book back to
the table and turned over on my cheek. Something or other I had come for, I had found.

* * *

It was characteristic of Hugo Bamman—with
whom I had gone to prep school (though we had
afterwards gone to different colleges), and whose
point of view, up to the night I met Rita, had, as
I say, so much influenced my own—that, at the
height of a convivial evening, he should take a
sudden and determined departure. Even at parties in Greenwich Village, with which he was in
principle more nearly sympathetic than with parties anywhere else, he would carefully isolate his
hat or hang it up in some specially conspicuous
place. He was never sure, even in the Village,
when he might not feel that it was urgently
needed, as had been the case on the evening I have
described, after his argument with Ray Coleman.

And when he once had his hat in his hands, it was impossible to keep him. It was at the same time as if he had suddenly become frightened, and as if he were under some obligation of reporting for duty elsewhere.

And it was true that he did become frightened, and that he was, in a certain sense, at the orders of a higher obligation. Hugo's father had been a well-to-do lawyer of a Philadelphia Quaker family; his mother, a Bostonian. The elder Bamman, after serving with distinction through three administrations at Washington as Solicitor General, had been dislodged by the advent of the Democrats; and had thereupon retired from public life and occupied himself with writing books. He knew Shakespeare and Milton by heart and was given to quoting them in conversation, and he already had a reputation for unconventional political views; but nobody had been quite prepared for the opinions which he now made public. His first book, which was called *Representative Government, and the Way and the Light,* began with an extremely realistic, and even cynical, discussion of American public life and ended, with quotations from Isaiah, on an unexpected note of religious clairvoyance.

It was said sometimes that Mr. Bamman had been embittered by his enforced retirement; sometimes, that he was insane. It was not that he had prophesied good of the Democrats: on the contrary, he had predicted the worst; but he had appeared also to repudiate the Republicans. He had asserted that, between the two parties, there was not a pin to choose—that both were lost in corruption and error; and, what was worse, that one could hope for nothing better from the society which accepted their leadership and from the religion which allowed them to survive. The book excited a certain amount of interest, was made the subject of editorials; then was completely forgotten by everybody. If I had not happened to know Hugo, I should never have looked it up and read it. Thereafter—his wife having died and his sons gone away to school— Mr. Bamman left Washington altogether and secluded himself on a lonely island in an Adirondack lake, where he lived on fish and game, cooked all his own meals and struck off another book even more realistically pungent and even more apocalyptic than the first. He had vowed to stay the winter out in his cabin, but in February he caught a bad cold which developed into pneumonia, and, despite his protests, he had to be removed to a town where he could have medical attention. His sons were telegraphed at their school; and Hugo, blinking at his sudden release from the agonizing life of prep school, where the boys made fun of his ebullient stuttering, his inability to pronounce *r*, his stiff intractable black hair, and his clothes, which were bought for him by an aunt and which always looked too young for him, lifted his goggles from the frozen ground and gazed about him with singular relief at the ice-ponds and white houses of the North; read nervously half a chapter of Meredith; and, at last, heard his father, dying, mingle texts from Isaiah and Ezekiel with anxious queries about the pump at his camp, which he seemed to fear was irremediably frozen, and with the names of his sisters and his wife.

Hugo Bamman, after his father's death, had spent his vacations with the aunt in Philadelphia who had selected his neckties and suits, and he had rebelled against her so violently, that he soon found himself under suspicion of having inherited his father's "queerness." But the more the aunt, who was an admirable person and felt her responsibility acutely, tried to inculcate sound principles in Hugo, the more resentfully did he shy away from them. Save for an occasional peevish outbreak, however, he remained generally docile; and his own docility increased his resentment. While he was still at school and college, his heresies were mostly confined to matters of literature and of minor social convention. But during the third year of the War, though he was to graduate the following spring, he suddenly left college and enlisted in the American Ambulance. In spite of his Quaker tradition, he was at that time full of romantic enthusiasm for the cause of the Allies, and had composed, for the college magazine, an eloquent editorial which began with Joan of Arc and ended with Villiers de L'Isle-Adam. When America joined the Allies, he went over to an American medical unit. Hugo served throughout the War; but he came out with different emotions from those which had carried him in. He never told me much about his adventures, and never indeed, at this time, talked much about himself, so that my account of his experience in the Army is derived largely from the well-known novel which he afterward wrote on the subject and which seemed such a striking contrast to the rather precious and exotic little poems, reminiscent of the eighteen-nineties, which he had published in the college magazine.

From Hugo's novel, then, it would appear that during the first months of his ambulance-driving, he was still sustained by his romantic faith and preoccupied with proving to himself his own capacity for endurance and courage. He tells us of the hero of his novel, that though most of the wounded men he had been carrying turned out to have died on the way, he had never felt so happy in his life as after successfully bringing his ambulance through the craters and geysers of a bombardment. At that time, after his first physical sinkings of nausea and fear, he had been able to line up corpses on the floor of the field hospital with less emotion than he had once arranged books on the shelves of his bookcases at college, and had incinerated amputated legs with less of real regret than he had once burnt discarded manuscripts.

But after America had entered the War, Hugo enlisted in the American army and found himself posted, with the rank of sergeant, during the dull and disheartened winter of 1917, at an American base hospital in the Vosges, some distance behind the lines. One afternoon, he had gone for a walk in the hills, and come out finally in the public square of a tiny mountain village. A circle of people were standing about the body of a wild sow which had been killed by a hunter and which, bristled like the piny ridges of her northern forests and with her jaws asnarl in death, lay flat, her belly ripped open and her little ones, brightly striped and in a day or two to have been far-rowed, stretched out limp beside her on the ground, while the hunter bargained over the car-casses and the dogs sniffed at the blood. A deep tenderness and sadness overwhelmed him for the little wild pigs; and he watched with horror the nonchalance of the hunter: he began to rage within himself against the violators of life. Then he was chilled with self-contempt. He took ref-uge in a little café and fortified himself with brandy. Then he went back to the base hospital.

There was a major of the medical corps who kicked and cuffed his patients, and who was in the habit of amusing himself, on his evening rounds of the wards, by tearing the zinc-oxide bandages off the raw and running wounds of the gas cases. Hugo complained of this major to the command-ing officer of the unit: he had always feared his superiors more than any amount of shell-fire.

Soon thereafter, returning in the morning, just before reveille, from the local château, where he often went to dinner and sometimes, by private understanding with the other sergeants and the guards, was able to spend the night, he was, to his surprise, picked up by the Military Police, put un-der arrest, court-martialled and convicted, and sent off under guard to a prison-camp. As a ser-geant he had been lax with his men; and, at the court-martial, he was accused of having abetted all their misdeeds: of these misdeeds he had never even known, but when he tried to explain this to the court-martial, the effect was equally unhappy.

On his arrival in the prison-camp, all his belongings, including private letters, his money and his watch, were taken from him. He saw the photograph of another man's sweetheart torn up before his face. The first morning, when he was led out in lockstep with the other prisoners, the ranks fell into disorder, and the sergeants set upon the men and clubbed them with what were known as "dizzy-sticks," while the officers looked on. This was repeated every morning, and Hugo learned that the confusion in the ranks was brought about by the sergeants themselves: the sergeant at the head of the line would order the prisoners to hurry up while the sergeant at the end would order them to slow down. Hugo was struck in the mouth one day and two of his teeth knocked out (he had the scar across his lips all his life). After this ceremony, which the sergeants called "morning exercise," the prisoners were drilled before machine-guns.

The food was scant bread and thin soup; and on the third day of Hugo's imprisonment, two colored boys got into the kitchen and tried to steal something to eat. One of the boys was caught, blackjacked, beaten and dragged bleeding to solitary confinement. When he had sufficiently recovered, an attempt was made, by order of the officer in command, to induce him to reveal the name of his accomplice: the boy was chained for four hours to a wall, while the sergeants threatened and cursed him, beat him on the soles of his feet and singed off most of his hair. In the meantime, however, the accomplice had cut his own throat with a razor-blade. Two days afterwards, a big

Texan, who had tried to strike one of the guards when the latter had assailed him with a blackjack, was shot down, in the presence of the men, by the commanding officer. At the end of three weeks, however, Hugo was finally released through the intervention of his elder brother, who was already a major in the Adjutant-General's department and to whom Hugo had managed to send a letter before he had left his unit.

Hugo's further participation in the War was of rather a half-hearted character. Now, it was no longer the Germans who were the enemy, but the governing classes of the world.

By the time he had been discharged from the service, he had become a social revolutionist; and his reaction against the complacent and conventional, the capitalistic, world from which he came, reached lengths almost grotesque. He hated this world because he feared it, and he feared it because he knew how much of it there was still left in himself. He was haunted by veritable hobgoblins which wore the aspect of doubles of himself. A visit to any of the members of his family was enough to throw him into a panic. He would afterwards describe it in terms which would almost have been excessive on the part of one resuscitated from drowning. "On a Sunday afternoon in Washington," he would gasp, "you go out into the stweet—and you see all those little bwick houses—and the weather is suffocating—and you look at the people on the stweet and they don't seem to be going anywhere—and you think that, if you stayed there long yourself, you'd probably get like that, too—and yet you haven't got the

mowal stwength to leave!" Or, "I was staying
with a cousin of mine at Cambwidge—my cousin
is being gwoomed for some big job at Harvard,
and it weduced me to such a state of depwession!—
Did you ever know any of these young men who
are being gwoomed for big jobs?—Well, first
their hair falls out—then they have to buy glasses
—then they have to appear at certain times and
places wearing a silk hat—then their teeth go and
they get false teeth—false teeth are almost as important as a silk hat, and it isn't everybody who
can make his teeth drop out just by auto-sugges-
tion—if they can do that, they've got the stuff!—
I'd said I was coming back to Cambwidge, one
night after I'd gone in to have dinner in Boston,
but I couldn't face it!—I couldn't get a berth at
the station, so I sat up all night in the day-coach!"
(This sort of thing was possible for Hugo, because he purposely never travelled with a suit-
case, but only with an old musette-bag, which he
had brought back from France.) Yet I have
heard him, when Boston was disparaged, unexpectedly come to its defense with a eulogy of
Thoreau and Garrison.

Whenever he introduced into his novels representatives of the "cultivated" class to which he
himself belonged, he would never allow them to
figure save in hideous caricature—the result of his
having discerned, seized upon and isolated in them,
those ignoble middle-class qualities which they
shared with the families of the *nouveaux riches*
manufacturers and railroad magnates whom they
ridiculed. And, on these occasions of visiting his
relatives, by the very force of his fixed intense be-

lief in their incurable perversity and prejudice, he
had a faculty for trapping them into absurdities
which did not at all represent their real views.
These Hugo would make careful note of, as he returned to New York on the train, leaving the
cousins and uncles a little blank. His aunt in
Philadelphia, for example, with whom Hugo had
spent so much of his boyhood, had been, by reason of her Quaker tradition, strongly disposed to
admire his war book, though she was offended by
the bad language of the characters: it always appeared, however, when she attempted to talk to
him about it, that, in deploring this particular feature, she was damning the whole book.

Hugo's elder brother, especially, though, unlike
the other members of the family, he did himself
profess progressive views, affected Hugo in a
fatal way. This elder brother had studied for the
ministry, but had found himself unable to accept
the doctrines of the Episcopal Church save in a
highly rationalized form: as a consequence, he had
gone in for sociology, and, after the War, had become a professor of sociology in a small New
England college. When Hugo went to visit his
brother, the latter would remonstrate with him se-
verely and unremittingly. He would, for example, point out to Hugo the serious impropriety of
the latter's having published certain scurrilous
verses in a radical magazine. He would argue
along lines of social responsibility: the real pur-
port of the objectionable metaphors would be understood by very few readers, whereas the rest
would see only obscenity and unpatriotic senti-
ments; this would hurt Hugo's reputation and

weaken his influence as a publicist, etc., etc. Such
discussions infuriated Hugo all the more because
his brother always went on the assumption that he
recognized the same evils with which Hugo was
so passionately preoccupied and that he had it as
much at heart to discover the proper way of rem-
edying them: Hugo's brother's social ideas and
Hugo's, when stated in a certain way by the
former, appeared indistinguishable. These visits
were further embarrassed by the apprehensions
of Hugo's sister-in-law: she seemed always on
edge for fear Hugo, whose manners were excellent, might advance, in the presence of the Dean's
or the President's wife, with whom she was
closely allied, some subversive opinion.

Another bugaboo which pursued Hugo—another monster which he lived in terror of allowing
to swallow him up—was the college dilettante—
that is to say, the superior undergraduate who
takes tea with the snobbish Latin professor, plays
Debussy at the club after the girls from the house-
party have left, and goes about with a small group
of friends who gossip over the politics of the dramatic club and giggle over the mustache of the
brunette who waits on the counter at the pas-
try shop where they buy cinnamon buns. These
friends, like Hugo himself, had been affected by
their experience in the War: but, in their case, it
had had usually the effect of leaving them merely
demoralized and dispirited, writing fragmentary
learned poetry, full of gall and resignation, in imitation of T. S. Eliot. These friends used to make
fun of Hugo for the obstinate persistence with
which—inordinately fastidious and shy—he had

trained himself to speak in public (overcoming his tendency to stutter, though not his inability to pronounce *r*), and had even attained a certain reputation as an orator at strikers' meetings and demonstrations for civil liberty. Hugo's friends, as a rule, disparaged the admirable literary gifts —the logic, the solid imagination and the feeling for pungent language—which were disguised by the deliberate plainness and the colloquial carelessness of Hugo's novels, pamphlets and appeals.

And Hugo himself would have been the last person to call their attention to his merits. Since the War, the discussion of literature had affected him like his memories of college, and the spectre of the modern literary man, whom he had encountered at New York parties and in Paris cafés, came to accompany, and to merge with, the spectre of the æsthetic undergraduate. Though he had in his youth been full of literary enthusiasms, he now habitually treated the great writers—including those whom he most admired, from Plato to James Joyce—in a manner cavalier almost to the point of hysteria. It was partly, I suppose, that Hugo had never forgotten young country boys from Arkansas and Georgia who could neither read nor write, bewilderedly drafted into the army and pitted against young Germans who had studied Goethe in the gymnasia—the accumulated masterpieces of literature having apparently not in any way affected the fates of either. But it was also that he continually tended, by some natural gravitation which enraged him, to find himself comfortably at home among the sallow-faced reviewers and the review-writing poets and novelists who relieved the mediocrity of their days by the gin-drinking and ribaldry of their evenings. At these gatherings, they were able to convince themselves that they were not merely dreary book-worms and hacks, but men of taste and wit, citizens of the world; and it was partly this anti-academic pose which made Hugo—himself violently anti-academic—eager at first to attend their parties. But he soon divined the pit of ashes at the bottom of the gin-bottle, and shied off as he had done from his family and from the companions of his college days; and literary society was soon added to his index of phobias.

When Hugo put himself into a novel, it was always in caricature—as the little Johnny Boston-Beans of the comic papers of his youth, or as some incredibly fatuous and inept young college intellectual who died of tuberculosis or fell into a subway construction. I have seen him shudder at the sight of a handful of volumes of Max Beer-bohm, whom he had himself enjoyed reading at college, which I was unpacking in a new apartment; and I have rarely heard him use bad language (though he admired it on the part of others) save when the name of Henry James was mentioned. This continual shying away made Hugo a little difficult, since he was constantly objecting, not merely to what you had said, but to what he thought you were going to say. Thus, if you remarked to him of W. Z. Foster that Foster had the barren rigid strength of a piston in a steel-mill, he would interrupt you with, "Well, I'd rather see an effective and hard-hitting machine like Foster than a jerry-built ornamental bank-

building in a phony classical style, like Harding!"
—and so plunge into a spirited tirade against the
industrial system, which you vainly tried to avert
with explanations that you did not admire Harding, that you did admire Foster, etc. Or if you
were going out to dinner with him and complained that the sentimental Yiddish soloist at
Zincovitz's restaurant was beginning to get on
your nerves, he would be off with, "Well, I can't
stand those little tea-rooms where they have copies of *Town and Country* lying around!"—little
tea-rooms of whose existence you had never even
known.

He was rather afraid of women, and seemed
never to fall in love. I suppose he regarded
women as the most dangerous representatives of
those forces of conservatism and inertia against
which his whole life was a protest: but I am convinced that he cherished, in his heart, the most
romantic expectations. I believe that he was always hoping for some straight, dark, spare, realistic girl revolutionist, who would be to him a
comrade and a partner; but that in fact, he was
invariably alienated from the types of emanci-
pated women whom he encountered in the Village, by an unconfessed but ineradicable instinct
which rejected them as not being ladies. He
would, of course, shy away from this instinct and
overwhelm them with politeness, with sympathy,
with determined good-fellowship; but this effusion masked a retreat. I think he was affected, in
this connection, by the same peculiar and incurable isolation which had made him seem to himself, during the War, almost indifferent to the

sufferings of the soldiers till he found himself
brimming with tears at the sight of a slaughtered
sow. So he would flee from even parties in the
Village, when an appropriate situation arose for
playing a rôle in some woman's life, and go home
to write with passion, almost with amorous feeling, of some girl bandit who had been harshly
sentenced and brutally denounced by a stupid
judge—of whom he had read in his evening paper.

For Hugo was really on close terms with no
one. As soon as he had sampled the conversation
and caught the social flavor of a household or a
group, he would simply go straight away and bottle a specimen for his books, where he would as-
sign it to its proper place in the economic structure. He distrusted his family and his early asso-
ciates, because he believed that they had sold their
souls to capitalist institutions; but though he chose
to live exclusively with outlaws, in whom he was
always discovering qualities heroic and picturesque
to the point of allegory, he never managed really
to be one of them and perhaps never trusted them,
either. So tough remained the insulation between
himself and the rest of humanity—the insulation
of his Puritan temperament and his genteel American breeding, reinforced by his artist's detachment and his special situation. Hugo once told me
of an illiterate Arkansas boy, lying wounded in
a field hospital, who, thinking Hugo a superior
person, had been unwilling to ask him to write a
letter, and who had finally had to beg the favor
of another wounded man nearly as helpless as
himself.

And so he walked among us like a human penance for the shortcomings of a whole class and culture—of the society which, in America, had paralyzed in his friends and himself half the normal responses to life; which had sterilized its women with refinement; which had lived on industrial investments and washed its hands of the corruption of politics; which had outlawed its men of genius or intimidated them with taboos; which so strangely had driven his father to his Adirondack lake and, on the rare and brief occasions when he returned for a wedding or a funeral, had seemed to Hugo's eyes to sadden him, as, to the latter's heartiness and wit, the other members of the family had returned only so much that was energetically arid, so much that was self-confidently timid and so much that was cheerfully cold; and which had desolated Hugo's own soul, when, through empty afternoons of boyhood, he had wondered why he seemed so impotent to break the spell of his tutoring in the morning, his aunt's nap after lunch, the people for tea in the afternoon and his late luxurious reading in bed, to work on a paper, to ship on a whaler or to live on a ranch in the West; and which had finally inflicted on him the shame of that day when he had found the crippled Arkansan dictating his letter to his wife to a man half-flayed with mustard-gas —the shame of knowing that a fellow sufferer and one who had suffered more than he, had been afraid to ask him to render what was perhaps the only service for which his education had fitted him.

I have said, a whole class and culture; but

Hugo had one other memory of his father, which was afterwards, he told me once, to take on for him a special significance. They had been lunching at the New York club of the university from which his father had graduated and to which Hugo was soon to go, and the elder Bamman had commented during lunch with humorous disapproval and with imperturbable surprise on the inferior quality of the men whom he observed in the dining-room about him: on their way out, as Mr. Bamman was getting into his coat, he had been violently jostled by a young man in a blue suit and bone-rimmed spectacles, who was in a great hurry, but who hurriedly apologized. Mr. Bamman was broad-shouldered and well set-up, and he still wore a fine Olympian beard and one of those flat-crowned derbies which were fashionable in the eighties (he remained something of a dandy even after he had become a recluse); but, at the moment of the impact, as Mr. Bamman looked dazedly around, Hugo had caught on his father's face the shadow of feebleness and pain. And he had realized then for the first time that his father had no longer the prestige of an acknowledged leader of the community, nor even of a distinguished person: he was a figure of isolation, bewilderment and fatigue.

In the America where Hugo came to manhood, there was, in a sense, only a single class and a single culture; one found it behind every façade, one felt it through every uniform—and not merely among those members of society whom it had already become fashionable to ridicule: the small business man, the hired reformer, the windbag

politician—but in the cramped mind of the clever
lawyer, for whom intellectual dignity and freedom had been forbidden by the interests which
he served; in the grandeur of the medical special-
ist's waiting-room and the impoverishment of
science which it masked; in the educated clergy-
man turned evangelist and vying with the mounte-
banks of Methodism; alike in the silk hat of the
labor leader and in the homely and hollow plain-
spokenness of the self-made industrial master;
and even in the universities, with their presidents
held in subjection by millionaire trustees, with
their middle-class timidity about raising, in class
or conversation, the real political, moral or æsthetic problems of the time; even in the best of
the theatre, where incompetence and indifference
almost invariably betrayed the beauty of the no-
blest text; even in literature, where an ignorant
criticism was ready to declare every apprentice a
master; in that whole machine of interrelated interests, which kept literature, theatre, learning,
church, medicine, politics and law, all fixed in
their mediocre functions, all constrained by the
fear of their neighbors, all intent on their bank
accounts—all that appalling susceptibility to regi-
mentation by "business" and that incapacity for
discipline of self, all that voracity for physical
comfort, all that pervading commonness of mind,
which, even in those sections of society from
which Hugo's father had come and which had at
least produced a few men like him, now debased
their distinction to luxury and made cowards of
their leaders. It was, perhaps, after all, hardly
necessary to find special explanations for Hugo's

fear of committing himself, of giving hostages to any group—which moved beside him like Pascal's abyss. It was, perhaps, after all, not unnatural that there should come a moment, in every company, when Hugo would want to snatch his hat, to say good-by and get away.

II

WE worked in silence, dismantling the walls and packing Rita's belongings.

Rita herself had left us: some one had knocked at the door, and she had gone into the front room. We had heard her receive a male caller and carry on a decisive, rapid conversation. And she had now been away so long that, deprived of her peremptory commands and made uneasy by the presence of the visitor, we no longer spoke to each other. Duff Burdan, the young man whom at Ray Coleman's I had taken for a baseball player, but who had turned out to be actually a painter, was laboring over Rita's suit-case, in the broken strap of which, with a great air of masculine effectiveness, he was gouging extra holes with a nail-file. The young Jew was taking down the pictures and wrapping them carefully in newspapers: we had only rarely seen him at Rita's and had not expected to see him to-day: he was very quiet, polite and well-dressed, and we resented as complacency his modest amiability. But Duff Burdan and I were also resenting each other.

And in the stillness which had ensued on hammering down the last boards of a packing-case, I heard the moaning of boat-whistles from the harbor; and my heart horribly sank. So we had used to hear them in summer—their sobbing, melodious and remote—in the late afternoon shadow; or at night, when the rumorous hum of summer came in through the open windows, when the summer world, which had already been sleeping gently by day, seemed scarcely to slumber at night: their trombone and oboe notes—so one night she had imagined Stokowski conducting a symphony of river-noises from the top of the Singer Building.

I stood up and tried not to hear them—tried to level on the objects about me a prosaic disenchanted gaze, as if by force of will I could insulate them and, impervious to the aromatic smell of perfume and cigarettes—the odor of her hair—so put myself out of reach of that current which had charged them with feeling and which still gave them the power to shock me. They were meagre and battered, it was true; the damaged electric heater; the little wooden cot, with the strip of batik above it; the sewing-machine; the potted cactus; the water-color of an Indian corn-dance, with its delicate red-and-black figures distinct against egg-shell white (it had been sent her, like the cactus, I never failed to remember, by an unforgotten admirer who had gone for his health to New Mexico and who was always on the point of coming back); the purple abstract painting of an eggplant taking shape amid a maelstrom of female membranes (which had been given her by another admirer about whom I had always wondered, but whose identity she had never revealed); the bookcase, with its rubbed and broken volumes, so fantastically miscellaneous, in which one could read, as in geological strata, the so various interests and tastes of the men whom Rita had known.

I looked away, and my eyes involuntarily sought the half-open door to the sitting-room. There I could see them standing at last by the

door which led out to the staircase: Rita was half
turned away, but I had a glimpse of the face of
her companion: he was an undistinguished, thin
and dingy-eyed young man, commonly dressed. I
saw him take some bills from Rita and put them
away in his pocket.

When she came back, she gave a sharp look
round. "Where's my little Buddha?" she demanded. I told her I had packed it in the box.
"Well, you just get it right out again! I didn't
want it packed! It will be smashed to bits!" I
assured her I had packed it carefully. "No: it'll
be broken in that box, just as sure as sure! I
think I'll take it with me—I'll carry it myself."

"I'll carry it over separately, when the other
things go, if you want me to," Duff Burdan vol-
unteered. "Will you promise not to break it?—
No, I think I'd better take it myself." "What do
you think I am—a smasher of images?" She
laughed on her precise little notes: "You promise
not to let it get broken?—promise!—If I come
back and find that Buddha broken, I'll never
speak to you again!—Oh, don't pack that Indian
corn-dance with the other pictures!" she inter-
rupted young Kaufmann. "I *do* want to take that
with me!—Can you get it in the suit-case, Duff?
—or couldn't you strap it some way on the outside?"

Duff Burdan dealt with this problem. "Everything here is to go, is it?" he asked, looking
round. "Yes, everything," she replied. "Are you
sure you'll have room for it all?" "Sure: I'm
throwing out a whole lot of my own junk." "It's
so sweet of you to offer to keep it for me!—Don't

let anybody borrow my books!" she admonished him, the moment after.

I looked at my watch and announced that it was time to get a taxi—Duff Burdan was storing her furniture, but I was to see her off.

Those stairs which I had climbed so many times to find, at the top, her little figure, intense and sharp even standing in the doorway and dark against the light of the door, so that it seemed sometimes like a knife on which I was running— those stairs where too often lately I had felt that, in answering the doorbell, she had been hoping for some one else—as I descended them this after-noon, it was not without relief at the thought that I should never have to climb them after to-day.

And was that he, that sloppily dressed reporter, that fellow from some insurance office, to whom Rita had been giving money—was that the visitor she had been always expecting, whom she would rather have seen than myself? I was glad of a new reason for disgust, of a new pretext for hat-ing those stairs—and yet that hatred, as I knew, was only fear, the fear of remembering how much I had loved them. And such bitterness was ig-noble, I knew—for houses were things to put away, like worn-out clothes, with the phases of our life, with the emotions with which life was clothed. And was not emotion here worn out?— on my side as well as on Rita's—had I not come myself to dislike the cold house, the sordid stair-case, the saloon with its hanging blinds, the op-pressive tunnel of the El, the bleak stony waste of the docks, where late one night I had walked so leadenly, not finding Rita at home? Had I not said to myself that afternoon, on my way to Rita's house for the last time: "Well, thank God, I'll never have to come back to this damned address again! I'll be out of prison at last!"

And now I could see that the winter sun was bright on a colored cigarette-poster, and that the school-girls returning from school were prettier than any school-girls had seemed to me for many months. I compared one of them with Rita, to the advantage of the school-girl—Rita had lately been looking rather badly. I should be free to love another girl now! I thought of Daisy, whom I had seen the night before and who had seemed to me unexpectedly desirable. If I could only keep up my spirit—if I could only play the game according to the sportsman's code which Rita had been trying to teach me so gravely and so sweetly —if I could only, I told myself, do that, then in the long run, all might be right between us—because I had not nagged her or wearied her, because I had proved myself her peer, as prompt to offer all for love and as brave to bear its passing. If I could only remember that the days were not bricks to be laid row on row, to be built into a solid house, where one might dwell in safety and peace, but only food for the fires of the heart, the fires which keep the poet alive as the citizen never lives, but which burn all the roofs of security! Be glad, be proud, to end so well—before that music of the harbor—I could hear it now again, as I came back to Rita's with the taxi—before that music had lost its beauty—for so one could hear it as beautiful forever!

Back in the apartment, I found that a new visitor had arrived to say good-by to Rita. It was a young man from Columbus, Ohio, whom I remembered having met with Rita one evening when we had gone to the theatre. He was one of those curious Westerners who dress like Westerners, but who speak like Philadelphians. The night Rita had recognized him at the theatre, she had seemed disquietingly glad to see him, and my first instinct had been to identify him as the admirer in Santa Fé who had sent her the corn-dance and the cactus, and of whose arrival I lived in dread. When he had turned out not to be this person, I had been exceedingly relieved, and as Rita had never afterward mentioned him, I had forgotten him completely. Now, however, his presence seemed ominous: it was evident that Rita had been seeing him. I remembered that, when we had met him at the theatre, he had said that he was soon going West, and that, I calculated now, had been at least a month ago. It had, it seemed to me, been just about a month that things had been going particularly badly between Rita and me.

She was hurried but gay with the partings—I thought that she had become more good-natured since the arrival of the new admirer. Just before she got into the taxi, she kissed everybody good-by. The Westerner, with unctuous heartiness, was all for seeing her off, but she explained that that was my prerogative—and she kissed him a second time. I felt suddenly that it was an impudence for her to have divided with such scrupulous fairness, between Duff Burdan and me, the honor of seeing her off and the honor of storing her furniture. —Yes: she had certainly got out of an engage-

ment with me a very short time after that night
when we had met the Ohioan at the theatre!

I saw, as I helped her into the taxi, that she was
carrying the little potted cactus, to which I had
taken an intense dislike: it had a stubby and prick-
led stalk, and it had with time come to wear to my
eyes a significance all too plainly phallic.

In the taxi, I at first said nothing: we had both
become, together, so tense. But when we had
turned into Seventh Avenue, I looked at her and
smiled and said, "Well!" She puckered her eyes
and mouth in one of her ecstatic grins and spas-
modically threw back her head in the movement
which had once made me feel that she was lifting
me into her ecstasy, but which now seemed to
draw her away from me: "Oh, it's so *wonderful*
to be going away where I won't have to see any
more people!"

Yes: she had left me already—long ago. She
would not let me come with her to that world. I
must return to the common world—and what
should I do there now? Those qualities of desperate independence and of intellectual passion
which had once exalted me so, could make me
now so glum!

Rita had decided overnight to leave New York.
One of her aunts, who still lived in the little up-
state town where Rita had been born, had lately
fallen ill, and Rita's mother, with whom Rita
shared her rooms, had gone to stay with her sister.
One evening, when I came to get Rita to take her
out to the opera, I had found her, not even dressed
for dinner, sitting amidst packets of old letters on
the day-bed, and passionately preoccupied with the

idea of returning to her native place, sustaining
the old age of her aunt, and consecrating herself
in solitude to the composition of a play in verse. I
saw, to my annoyance, that she had been crying.
And at the *Rosenkavalier* she had relapsed into
that punctual responsiveness, with its effect of
deliberate polite effort, which I had noted in her
the night I had first met her, but which she had
dropped when I had got to know her better. She
had intimated, on the way home in the taxi, that
she considered the *Rosenkavalier* a little cheap.
And I had expected her to like it so much!

I had hoped then that her intention to leave
town, which I had applauded with insincerity,
would evaporate like any other of those suddenly
excited desires—to go West, to go to Paris, to return to the stage again—which she would as suddenly forget; and I was dismayed when I found
that she persisted in it. She had sat down and
written half-a-dozen stories for a popular magazine, and had succeeded in getting an advance from
the editor (who was also wildly in love with her),
on the strength of a promise of more stories. She
had then paid her arrears of rent and had persuaded the Italian landlord to allow her to break
her lease.

I had made to Rita's sigh of relief, in the taxi
on our way to the station, some appropriate reply,
conscientious and devoid of conviction; but I saw
now that we were already at the Waldorf, where,
with the traffic cut across us, we stopped.

I looked toward her and saw that her face, with
her old fur collar close about her neck, was pale
and demoralized and ill, staring and pinched. For

the first time since that night in Bank Street, when her cheeks had flushed a hot pink and, leaning back against my couch, she had revealed her long Muse's throat, her face seemed sharp-featured and tarnished. And though I knew well enough, even then, that, if all I had once adored in that face—passion, intelligence, daring—seemed now to have disappeared, it was strained nerves and hard living which had killed them—her poverty which had put her at the mercy of all that importunate pack—myself among them—who had been forever ringing her doorbell, and all that alien life of the city which had taxed her almost to dementia (the crosstown traffic stopped; our own commenced to move: she had told me once that the traffic terrified her)—though all my conscious feelings were of horror that some one I so honored should be injured, that I should ever come to find unlovely a being I had once so loved; yet that savagery of the human animal which makes us fall upon our wounded fellows, especially those whom we have feared, impelled me to say cuttingly and abruptly: "You have no faith!"

"What do you mean—religious faith?" she asked, as if she had been talking to a stranger—but I cut her short with, "No: the other kind—good faith, I mean!"

"You know very well," she replied, suddenly speaking to me directly, "you know very well that I know what sort of person I am—but if I wasn't that sort of person, I shouldn't be the sort of person who would do what I did with you. . . . I was cruel to other people then."

"Yes," I said, "I know: but when I see some

of the people you care about, you can't blame me
if I take it a little hard!"

"What do you mean?" she demanded.

"I was thinking of this afternoon."

"Duff Burdan and Max Kaufmann are both
nice boys—I thought you liked them. And I'm
not in love with either of them, if that's what you
mean!"

"I wasn't thinking about them—I think they're
all right."

"I hadn't seen Max Kaufmann for months,"
she went on. "He came around to see me just because he heard that I was going away. It was nice
of him to come."

"Who was that fellow that needed a shave?"

"Who do you mean?" Her wonder made me
angry.—"You don't mean my brother?" she added, after a moment.

"Was that your brother?" I pretended to be
amused by my own jealous suspicions. I had forgotten she had a brother, though she had told me
about him once.

"Yes," she answered. "My brother came in
this afternoon."

"What does your brother do?" I inquired.

"He drinks," she said bitterly, without humor.

As I remembered the visitor's face, dim-eyed
and devoid of personality, I could see now in it
Rita's sharp nose and her eyes of indefinite color.
And my first feeling was one of relief that the
shabby nonentity I had seen, to whom Rita had
given money, was merely Rita's brother. But the
discovery, as I found in a moment, had the effect
of increasing my resentment: if my worst suspi-

cions had been justified, I could at least, to that
extent, have despised her, could even perhaps have
washed my hands of her. But now I knew that
if it was not the unknown visitor, as unconsciously
I must have hoped, with whom Rita had been lately preoccupied, it must have been the young man
from Columbus, who was obviously attractive and
eligible.

"At least," I brought out after a pause, "this
big-hearted guy from the West isn't a relation of
yours?"

She was silent. Then she began, with her effect
of dramatic sincerity which I had come to resent
and dread: "It's so false of you to nag me and
scold me like this. You ought to understand how
I feel! You ought to be able to see what I've been
going through. If you really loved me, you
wouldn't want to say hateful things to me!—But
I don't care now—I don't care about any of you!"

"I know: I do understand," I replied. "I hope
that you get a lot of work done." But I wanted
to say, "That's nonsense, and disingenuous besides,
to say that my being jealous means that I don't
love you enough. And then you accuse me of
being 'false'!"

I stared out at the motor-cars and taxis which
were mounting the enormous driveway of the via-
duct that girds the Grand Central. They had still,
I found, the power to stir in me, like those taxis
I had heard from the window the night I had
first met Rita, the excitement and hope of the city.
They were urgent and expectant now, crowding
up-town along their private gallery, to dinners in
apartments and hotels, where romances and ad-

ventures were beginning, where people were drinking cocktails and becoming amusing and gay (as I had not been able to be for so long)—to parties, to night-clubs, to plays, to the theatrical iridescent Forties, which I had never properly explored and where I knew that Daisy was living.

"Did you know Daisy had left Ray Coleman and gone back to the stage?" I asked.

"No," said Rita. I could see that her hands were quivering with tenseness.

"I think it's probably a darn good thing, don't you?" By approving of Daisy's vagaries, I perhaps hoped to make reparation for my harshness about her own.

"Yes," she answered, "I suppose it is."

"I like her so much," I continued. "I saw her at Sue Borglum's last night. She has a wonderful sort of good-natured frankness. I really think, in fact, that she's one of the girls I know that I like best."

I hoped, no doubt, to make Rita believe that I had been happy the night before without her. She had told me—what seemed to me improbable—that she wanted to be left alone, that it always made her nervous to have people around while she was packing. I tried to fix my mind on Daisy as I had seen her at Sue Borglum's party: with bare arms in a girlish black evening-gown—with her candid American smile and her continual spark of wisecracks. And it occurred to me now in the taxi that, as soon as I had seen Rita off—I had never hitherto been able to think beyond that event—I should be free to cultivate Daisy. I could go at once to her place on Forty-fourth

Street—I could ask her to dinner to-night! And this realization sustained me.

We had been silent, but now Rita began again: "It's so *false* of you to talk to me like that! You used to understand things so well! You know that the first time I met you, you said that Ray Coleman was bitter because he hated his newspaper work, and that that had made him harsh with Daisy. Well, don't you think that *my* life makes *me* bitter? Don't you think *I* hate the way I've been living?"

"I know: I'm sorry," I replied, and I took her hand and pressed it, without tenderness or warmth.

We had stopped at the station door. I gave Rita's suit-case to a porter.

"Don't you want him to carry that?" I asked, nodding toward the cactus.

"Oh, no!" she guarded it, grinning. "I wouldn't trust it to anybody—I'm afraid that something might happen to it!"

All the rest was mechanical—when we kissed good-by, most of all. I sat down in the train for a moment, and told her what an excellent thing I thought it for her to go away alone and write: I hoped that she would accomplish a great deal. "You must produce a masterpiece," I said. "Let me see it when it's done, won't you?"

I plunged out into the hurrying concourse and made straight for the door to Forty-fourth Street.

On my way—as I was passing a news-stand—at the sight of a bright red magazine-cover, I found myself shocked by that terrible current of which the furniture and pictures of Twelfth Street, of which everything connected with Rita,

had for so long been such active conductors. It
was the second-rate fiction magazine for which
Rita had written the stories that had enabled her
to leave New York. She had never been willing
to sign them—I remembered that now—though
they were really not at all discreditable: she was
incapable of writing badly. But as she had never
taken them seriously, as she had written them
merely to make money, she had always hated them,
and had insisted on signing them with a pseu-
donym, though she could have gotten a far better
price for them by publishing them over her own
name.

I turned suddenly back toward the train, as if I
could still have redeemed our farewell from the
memory of my bitterness and spite—but the man
was taking down the sign.

* * *

The news of her aunt's illness had deeply affected Rita; and though I was sceptical and suspicious at the time, I see now that it had really
preoccupied her to the exclusion of everything
else. Aunt Sarah, who was always called "Aunt
Sadie," had been the artistic member of the family; and Rita had originally been named for her.
But when Rita had first come to New York, and
had acted for a short time on the stage, she had
substituted "Rita" for her real name, and she had
never afterwards been able to bring herself to be
known as Sarah again. Her first poems had been
published over her stage name. And now she tor-
tured herself with the fear that this might have
hurt Aunt Sadie's feelings. With her passionate

concentration, she had talked to me of that extraordinary little woman with the birdlike nose and neck, and the square enormous brow (which Rita had inherited).

Aunt Sadie had, in her youth, been the organist in the church and the gay getter-up of church "sociables"; she had wanted to go to Paris to study music, and had nearly succeeded. But the men of Aunt Sadie's family—like Rita's brother—had not made life easy for the women: some drank; some had broken down; some had simply disappeared. When she had found she could not go to Paris, Aunt Sadie had decided to move to Watertown and teach music; but a last brother, who kept the general store in the little town where they lived, had been disabled by a paralytic stroke, and Aunt Sadie had had to take care of him and help with the store, for which she presently found herself assuming the whole responsibility. But as she had always been hopelessly perplexed by the local problems of supply and demand, she was gradually deprived of her trade by a newer and more modern store, which had a soda-fountain with tables. Now she had come down with a bad case of pleurisy, and was unable to work at all.

And Rita, brooding on the slow extinction of Aunt Sadie's personality, tragically reproached herself for having suppressed Aunt Sadie's name. She talked to me about Aunt Sadie till I could see the chipped and yellow keys of her little upright piano, and the elegantly engrossed scrolleries of the old-fashioned black-and-white music-covers, more clearly than the objects in the room in

which we were, and could hear those other scrolleries, both elegant and noble, of the voices of
the fugue, weaving an indelible watermark of
beauty in the air of the cramped little parlor behind the general store. Aunt Sadie had taught
Rita to play; and Rita still remembered some
fragments of Handel and Bach, which sometimes
tumbled out without warning when she found herself beside a piano, all rumpled, as it were, but
still fresh, from the disordered wardrobe of her
mind. These gusts of music surprised me at first:
they were so spontaneous, light-hearted and
lovely—so different from the sometimes tight,
and always sober, style of her poetry; and I have
thought since that they were perhaps the only
thing which I ever knew of Rita as she had been
in her girlhood.

For Rita, too, had spent long years in the little
up-state town; had sung in the church choir and
known all the hymns by heart; had studied French
from the book, where there was no one to teach
her to speak it, and had read Baudelaire and Gau-
tier when she could not pronounce their names.
And before she had finally gone to college on the
scholarship which she had won by fierce solitary
effort, she had almost, she told me, abandoned the
hope of ever sloughing off that life of the small
American town, which she put on when she woke
every morning, like some cursed indestructible
dress of girlhood, too worn, too soiled, too small.

Yet, I never heard her speak with resentment
of her early environment: it was herself, and not
the place or its people, which, when she told me
of her youth, she made me see. When Sinclair

Lewis wrote his famous novel, in its own way so intense, he made one feel that the American small town had rendered the whole of American life unpalatable, had flavored it with a rank flat taste, like some minute organism which spoils the drinking-water. But my impression of the town from which Rita had come was made up merely of those moments in Rita's life which she had told me of passing there and which seemed to me, like everything else about her, to have taken place outside the common world. She had described to me once, for example, how, lying late awake at night, she had heard some drunkard, returning from the town, singing clearly in the empty country road, dark-and-clear with the autumn moon:

"I wooed her in the summer-time
    And in the winter, too;
 And all night long I held her in my arms,
    Just to shield her from the foggy, foggy dew!"

To-day, when I can sort out the drunkard, the song which every one knows, the little New-York-State town, the girl who wants to get away—though I summon all the drunkards, all the bawdy songs, all the discontented girls, all the towns, that I have ever known—I can see nothing but that moment of Rita's girlhood, of her girlhood too long detained, which seemed to hang half clear black and half a turbid crystal, in the radiant-dark country night, like a drop of foggy dew —I see all through the eyes of the poet, to whom our social history is invisible.

I made differences between New York and Paris; between New Orleans and New York. *I* had wondered, at Ray Coleman's party, whether McIlvaine were a Scotchman or a Jew; I had insisted on finding out from Hugo in what city Daisy was born. And though I did not, like Hugo, compute incomes nor peg out the people I encountered in the economic web, I marked degrees of education and was always trying to identify accents. I had noted, in this way, in Rita, the Irish fickle-mindedness and sharpness; the traces of the superior person in the small provincial community; of the bold and original personality in the community of college girls, who had, however, learned the language of the rest—that savorless language of young segregated women constantly dosed by older women with the highest feminine ideals; the intonations of the American actress of English light comedy; and, finally, dominating all, her rôle of princess and rake of the Village. But it made no difference how she talked, where she had been, what she wore, where she lived, what boors she caught up in her life, what threadbare images she used—the being who filled my mind had little relation to all this. I first learned from Rita that the importance, the significance, of what we see, is supplied by the mind which perceives them—that the power which creates, through imagination and passion, never stops to appraise the value of the materials with which it works, but itself assigns them value.

And just as, despite the fact that Aunt Sadie presented herself as an obstacle to my happiness, that I was by no means, at the time of which I write, in a mood to share Rita's anguish for the muted and dying vibrations of that steel-silver and

tight-strung soul—so she had compelled me,
against my taste and interest, to accept all her
friends and admirers at the value she put upon
them herself. These friends, when I came to meet
them, almost always impressed me at first as quite
unlike what I had heard about them from Rita—
as insipid, ineffective, or underbred. And I used
at first to find my jealousy allayed at discovering
that Rita's swans were geese—(though I suppose
that I still felt, in the case of the Greenwich Villagers proper, a sort of jealousy at their having
participated with Rita in the braver exploits of an
earlier day—a day which I myself had come too
late for: I had the sense that even the worst of
Rita's friends had at least "fired one ringing shot
and passed"). But young journalists cheapened
by their work; pottering young writers, like myself; debauched or epicene young poets, with neither genius nor self-respect; mediocre middle-
aged literary men, with bald heads and stale
reputations; and all that odd mixed company of
lawyers, contractors and brokers—I was obliged to
grant even to these each his gift or his special distinction—and, even then, I could never be sure
how far they were distinctions or gifts which Rita
herself had lent them. So constant and so acute
was her need to intensify experience that, just as
she would cherish the timbre of certain boat-
whistles which she heard from her apartment in
Twelfth Street, just as she would sometimes keep
for days a tangerine or an apple which she had
bought at the grocer's on the corner, but of which,
when she had brought it home, she had become
fascinated by the color or the shape—so she had

the faculty of endowing her admirers with qualities which they themselves may hardly have hoped
to possess. With Rita, the vagabond poet would
prove to have an interesting temperament; the
journalist, an honest conviction; the obsolete editor or essayist, something of the grace of a man of
the world; and those bewitched business men and
brokers, who so furiously pursued her, seemed to
have caught from Rita's own imagination some
disturbing conception of themselves which they
were straining to realize—she told me once how a
man who had seen her on but a single occasion,
and whom she had afterwards succeeded in evading, had recognized her again, after years, merely
from hearing her voice over the telephone, when
he had by mistake been connected with a wire on
which Rita was talking to some one else.

But it was not merely that Rita disregarded all
those social and moral considerations which oc-
cupy so large a place in the minds of ordinary
people. It was not merely that she was free from
prejudices; but that character itself, in the sense
in which it may amuse us, stimulate our curiosity
or appear to us picturesque, did not interest her.
She was not at all the sort of woman who enjoys
collecting celebrities or types: gossip did not entertain her; she had little taste for novels. In her
own stories and plays, there were no characters,
but merely situations and emotions. And so, not
seeing at all in her friends what most of them saw
in each other, she made it possible for them, in
their relation to her, to play rôles for which the
world would never have cast them. It was as if,
in their contacts with Rita, they had become some-

how facets of herself, their longings given body
by Rita's imagination and their vitality doubled
by her force. They had become aspects of her own
personality; and so wear for me even to-day—the
middle-western journalist with the Abraham-Lin-
coln voice, the snow and quiet of the diamond
winter night when she had spoken to me, after he
had left, of the purity and peace of his spirit of
which she suggested that the longings were yet so
poignant—the international vagabond, the muffled vagueness of the August dusk when we had
carried him part way up Fifth Avenue in the vic-
tòria in which we were riding, and she had afterwards, in Central Park, among the asphalt wind-
ings and dark walls, where the lovers embraced
mute on their benches, sung some Spanish songs
he had taught her—and the man in New Mexico,
alas! the sweet pathos of the short days she had
known him and which she had described to me
with her brief telling eloquence on the very afternoon in Bank Street when I had counted on finding eloquence myself to persuade her to marry me
—the bare two days and a half she had spent with
that tubercular landscape painter whom she had
loved, she said, the best of all!

I myself had good cause to be grateful: when I
had read Rita my indifferent verses, she would
always afterwards take them from me and go
through them intently herself, repeating aloud the
lines which pleased her, so that they had the sound,
brought to life by her voice, of being a great deal
better than they were; and, at the time, I never remembered that she had also a knack of reading
certain poems by Coventry Patmore and Arthur

Henry Clough, poets whom I detested, so that
they sounded as if she had written them herself.
—Even during our last conversation when I had
scolded and complained in the taxi, she had appealed to a generosity for which I was really by
no means remarkable by reminding me of those
excuses, perfunctory and largely hypocritical,
which I had made long ago for Ray Coleman.

In any case, we swarmed to her apartment, de-
voured her time and her force, and finally, at the
period of which I write, had rendered her life
intolerable. I had told her once of something that
Hugo had said of literary people together, as one
saw them in New York or Paris—that they were
like the leeches in a druggist's jar: dependent for
nourishment on blood, but reduced to the desperate extremity of preying on one another. Rita
had added: "Yes, and I'm the druggist, when he
puts his hand in the jar!"

So I had learned in half a year from Rita that
from another point of view than Hugo's, the
world may present quite different values, and give
rise to quite different problems. But I had learned
something else from Rita, which it had cost me
more pain to learn. When I had taken her to task
in the taxi, reproaching her for lack of "faith,"
she had forced me to confront a principle which,
since I had known her, had haunted and tormented
me, but which I had hitherto tried to evade; and
even she, who must have lived with it so long, was
reluctant to confess it to me: she had pretended
for a moment to mistake what I meant. As Hugo
had learned from his weeks in the prison-camp
that men who are beaten become brutalized and
that poor men starve; so I had been obliged to

learn from Rita that any great strength or excellence of character must be, by its very nature,
incompatible with qualities of other kinds—that
it carries with it weaknesses and ignominies in-
separable from excellence and strength. I should,
I dare say, like every one else, always have been
willing to admit both these truths: they would,
in fact, have seemed to me platitudes. But I had
had to learn them both from experience, and once
I had felt their reality, it had seemed to me that
all our social and moral conventions had been
based on the opposite assumptions—that a person
who had had either revelation (either Rita's revelation or Hugo's), and who uncompromisingly
met life on that basis, must, like Hugo or Rita,
be a rebel, and in consequence, an enemy of society.

For Rita, who exalted every impulse and made
dramatic every relation, neither happiness nor
drama could endure. I taunted her once, in those
later days, with Wilde's saying that, *"He who
lives more lives than one, more deaths than one
must die."* But it was not deaths of the body that
she suffered: it was the deaths of all those human
relations—it was her rejection, day after day and
year after year, of all the natural bonds and un-
derstandings which make up the greater part of
human life—comfort, security, children, the pro-
tection and devotion of a husband, even simple
comradeship and affection—so that she was still,
at the time of which I write, an outlaw living from
hand to mouth, always poor and often ill, be-
devilled day and night by all the persons she no
longer had the energy to excite to her own pitch
of incandescence. And even at the time I had

taunted her, even at the time I had denounced her in the cab, it was my consciousness of this strength which had continued to keep me in subjection. For I knew now, in spite of all my pain, in spite of all my complaints and indignation, that if we have the instinct to admire what is admirable, we must also have the courage, and must not rage against—nor even try to minimize—that which makes it possible and mars it.

* * *

Outside, the light had grown cold; but the white and orange power of the lamps was beginning to dominate the town. The day seemed hardly now to have been serious: it was withdrawing, by arrangement with the city, which had so much to do at night. The taxis on Vanderbilt Avenue were wedging, honking and hitching, in their efforts to turn and to pass; but I dodged energetically through them and headed west.

If I could only find Daisy home! If only she were free to-night! I had refrained from telephoning on purpose: I wanted so desperately to see her, even if she were going out.

I could still feel the thrill of Fifth Avenue—I scarcely glanced a second time at a face which looked a little like Rita's. And that fascinating region of the Forties, where I had lately gone so rarely—I found that I could still peer with interest at the photographs in front of the theatres and at the faces of the passing women, who seemed sometimes, with their theatrical make-ups, as miraculously, ideally pretty as women on the stage.

The apartment-house where Daisy lived was narrow and very plain: there was merely a bare hall, with a telephone man, who also opened the door and ran the elevator.

He took me up to her floor, and I knocked at her room, but no one answered; then, as the door had been left half-open, I went inside. The lights had also been left on, and the chairs and the floor were littered with a débris of stockings and chemises, as surprisingly slight and as sordid as the shreds of exploded balloons. On the table stood an empty spaghetti can, two plates gummed with cold tomato sauce, several tumblers with the stale remains of drinks, and an empty gin-bottle. It seemed to me from the contents of the tumblers, that they had begun by drinking gin and ginger-ale, fallen back on gin and bathroom water, and probably ended up with raw gin.

It would be hours now, no doubt, before her rehearsal was over: I had come far too early, had better go away and come back. I looked about the room, and then searched in my pockets, for paper to write her a note, but could find nothing except a letter from a distinguished professor of philosophy whom I had greatly admired at college and to whom I had sent a book of Rita's poems: he had written me, thanking me for the poems and inviting me to come to see him. I had thrown the envelope away, but my respect for the professor had been so strong that I had never destroyed his letter, though my preoccupation with Rita had prevented my answering it.

But now, as I could find nothing else—finally reflecting that colleges, after all, were places where poets were put to sleep—I tore off part of the back page of the letter, just below the signature, and sitting down in a mission morris-chair, I wrote a note to Daisy.

When I had finished the note, however, I turned over the pages of the magazine—it was a movie magazine called *Photo-Life*—which I had picked up to hold the paper on. Suddenly becalmed in that abandoned apartment, high aloft on that inaccessible floor, with the elevator between me and the street, I found that I had dropped into a pocket of inertia and lassitude. When I had exhausted *Photo-Life,* I looked carefully, with the same serious interest, through *Zit's Weekly,* the *Cosmopolitan* and a tabloid of two days before. Then, with the magazines in my lap, I remained blank and incapable of rising: I apprehended the onset of despair. What motive had I for moving? I could no longer go to see Rita, and was there any one else in New York whom I really desired to see? It was as if the emptiness of Daisy's room had represented the emptiness of the world where I had been left by Rita's departure. I had not slept much for several nights, and I felt that my joints were heavy. The telephone rang: I did not answer it.

There was a phonograph beside me on the table: it was a small cheap portable one. I regarded it with hebetude. Without Daisy, it seemed as depressing as the glasses, as the garments, as the magazines. But involuntarily grasping at a last resource against despair, I picked up the heap of phonograph records, lying half-shuffled, like a battered pack of cards. Scrupulously I pushed them even and ran through them, reading all the titles: *With You in Paradise,* from *Pretty Kitty,* sung by Bee Brewster; *Ben Bolt,* by John McCormack; *Chanson Hindoue,* Saxophone solo; *So's Your Old Man,* Fox Trot, by Fred Casey and His Burglar-Alarm Boys; *La Forza del Destino,* Red Seal, Duet by Caruso and Scotti; *Mamie Rose,* Fox Trot, by Jake King and His Eight Kentucky Mocking-Birds. I remembered that *Mamie Rose* was the fox-trot which Daisy had so offended by playing, the night of Ray Coleman's party, when Rita had been reciting her poems. I got up and put it on the machine.

The record, I noted, as I wound the crank, had been made by the American Melody Company: it was a pale and unpleasant brown and seemed to have been moulded in river mud. Remembering the handsome victrola which I had seen at Ray Coleman's apartment, I pitied Daisy a little; yet she had had the right sort of bravery, the bravery to go free when love had passed! The only needles I could find were in an ash-tray, under the débris of cigarette-butts and burnt matches, and it was impossible to tell the used from the new: the first I tried began with a blurt, a hideous stuttering blur. Still dominated by Rita's tastes, I began to feel that turning on the phonograph would be like applying to myself a dental engine: Rita had not cared for popular music—had thought lightly of even the *Rosenkavalier!*

The second needle turned out no better, but I let it go; and presently *Mamie Rose* emerged as a kind of fiendish jig, running itself off at impossible speed: too fast, too nasal, too shrill. I made an effort to regulate it and only effected a harrowing descent of pitch, like the gasping and discordant howl of some demon inside the machine crying out in intolerable agony at being compressed from one tempo to another. I listened for the first night I had met Daisy, but merely succeeded in having my heart wrung by the first night I had heard Rita's poems. The spring of the little phonograph held only for a single winding, so that the record began too fast and was already running down before it came to the end; but, what was worse, it had no horn, so that the demon inside the box, beating in its cramped black prison like a panic-stricken bat, had to squeeze out, as it were, through a crack—the little aperture at the base of the "arm." No wonder it chittered and squealed so thinly, like an unwinding wire of sound, like a wire, rusted, wry and eaten, worn away so that it seemed almost snapping, or so rough that it would stick and stammer over some echolaliac phrase! So completely had the music been robbed of resonance that it seemed a mere memorandum of music, as if some writer in sound had scribbled down the skeleton of an orchestration, with the brasses brief tin-whistle blasts and raspings, the strings a jotted jingle of cicada-chirpings, and the tympani scored as tiny explosions and echoless crashes of glass. And the "vocal refrain," when it suddenly began, had as little in common with the human voice as the noises of the instruments had with music: it gave the effect of some mere momentary modulation in the quick mechanical jigging of a railroad train—it was simply a sharper shrillness, a more insistent iteration: *There she goes— Mamie Rose—She—loves—me!—Don't seem to show it!—How do I know it?—It's A. B. C.!—*

She's a crackle of high-pitched syllables ending
with *aggravatin'. But when I want a little lovin'
she don't keep me waitin'!—She's proud and
snooty—But she's my cutie!—She tells me* a second slip of dulled and driven cogs—*That's how
I knows—Mamie Rose!—She—loves—me!* The
jazz departed, with redoubled violence and com-
plexities of deformation, into a last frantic chari-
vari—then, after a brief unpleasing flourish, was
bitten off as abruptly as it began.

I lifted the needle, clicked the little catch and
went over to the window. Outside, gaped a blank
abyss: several buildings had just been demolished
and the vacuum of vacancy they had left seemed
to be sucking with its blind raw walls for some
structure to rush in and fill it. I felt again the
horrible imminence of despair, and I tried to summon against that blank outlook and against the
mechanical voice of the phonograph—those ne-
gations of flesh and blood—an intensified vision
of Daisy: her alert little yellow head, with its
deep stainings of Irish rust, her lips still moist
through carnation rouge, and the robust little organism of her body, which made its home among
those stone and metal cells, not merely resilient to
their surface, but making their grindings quicken
and feed it.—Then a sudden voice said, "Hello!"
and with a start I turned round and saw her.

I asked her to come to dinner with me. She
had on a dark blue street dress, and she looked
tired; I had been imagining her animated and
hearty, but it seemed to me now that she was frail:
her eyes, a lighter green than Rita's, looked colorless and dim.—"Why—I'd like to," she demurred,
"but I've got a sort of a date."

The telephone rang again and she answered it:
I heard her begging off with her little-girl-like
"Well, I don't think I will—I'm so tired—I just
got back from rehearsal—I think I'll go to bed—
well, I don't think I will—you go—well, I don't
want to—all right, see you to-morrow!"

And I felt, not merely flattered, but also reassured, to find that Daisy seemed to think it natural
to set aside her previous engagements in favor of
those higher obligations—of which I had learned
the importance from Rita—of following one's
own inclination.

"I'm glad you came," she explained. "I didn't
want to go to that party and if you hadn't come,
I would have gone." "Where was it?" I asked.
"At Myra Busch's." "Are her parties any fun?"
She shook her head contemptuously: "No: she
just has a lot of twirps.—I can't stand 'em!"

"How cute you sounded talking over the telephone!" "Yes: strong men weep!" "No, really:
you're awfully cute!" "You don't mean it really,
do you? It's a panic, isn't it?" "No: I do mean
it! You sounded cute." (Now that I had to re-
new my assurances, I began to feel insincere—I
had so long praised no one but Rita, and had
praised her with such passionate conviction, that
I found now that it cost me an effort to compliment any one else.) "Ray Coleman used to say
that I had the world's worst voice on the telephone
—he said I sounded like some awful whining
cash-girl." Another proof of Ray's stupidity! I
could see what he meant, but there was about
Daisy's speech something finely chiselled like her
features, so that I had scarcely been aware of her

voice; and my resentment at Ray's stupid taste
imparted to my compliments a new fervor.

"Shall I go out and get a drink?" I suggested.
"That would be fine!" said Daisy, brightening,
and with the humorous consciousness of brightening, that irony of the city I so liked in her. "As
the English actor said, when the girl said, 'How
about twenty-five dollars?'—'That would be a
godsend!'—I'll be getting dressed while you're
gone."

When I came back, she was still in the bathroom, and called out to me: "You might pass me
a drink in here, if you don't mind." I poured the
dregs out of one of the glasses and handed in
some gin and ginger-ale: her little naked arm,
reached out from behind the door, had the prettiness of a child's.—"Now, you turn on the phonograph," she called to me, "so you won't hear me
use the what-not!" I started *Mamie Rose* again
and poured out a drink for myself: the music
seemed almost gay and, when the record had
come to an end, I put on another record.

When she came out, she looked a good deal
rosier and extremely clean: she was dressed in a
light blue dress, with a blue scarf dappled with
white, and wore straw-colored stockings. "How
nice you look in your blond clothes!" I told her.
"Oh, this is just an old rag!" she squeaked in a
burlesque hen's voice. "Well," I insisted, "you
look sweet!" "I probably look like the Collapse
of Western Civilization!" she replied—but with
a particularly charming smile.

She turned off the phonograph, which had been
gibbering like an imbecile over a single unintelli-

gible phrase. "That phonograph's a delight, isn't it?" she said. "I took it with me when I left Ray, because it was one of the only things I had left that had belonged to me before I lived withum. Phil gave it to me on our honeymoon. Some of those records are Ray's, though, I guess." I remembered Rita's bookcase.

"Phil was your first husband, was he?" "Yes: he's my ex," she said.—She went on, after a moment: "Did you think I was really married to Ray?" "Yes," I said, "I did." "I guess a good many people really did. But we weren't. It was a lucky thing, too: if I'd marriedum, it would have been harder to leavum." "Did you have a pretty trying time?" I asked. "He wouldn't let me do anything or go any place. If I went out with anybody else, he'd burn up one of my dresses—he was great on burning things up—I used to tellum that if he'd lived a little longer ago, he'd have been burning witches.—He'd say that he didn't buy me clothes to have me go out with other men. And then when I did stay home withum, I'd just have to listen to-um read to me out of the *Oxford Book of English Verse*.—Finally, one night I got reckless and stayed out for two days with Pete Bird"—(Pete Bird was the little man with whom I had seen her talking at Ray Coleman's and in whose company I had found her the night before)—"and when I came back, he wouldn't let me in, so there was nothing to do but go looping again—I was plastered for a week. Finally Gus Dunbar offered to let me stay here—it was awfully decent ofum and he just did it out of friendliness. He helped me get a job, too. I understand that Myra Busch is telling it around the Village that I'm having a love-affair with Gus —but that's just absurd—he's my oldest friend in New York: I knew him back in Pittsburgh. He's just my yes-man. He lets me sleep in the bed and he sleeps on the couch. And besides, he's sick!— He's gone out of town and I'm going to get a good rest. Oh, how I'm going to rest!"

We continued the conversation in a chop-house, with red-and-white checked table-cloths and the smell of a butcher-shop, where very large sour pickles were served with every order, on the side.

"What sort of a fellow is Pete Bird?" I inquired. "Isn't he more or less of a twirp?" "Well," she said, "he did pretty well the other night: he spent about a hundred and thirty dollars." Even allowing for the tremendous prestige which always attached in New York to the spending of large sums of money, I felt a little that she was evading my question, but I didn't pursue the matter further: I seemed to divine that Pete Bird was the man with whom she had broken her engagement to go to Myra Busch's that night.

I asked Daisy how she had ever happened to run away with Ray. "I metum in the Ritz Bar in Paris," she explained. "Phil and I didn't care anything about each other, by that time—Phil was in love with a French girl. I didn't resent his having affairs with other women, but he used to give her my clothes.—Besides, I didn't want to have people saying: 'That poor little Mrs. Meissner, sitting around crying her eyes out, while her husband goes with other women!' Besides, Phil and I had just been thrown out of our hotel.

Phil had a lot of money when I marriedum, but we spent it all. Ray came along and he seemed to be pretty affluent at that time, and I was so tired of not paying any bills.—I will say about Phil, though, that he did everything with a grand air. Ray would get worried if a bill ran for as much as a week—whereas Phil never thought of paying a bill, even if he had the money. It was funny: when you were with Phil, you felt that you were swell, even though you didn't have a cent—but when you were with Ray, even though everything was paid for and all the bell-boys and everybody tipped, you felt you were only trying to be swell."

I asked what Phil did. "He was a photographer," she replied. "Not an ordinary photographer, but one of these super-photographers. He only took a picture about once every two months —he'd charge a hundred and fifty dollars for a sitting. At least that's what he did when he did anything. He had money—at least, he did till his family wouldn't givum any more—so he didn't really have to do anything.—He composed songs, too.—But what he really worked hardest at was getting up practical jokes. He'd spend hours sending out invitations to all the worst bums in Paris, asking them to come to dinner at the house of one of the social leaders of the American colony." "What happened?" I asked. "Well, they all showed up—all the dope-fiends and dead-beats, and all the old drunken bozos that hang around the bars—all the most undesirable Americans in Paris—and Mrs. Tilford was furious and almost gottum arrested. Then another time, when he had to have lunch with some friends of his family's from Pittsburgh, he put camphorated oil on the seats of all their chairs—well, camphorated oil makes you feel as if you were freezing—so they all had to sit there at the table with their fannies freezing and not knowing what was the trouble."

I laughed. "Well, that sort of thing," she explained, "can get to be pretty tiresome, if you live with it all the time. And I was his wife, so I felt partly responsible. When some guest almost broke his back on a chair that flattened out when you sat in it, I'd feel pretty humiliated.—And then he'd work his gags on me. One day he left a note for me, saying that he'd committed suicide. And I suppose he thought it was a joke when he took half my clothes away and told me that he was sending them to the devastated regions, and then gave 'em to-uz little French twirp!"

We had ordered ginger-ale, and had had some more gin: "You really look marvellous in blue!" I said. She knocked herself under the chin: "That sets me all up," she said, meeting my gaze without blinking. Then she dropped her eyes and added: "Phil really had a lot of charm, though."

"What shall we do after dinner?" I asked. "Take me to the movies!" she said, smiling. "I've had a yen to see some movies all day: I want to do something restful.—Take me to something funny. —I'm so glad you came to-night! I've been beginning to feel like a twirp. If I keep getting plastered like I have been, I'll lose my job.—It's so long since I've been alone or had any place where I could go and be by myself. It seems to me I haven't done anything for weeks but sit around and be funny for people I didn't really care about.—Gee, I don't know what to do! When I begin to get paid, I can live on what I make. But I've been afraid to sober up, because then I'd have to face the future." (She always gave to all her clichés—"facing the future," etc.—a special ironic emphasis.) "I can't think of anybody I care about —I haven't even got a girl-friend any more: all the ones that I had are off me now because Ray wouldn't let me have 'em around. So I haven't even got anybody to laugh about things with.— Business of twisting handkerchief.—Let's go, before I have you in tears!"

We had a reckless taxi-driver; but to me, strong with accelerations of gin and with my normal masculine self-assurance, which Rita had done so much to demoralize, now gratifyingly re-enforced by Daisy's feminine confession of helplessness and distress—it seemed to me at that moment that I occupied a position of unchallengeable supremacy—it seemed to me now that it had become possible for our taxi, at its exhilarating giddy speed, to plunge through every opposition, to make every obstruction give way. I marked with intensest vision the objects which we seemed to ride down: an American Railway Express truck; a woman with a German police dog; other scuttling and inferior taxis. Rita had always been nervous about El posts; but, as we ripped our way through the traffic, Daisy merely remarked: "Madcap Joe: the Demon Driver!"— and as we erupted into Broadway: "You better stop him or he'll drive into the lobby!"

I thought scornfully of Duff Burdan, who had been barking so long on Rita's doorstep, and who, for the privilege of storing Rita's furniture, for the certainty of seeing her again, had been willing to render his studio uninhabitable.

In the darkened moving-picture house, we found the news-reel passing before us like a gray inconsecutive dream, and its images, as I watched them, seemed to swell with the significance of dreams.—A handsome buxom Sixteen-Year-Old Girl winning a Florida yacht-race in a bathing-suit to the blaring triumphant pace of a red-white-and-blue Sousa march. "She's cute," whispered Daisy, "isn't she?" Yes: there was the real native American poetry!—my spirit flashed again at the thought of it—it had the daring and excitement of a poem!—and such a spirit, which abandoned itself to the water and the wind, to the speed of the flying yacht, would she not give herself also to love beneath the nights of southern waters!—Mayor Hylan—*East Side, West Side* —making a speech in New York: the flat-faced official visage, the senseless savorless words of the American public figure—while the brave filled the air with words of fire or slashed with white sails and tanned arms the deep blue of Florida seas!—free America that flew above those drones, that never paused for a thought of Mayor Hylan and his imbecile servile speeches; in our eagerness, our taut attention, stimulated more by the drinks than the film, Daisy and I were sitting forward and our arms were pressing each other.— An aeroplane wafted by a waltz—I had missed the title, my mind ablaze with the beauty of poetry and sportsmanship—below, the city, flat as a map, a plane shifted, not haphazardly, but with some underlying harmony and balance, to a jerky succession of angles.—Laddy Boy's Rival, a husky brought to Washington, to the gallop of some lolloping dog music, by one of Harding's Secret Service Men—I whispered, "I believe that that husky would make good presidential timber!" I glanced aside at Daisy and saw her profile pale and clear as porcelain in the pale light from the film, in which her pert little nose and chin showed a fineness and purity of outline—an outline prolonged by the frail hand which, with the fingertips lifted to the chin, received also, along fingers and wrist, a pale porcelain border of light.— Members of the Municipal Council at Baka, Japan, to the tune of *We're Gentlemen of Japan,* visit the city's reservoir; they jump in and catch carp with their hands: "I should think it would be bad enough," whispered Daisy, "to have to drink the carp, without drinking the municipal councillors," and I so threw myself forward in laughing at this that Daisy became self-conscious about the pressure of our arms on the seat, and drew a little away.—A slow-motion diving picture of champion woman swimmers—they turned along the sweet lengthened rhythms of *All Alone with the Telephone,* curving wonderfully through the air in moulded recumbent postures and sending up, when they had slipped into the water, a slowly condensing cloud of spray—how Rita would have loved those slow parabolas, stripped clean of the flashiness of speed, as tight-strung as the curve of a bow—she would have exclaimed of the cloud of spray, "It's like some lovely sort of punctuation—as if you could punctuate a statue with some solid effect of light!"—The Prince of Wales—*It's a Long Way to Tipperary*—joking with a paralyzed soldier—I wondered whether Rita would find the Prince of Wales attractive, then reflected that, on the contrary, she would probably be just perverse enough to prefer the paralyzed soldier: it occurred to me now to consider that I was becoming too much preoccupied with Rita and not paying enough attention to Daisy, so I moved my arm back against hers.—Jo LeBlanc, Head of the New Central Ticket Office, playing tennis to the jigging tune of *Tea for Two and Two for Tea,* to decide who shall pay the religious expenses of one hundred Jewish children to aid the Jewish Education Association Drive— "I bet the other man loses, don't you?" Daisy remarked. I wondered whether perhaps, after all, I hadn't been unfair to Max Kaufman—whether, perhaps, what I had taken for complacency hadn't been, after all, merely modesty—I had a pang as I was revisited by the feeling that I had behaved badly with Rita in the taxi.—Bishop Manning, to the firm exaltation of the *Pilgrim's Chorus,* receiving an emblematic pastoral staff, a huge encrusted crozier, from the Chaplain of the House of Commons—Daisy and I thought that Bishop Manning had the look of a priggish baby being handed an enormous rattle: I put my hand gently over Daisy's, which lay beneath it cool and friendly.—A Chimpanzee Chauffeur: roguish monkey music: *Yes, We Have No Bananas;* but I had fallen to reflecting that, like some hero of a

mediæval legend—the *Pilgrim's Chorus* and the
pastoral staff had made me see myself in that
image—I had, for a dreamlike space escaping
measure, been shut away with Venus under the
hill, or, like Oisin, with some goddess of fairyland—that I had been gone from the world of
men, and only now, still blinking from the Venus-
berg, still with the music of fairyland in my ears,
still knowing how the ache for the ideal may torture us like the ache for a drug of which we have
been deprived, beheld with joy, with bewildered
relief, the vision of Senator Oscar W. Under-
wood, who—to the rousing music of *Dixie*—was
making a speech at a Monster Barbecue in Mont-
gomery, Alabama—and found myself almost safe
again in that familiar American world, hetero-
geneous and absurd, which had ceased for so long
to seem real to me, of which I had never for so
long been aware save to repudiate it with scorn
and impatience. The Oldest Human Remains, a
Skeleton of the Stone Age Discovered in an Oys-
ter Bed: black bones embedded in oysters: dull
sombre chords—Rita could have done something
with this—something bitter about the fatuity of
the twentieth-century traveller who was pointing
at the bones with his stick—or better—what I
could never have done: it was I who would have
made easy capital out of the traveller with the
spectacles and the stick!—something simple, troub-
ling and hard about the bare black bones themselves.

And the smoothly revolving globe, supported
by a kneeling goddess and scrolling suddenly and
rapidly out—as if in the burst of an exciting rev-

elation—the title of the comedy that followed—
affected me, in a drop equally sudden, as idiotic
and insupportable: now that I had been brooding
on those blackened bones, I had become impatient
with everything again—and I crushed my way
across to the aisle, over overcoats, seats, and
knees. I got some waxed-paper cups from the
smoking-room, and Daisy and I, in the half-dark-
ness, had a drink of water and gin. The paper
cups leaked, and we had to get it down at a draft.

On the screen, a dough-faced comedian with
goggling horn-rimmed glasses was enlisting in a
fire-brigade.—An alarm!—he is the first to respond—he rushes headlong for the fire-house
pole, slides down it head-first and remains at the
bottom stunned: the firemen who follow fall over
him and pile up like a football scrimmage. We
laughed at this; and, on the way to the fire, the
long hook-and-ladder truck, whisking briskly
around a corner with impossible nimbleness,
caused Daisy to laugh so violently that I thought
again, as I had done on the night when I had
heard about her motor-cycle honeymoon, of that
American sense of motor-traffic which we had developed to such an extraordinary degree—and
which was now further played upon, in the film,
when the hero, in goggling innocence, allowed his
hook-and-ladder attachment to swing around at
right-angles to the truck, so that it swept the
boulevard like a scythe, mowing the tops off all
the Fords, and never failing at every disaster to
make Daisy laugh with delight.—On the scene of
the burning building, the hero was contending
with the hose, which enmeshed him like a boa-

constrictor. The owner of the building appeared, a pompous and imposing dignitary, in a frock-coat and silk hat. "Oh, I hope he turns the hose on his hat, don't you?" whispered Daisy. And in a moment, just as the dignitary was denouncing the clumsiness of the hero, an unexpected leak in the hose cleanly squirted off the silk hat, which landed on an organ-grinder's monkey and gave rise to a fantastic chase.

Such was our wild exhilaration over this that I reflected, as the chase began to flag, how, only half a year ago, if I had gone to the same film with Hugo, I should, in laughing at the ruin of the hat, have been moved by something more than the impulse, the mischievous impulse of a child, which I shared to-night with Daisy: I should have laughed with both savagery and zeal. I should, like Hugo, have taken the silk hat as a symbol; I should have made of its destruction an issue. And now at last I became aware how completely my point of view had changed since I had fallen in love with Rita and ceased to see much of Hugo. Had I not myself, only a few days before, taken out my own silk hat to go with Rita to the *Rosenkavalier?* I knew now that I no longer cared to imitate Hugo's intransigeance in matters of this kind: his rejection of all the amenities of that civilized life of which he was himself the product; his fixed belief that society was divided into two mutually hostile classes, a proletariat and a bourgeoisie; his unquestioning acceptance of the catchwords of the social revolution, and his hostile and suspicious unwillingness to arrive at a human understanding with people who lived by different catchwords—all this seemed to me to-night the product of a superficial point of view, or, almost, of an arrested development. For Rita, despite the revolt against conventions which all her life implied, despite her long association with radicals, had had really but little interest in politics: her revolt was a revolt of the individual—and I had discovered to my surprise, when I had come to discuss with her the personalities of the Village, her complete lack of interest in, and, in some cases, her positive contempt for, certain of the radical leaders who most generally commanded admiration; and that, despite the atmosphere in which she lived, it was actually possible to strike fire from her mind by reactionary or conventional views, if they were delivered with the right ring of bravery. And I had myself, oblivious of the film, taken to meditating so exaltedly on the vanity of people's opinions beside the deeper realities of character, the insignificance of politics compared to clairvoyance and passion, that I began to laugh only belatedly when I had already become aware that Daisy was roaring over one of the captions. The hero with the horn-rimmed spectacles had just been bitten by a small bull-terrier, and had picked it up and bitten it back: the caption read, "See how you like it yourself!"

"Oh, I'm so glad you took me!" said Daisy. "I think it's swell! I just wanted to see something funny!" I slipped my hand over hers again with sympathetic affection, and watched the rest of the comedy leaning toward her and paying closer attention. We followed the picture together, with a lively interchange of comment.

"Well, I suppose you want to go to bed," I said to Daisy as we walked out into Broadway. I suggested that we might stop at a restaurant and finish up the gin. "No," she said, "I'm too tired for a restaurant.—Why don't you come up to my place and we can drink it up there?—'Should she ask him in?' If he's got anything to drink: Yes!"

When we reached the room, the telephone was ringing. Daisy answered it, speaking with some vehemence: "No: I don't want to come—I'm tired, I've gone to bed—well, I went out to get something to eat.—No, I *don't want* to come!"

She lay down upon the bed, propping her head on the pillow and crossing her feet: she was wearing lizard-skin shoes, light brown and very small, but quite different-looking, I reflected, from any shoes that Rita wore: Rita's feet, like everything about her, seemed to manage to be attractive in a curious personal way quite apart from current fashions of prettiness, whereas Daisy's feet were pretty in an almost perfect ideal way, like the small feet of the girls with slim ankles in the drawings in magazines.

"Well," yawned Daisy, "this is where Mother takes a long refreshing rest!" I handed her her gin and ginger-ale and sat down beside her, drinking mine. "But I'm afraid I'm not going to be able to," she added, after a moment. "That's why I want a drink."

"What's the matter?" I asked. "Are you worried?" "No," she replied. "I've just got the heeby-jeebies!" "What's the matter?" "I think everybody's a twirp!" "Are you in love?" "No;

that's the trouble." "You ought to be glad you're
not," I said. "You have been, haven't you?"
she asked. "Yes." "You still are, aren't you?"
"No," I answered—"not any more." She was
trying to kick out of her shoes without unbutton-
ing the straps, and I undid them and lifted them
off. "Thanks," she said. "As soon as I lie down,
I'm dead!"

I held her firm little insteps for a moment in
my hands: in pale stockings, her tired and sweaty
feet were like two little moist cream-cheeses en-
cased in covers of cloth: her body, which seemed
now so slight in its pale blue dress, lay as limp as a
lettuce-leaf soaked by the summer rain.

"No," I said. "You oughtn't to be sorry if
you're not in love." "I know: that's what I keep
saying to myself when I think what damn fools
people make of themselves. But sometimes you
feel the old aching in the arm-pits—and it's not
just because you want to sleep with somebody
either.—You know the real reason that I asked
you to come up here? It was because I knew it
would give me the willies to come back alone. As
soon as I get alone, everything seems so empty—
I begin to get panicky. Of course, it's just the
heeby-jeebies, though—after I've had a good
night's sleep, I'll be all right again."

A deep tenderness of sympathy seemed to flush
my very mind, and I almost felt she must feel
its warmth as it brimmed from my soul and
bathed her. I put one arm about her shoulders
and with the other hand covered her breast—it
was low and lapsed a little—Rita, for all her small
head, her small hands and feet, had had the bosom

of some divine being—and from Ray Coleman's
gesture at the party, when he had put his arms
about Daisy, and from McIlvaine's plump little
Venus, I had been imagining Daisy's breasts as
little firm globes. I kissed her on the neck—
which was round and short and had no sculptural
contours like Rita's—and she kissed me back on
the cheek: it was like the kiss of a little girl, some
cousin or playmate from next door, whom, at
ten, one decides to marry, and the relief of that
human kiss, that embrace of simple comradeship,
soothed the strain with which my spirit, with
which my body itself, had ached.

I stretched myself beside her. If I had ever
had any idea—playing the part I had learned
from Rita—of making love to Daisy that night,
I knew now that it had never been real, I could
not now even conceive it—it was so long since I
had heard the boats as they moaned from the
harbor in Twelfth Street and the thought of them
no longer moved me, yet to try to love another
woman on the day one had parted from Rita! . . .
And there began to take music in my weary, in
my half-drunken, mind the falling rhythm of a
poem, the beginning of a sonnet of which, the
night before in my wakefulness, I had with obstinacy fixed in their target the accurate shafts
of the end. It took the form of an answer to
Daisy, and I found now that what had then been
unbearable, because written of myself for myself,
now that I could write from the point of departure of another's fate than mine, now that I could
dramatize my fate for another—dignifying, or
rather creating, for another person's mind—another's mind which I merely imagined, since

Daisy, it seemed, hated poetry—a romance which should somehow console me for the wreck and defilement of romance—now I could bear to return to the poem, and to the pain which had stamped its images, putting another between them and me—*"Ah, never sigh for love, for love is death!"* . . .

She was asleep—I could hear her breath: it seemed so slight to supply the fuel for that warm body I felt against my arm, that engine of activity and desire!—I turned off the electric light, covered Daisy over with a blanket, and lay down myself on the couch—and with the silence of the mind, love was still.

III

I HAD made a dinner engagement with Daisy for the next evening but one after the night when I had taken her to the movies; but the sudden death of one of my aunts, who had for many years lived with my mother, prevented my keeping it. I was obliged to go down to the country, and for several weeks I commuted between my mother's house and my work. Sustained by the vision of Rita renouncing the vanities of passion and vowed in solitude to her play, I applied myself to reading Sophocles, who at college had always bored me, but of whom I had so often heard it said that he saw life steadily and saw it whole that I wondered whether, in my present situation, I mightn't perhaps be able to benefit by his wisdom. Rather, however, than risk a first evening alone in my Bank Street apartment, where for so long I had seen no one but Rita, I had asked Daisy to have dinner with me the night of my return to town.

When I dropped my suit-case in the darkened sitting-room, with its drawn blinds and its frigid radiator, I felt for a moment, with a shudder, the shock of that current of emotion which I had hoped had been for ever disconnected when Rita had moved out of Twelfth Street, but which I found now that my own possessions, themselves saturated with Rita, had also the power of conducting. At the sight of the couch, the Leonardo (which Rita had admired), the Pernod peach-brandy bottle on the little marble mantelpiece (I had kept it there ever since the night when Rita had spoken of the label)—my heart sank as it had done in Twelfth Street the day when I had heard the boat-whistles. But I resolutely thought of Daisy—and as gaily as I had ever done, it seemed to me, I took my bath, changed my clothes, picked out an appropriate tie. I threw away the peach-brandy bottle, which the last time I had looked at it on the mantel on the occasion of a ghastly scene with Rita, I had had a violent impulse to smash as an outlet for my exacerbated passion: it fell in the waste-basket with a thud which astounded and routed my nerves. I was throwing in, as if to cover and conceal it, all the circulars which had accumulated during my absence when, on the tightened silence of the room, the telephone suddenly blazed.

It was somebody speaking for Daisy; I was to meet her now, not at Gus Dunbar's, but somewhere else—I couldn't make out where: the voice—it was a man's—kept instructing me just to walk right in and to ask for Mr. Somebody's—he was at once so indistinct and so admirably polite that I concluded he must be drunk. I asked if I could speak to Daisy, and her voice was presently heard through the receiver—she seemed far-away, facetious and vague. I tried to find out whether the place I was to go to were a speakeasy or a private apartment—but she only answered, "Yes," and laughed, and then insisted that I should walk right in and go right up to Somebody-or-other's. I begged her to spell out the name—and she began with loud-vibrating emphasis: "M for mother—I for 'ighball—C for

seasick—K for—Oh, you know K!—L for lar-
yngitis"—She began to laugh again, evidently
at some suggestion from somebody else in the
room. I tried to check up on the letters which I
had already heard, but she broke in: "Just put
them all together and they spell love!"—then,
with no relation to my further questions: "Yes,
'Mick'—just ask for Mick!—All right!—hurry
up!—Good-by!" She hung the receiver up: I
had, however, got the address.

The taxi carried me far, too far—beyond
Lexington Avenue—along East Thirty-fourth
Street: the neighborhood seemed to me sordid.
I had hoped to find Daisy, clean from her bath
and with her lovely candid smile, as on the night
when I had taken her to the movies: I had looked
forward to watching her in the light of the little
pink table-lamp, over the white cloth and yellow
wine of a brisk and bright French restaurant.

We drew up at a narrow entrance which the
driver located with difficulty between a manufac-
turer of nasal syphons and a merchant of rebuilt
typewriters. It was the meagrest pretense of a
doorway: a layer of livid imitation marble, a
length of blue-and-white rubber tiles. I looked
above the bells in vain for a name which began
with Mick; but then, in some of the grimy little
frames, there were not even any cards. I rang
one of the nameless bells—but it awakened no responsive click, and I rang another.

A man was coming out of the hallway, and I
asked him whether he knew of a Mr. Mickle. I
looked into dim and evasive eyes: I was appalled
to see that he had no chin, that his nose was an

almost elephantine proboscis and that his ears
stood out from his head like those of an elephant
listening; he wore an old shabby overcoat and a
curious gray felt hat, which tended to be conical;
his hands were non-prehensile, and trembled. He
shook his head without a word, in answer to my
question—and passed on like an apparition. I
thought: He must live alone!—he must have lived
alone for so long that he is numb and can no
longer feel loneliness, can no longer feel even irritation at strangers who are looking for friends
and who hurriedly break in on his solitude. And
I resented such an existence, solitary, dismal, and
uncouth, resigned to drop out of the world, hoping only to be noticed by no one; and I was re-
pelled by his strange trunklike snout: my own
nose, I remembered, was bulbous, and, as I
mounted the narrow staircase, it seemed to me
more bulbous than ever.

The stairs turned above the typewriter shop,
and I was confronted by the cramped and
crowded doors of cheap dentists and real-estate
offices. I explored the corridor, and found another staircase, and climbed to another and darker
hall, where there were no longer, as below, any
names painted on the doors. That was evidently
where people lived: it was as if the occupants had
made their homes in the chinks left by petty business: they seemed as narrowly confined, as dis-
couragingly inaccessible, as the inhabitants of a
jail—and they lacked even that common bond,
that limited intercommunication; each had stowed
himself dumbly away at the bottom of his little
slot, in oblivion of the others; each asked only to

be let alone at the end of the herded day—behind
the locked and anonymous door, presenting a
blank to all the rest, as they presented blanks to
him.

At random, I rang a bell—and, as if in confu-
tation of my vision of benumbed and sullen re-
cluses, after shuffling precipitate noises within,
the door was suddenly flung open and there appeared a lady with bright dyed red hair and a lacy
dowdy dressing-gown who, at the barest suggestion of a name which began with M-i-c-k, seemed
transported by enthusiasm. Yes: they lived just
across the hall—just opposite her own apartment.
"Yes: they're just in now," she ran on, slopping
over with friendly helpfulness and with a simper-
ing ladylike smile. "If you'd come a little later,
I don't think you'd have found them home, because they most always go out to dinner about
seven o'clock!" She eagerly crossed the hall in
her voluminous negligé and rang the bell herself.
I thanked her, but she did not withdraw. She
waited, repeating herself and beaming. I thought
her a little insane—from loneliness, I supposed.

Some one was hastening from the depths
within. Then Pete Bird opened the door and confronted me with a goggling stare. The red-haired
woman still lingered in the hall as if she hoped
for a little general conversation, but Pete Bird
merely asked me in, and shut the door behind us.

We passed through a little dark hallway and
emerged into a narrow sitting-room. I saw
Daisy in a morris chair with her legs dangling
over one arm and her back against the other: she
greeted me with an odd unsmiling daze. And,

still charmed by the memory of her paleness when
she had lain along the bed like a moonbeam the
night that I had taken her to the movies, I was
horrified to find her now with touzled, muddy
hair and a sallow, puffy visage, in which the nose
was an ignoble little knob, blobbed in candle wax,
and the eyes were two protruding gooseberries,
scored about with discolored skin: she was wearing a greenish-blackish plaid. I took her hand:
it was a cold little claw.

I remarked that she looked quite different, that
having her hair done differently had transformed
her: I saw now that the ragged effect had been
originally intentional. She said: "Yes, and I
suppose you're going to tell me that it looks terrible, too." "You look like a French whore!" said
Pete. "Well, you know what you look like?" said
Daisy. "You look like some kind of a goblin
that's been drowned at the bottom of a well!"
And it was true: with his gargoyle gaze, his hag-
gard, greenish cheeks, the deep furrows in his
forehead and the ape-like lines to his wide mouth,
he had an aspect half immature and half prema-
turely old, at once disaffected and aghast. There
seemed to have occurred, since I had talked to
them on the telephone, some abysmal lapse of hi-
larity. Yet Pete Bird's double-breasted jacket, his
spats, the handkerchief sticking out of his pocket,
and the collar of his blue shirt fastened together
by a small gold pin, gave to his appearance and to
the whole situation an odd indestructible note of
urbanity and smartness.

In that atmosphere clouded by drunkenness, I
glanced instinctively about for a drink, and saw

nothing but empty bottles and a débris of the enormous thick crusts of delicatessen sandwiches, with the oiled paper in which they had been wrapped. "There's nothing to drink," declared Daisy with what I thought was a note of asperity. "What is this place, anyway?" I asked. "Listen to-um!" said Daisy, indignantly. "He expects us to tend bar for-um!"

"No," I explained, "I just meant, who lives here?" "It belongs to Larry Mickler," she replied, as if she had already, over the telephone, made all this quite clear enough. "Mr. and Mrs. Lawrence Mickler," said Pete, with the invincible gentlemanly instinct to be informative and agreeable from his grave at the bottom of the well.

I inquired where the host and hostess were. "Well," said Pete, as if his own extinction, though powerless to impair his politeness, had rendered him uncannily detached toward the catastrophic fates of others, "Mr. Mickler's in the bathroom, probably unconscious, and Mrs. Mickler's in the bedroom, sore as a crab." "I insulted the hostess," said Daisy. "Well, anyway," concluded Pete, "that leaves the drawing-room to us!"

The drawing-room, like everything else in that place, cooped one up and made one uncomfortable: I saw, at the other end, a contracted fireplace, like a large square-cornered rat-hole, with, above it, on the shallow mantelpiece, a plaster cast of the Winged Victory; and between two narrow windows, which looked down on the Thirty-fourth Street car-tracks, a bookcase containing, I noted, volumes of D. H. Lawrence, Cabell, Dunsany, and Shaw; George Moore's *Memoirs of My Dead Life;* Freud's *Interpretation of Dreams;* Frank Harris's *Oscar Wilde;* several volumes of Levy's *Nietzsche* and a whole shelf's array of Dostoevsky.

"Come on," exclaimed Daisy abruptly, swinging out of the morris chair. "Let's get out of here right away!" I asked her where she wanted to dine, in the hope that we might now be able to effect a separation from Pete. "I don't want any dinner!" she replied, as if nothing could have seemed more revolting. "I've just had some sandwiches.—What I want is a dirty big drink!"

"I'd better say good-by to Larry," suggested Pete Bird. "I wouldn't say good-by to-um," said Daisy, "after the way he acted with us."

Pete went into the little corridor and knocked on the bathroom door. "We had a fight," Daisy explained. "We would have left before, if we hadn't been waiting for you. Larry sent Pete out to the delicatessen's to get some sandwiches for supper and gave him a ten-dollar bill—and Pete brought back six sandwiches and Larry didn't think that Pete had given-um back enough change and accused Pete of keeping the money—when they'd actually cost that much!" We could hear the voice of Pete in the bathroom, pleading with the host on a tone of gentlemanly reasonableness. I asked how the *Frolics* were going. "Oh, I got canned!" she replied, sullenly and shortly. "I stayed away from too many rehearsals."

Pete returned with Larry Mickler. He was a young man with dingy skin, a round head and a small dark mustache, very smartly and cockily waxed: he bent forward from the waist when he shook hands with me, and I took an almost immediate dislike to him: he was taller than Pete Bird, but not so tall as I.

Pete was urging Larry Mickler to come out with us, and I seconded him insincerely. "Get Alice out," Pete insisted, "and make her come along, too!" "Oh, she's tired," Larry Mickler perfunctorily assured him—"she doesn't want to come!"

"I'm not out for any looping," said Daisy, with what I thought—with what I hoped—was an intention of discouraging this idea. "I think I'll go home and go to bed." "You're not going home yet, little woman," Pete asserted, with a firm, though humorous, accent of masculine domination. "You're not going home to bed till you've had a little insomnia-medicine, a little touch of the magic elixir that causes the lame to see and the tongue-tied to run like rabbits! The old miracle-scattering scamper-juice!—Am I right?" he appealed to me.

"Let's go to Tony Scallopino's," suggested Larry Mickler. "Let's not!" said Daisy promptly. "You see," Pete Bird explained, with dignity, irony and ease, "Tony raised a check of mine once and I've never felt quite the same about him since." I proposed Harry Heinz's. "Well, Harry Heinz and I are not quite the best of friends either," Pete casually replied. "In my opinion, a restaurant is a place where the patrons are supposed to drink while the man who runs the place stays sober: when the guests have to take care of the proprietor and put him under the pump, I consider that the time has arrived to seek recreation elsewhere!"

"Let's go to Sue Borglum's!" said Daisy, with a sudden inspiration. "To-night is Thursday night, and she has a party every Thursday. I saw her the other day and I promised that I'd come.—Oh, I'm so glad I thought of that!" she added, smiling for the first time. "I want to see Sue Borglum!"

"All right: Sue Borglum's it is!" Pete approved, with rollicking decisiveness. "Come: snap into your coats, ladies and gents! Let's be off to some place where there's stimulants!"

I helped Daisy on with her coat, and as I caught a momentary glimpse of her pale watery-yolked poached eyes, it seemed to me—(Rita and I had read some scientific books together: the vision of human futility which she derived from scientific ideas exercised upon her a strong fascination, and threw her back with an exacerbated appetite on the gratification of the moment—and to-night it was these scientific images which rose to my own imagination at the expense of both Sophocles and Rita's poems themselves)—it seemed to me as if the Daisy whose profile had appeared to me in the theatre, so fragile, pale and chaste, whom almost with the tenderness of tears I had covered with a blanket in Forty-fourth Street —as if that Daisy had been merely the spray of which I had happened to catch a glimpse for a moment on a wave of common human colloids, the unstable fluids of the body, continually gluing and ungluing—or a cloud which had for a moment taken symmetry from those atoms of carbon and the other things, but which to-night had been blown awry. I turned Daisy's collar down carefully.

Larry Mickler had been getting into his coat, a garish rust-red ulster, and Pete Bird had been helping him on with it. Now Mickler pulled up his collar, which completely covered his ears, and slapped on a rakish felt hat, pulling the brim down over his eyes.

"You know, that damn statue annoys me!"— he indicated the Winged Victory: I saw that he was drunk. "Alice's had that goddam thing ever since we were married: she acquired it at college. It always reminds me of a chicken running around with its head cut off!"

He produced a revolver from his pocket and, almost before we had seen it, had fired before him point-blank at the little plaster cast: it fell from the mantel, and lay shattered in chalky fragments and flakes.

"Well," said Mickler, "so much for Nikky! Alice may miss her at first, but I'm sure it'll be a splendid thing for her to have to get along without her.—I feel almost," he added, grinning at us, "as if I'd committed a murder, though! 'Ad Writer Slays Phi Beta Kappa Girl!'—Well, let's go! The neighbors may be coming in to find out who's been shot!"

He turned to me, grinning, and explained, as if in friendly humorous confidence: "No disrespect to the Greeks!—I'm a Dionysian myself!—sometimes a Dionysian and sometimes an Apollonian!— it all depends on metabolism!" He began to sing, parodying the popular song:

"Sometimes I'm Dionysian!—sometimes I'm Apollonian!
My disposition depends on metabolism!"

Then, finding me a little unresponsive, he changed
his tone and addressed me more earnestly: "I just
wanted you to know," he insisted, "that I don't
mean any disrespect to the Greeks. The Greeks
knew what it was all about: they danced with
arms and legs—but we lock ourselves up in the
bathroom because we're afraid to face life!"

"Say, listen," declared Daisy, "if you're going
to go out with us, you've got to leave that thing
behind! I can face life without it." "Take it
along to protect you!" said Mickler. "Never know
who's going to stick you up nowadays!" "Don't
be a fool," said Daisy. "I won't, sweetheart," he
retorted. "Never you worry about that!"

"I'm going to say good-by to Alice!" said
Daisy, as if with a sudden resurgence of sympathy. She went out into the little hallway and
knocked at the bedroom door, but there was no
reply. "Oh, she's all right!" insisted Larry Mickler. "She probably thinks I've shot myself—let
her enjoy a few moments' happiness!" Pete and
Mickler put their arms around Daisy, propelled
her along the little hallway and pushed her out
through the apartment door.

Outside, we found the lady in the dressing-
gown, who giggled ingratiatingly: "I thought I
heard a shot." "I was just shooting a cat," said
Larry Mickler. "It was keeping my wife awake!"

I finally, standing in the slush, succeeded in
capturing a taxi; it couldn't draw up to the curb,
and Daisy got her feet wet. She seemed worried
and morose.

"That old hag'll lie awake all night," remarked Larry Mickler, with a chuckle, "thinking that I've killed Alice!" "Well," said Pete, "it will doubtless afford her a great deal of entertainment. I'm sure her life is far too tame!" "Yes," said Mickler, "how they lick their chops in vicarious enjoyment over other people's murders! How all the world loves a murderer!" "It would take more than that," said Daisy, "to make me love you!"

"I hear," said Larry Mickler, changing the subject and evidently attempting to talk more soberly —"I hear that Bobby McIlvaine has given Sue Borglum the air.—Is that true?" he inquired of Daisy. "Guess so," said Daisy. "I don't know." "I guess he decided that she'd done all she could for him," Larry Mickler continued, "and that it was time to move farther up-town!" (Sue Borglum, who knew every one, more or less, had taken Bobby McIlvaine up soon after the night that I had met them at Ray Coleman's, and had smoothed his way among the managers and dramatists.) I remarked that I considered Bobby McIlvaine a very gifted fellow, none the less, and that I admired his designs for Homer. "Yes," said Mickler, "but why not make designs for Wells's *Outline of History?* Why not try to produce the *World Almanac?*—Bobby McIlvaine's all right on paper, but did you ever see a show that he'd staged that was worth its space in the storehouse? Look at *April Showers,* for instance: Fritz Fishbein, Al Leiper's publicity man, blames Bobby for the show being a flop. It seems that Bobby insisted on putting in a trick ballet, where the chorus had to wear papier-mâché bodies. Al Leiper wanted to throw it out at dress rehearsal, because the papier-mâché bodies took up too much room behind—they could hardly change the scenery. But Bobby hit on the brilliant idea of sending them downstairs in an elevator—it seems they use elevators in Berlin. The first night, the elevator got stuck just before the second act and they couldn't ring the curtain up—they had to hold it twenty minutes. Finally, Al Leiper sent some stage-hands down with great big mallets and—zongo! zongo! zongo!—they just smashed in the elevator doors and threw all the papier-mâché bodies out in the alley—and then, when that was full, they threw them into Beattie's drug-store. There were all those pop-eyed dummies which Bobby had been working on for God knows how long lying around Beattie's—though I don't suppose you could have told them from the customers!—What a civilization, eh?" he turned to me again. "Bring slavery back, I say—it never should have been abolished! Bring slavery back and make nine-tenths of the people slaves! Then the superior man would be free to live life like it ought to be lived! As it is, the civilized man has got to black the peasant's boots!"

We had come to the end of Fifth Avenue, and Daisy, sliding back the glass panel that opened in the front of the cab, directed the driver to turn to the right.

Among those tangled irregular streets to the west of Washington Square, I caught occasionally, from the taxi, a glimpse, almost eighteenth-century, of a lampless black-windowed street-end where the street-urchins, shrieking in the silence,

were stacking up bonfires in the snow—those lost
corners of the old provincial city, where the traffic of the upper metropolis no longer gnashed iron
teeth, no longer oppressed the pavements with its
grindings and its groans—where those soft moans
and hoots of the shipping washed the island from
the western shore. There they had come, those
heroes of my youth, the artists and the prophets
of the Village, from the American factories and
farms, from the farthest towns and prairies—
there they had found it possible to leave behind
them the constraints and self-consciousness of
their homes, the shame of not making money—
there they had lived with their own imaginations
and followed their own thought. I did not know
that, with the coming of a second race, of which
Ray Coleman, without my divining it, had already
appeared as one of the forerunners—a mere miscellaneous hiving of New Yorkers like those in
any other part of town, with no leisure and no beliefs—I did not know that I was soon to see the
whole quarter fall a victim to the landlords and
the real-estate speculators, who would raise the
rents and wreck the old houses—till the sooty
peeling fronts of the south side of Washington
Square, to whose mysterious studios, when I had
first come to live in the Village, I had so much
longed some day to be admitted, should be re-
placed by fresh arty pinks—till the very guardian
façades of the north side should be gutted of their
ancient grandeurs and crammed tight with economized cells—till the very configuration of the
streets should be wiped out, during a few summer months when I had been out of New York

on vacation, by the obliteration of whole blocks, whole familiar neighborhoods—and till finally the beauty of the Square, the pattern of the park and the arch, the proportions of everything, should be spoiled by the first peaks of a mountain-range of modern apartment-houses (with electric refrigerators, uniformed elevator boys and, on the street-level, those smartly furnished restaurants in which Hugo was soon to be horrified at finding copies of *Town and Country*), dominating and crushing the Village, so that at last it seemed merely to survive as a base for those gigantic featureless mounds, swollen, clumsy, blunt, bleaching dismally with sandy yellow walls that sunlight which once, in the autumn, on the old fronts of the northern side, still the masters of their open plaza —when the shadows of the leafless trees seemed to drift across them like clouds—had warmed their roses to red.

Sue Borglum, at any rate, at the time of which I am writing, had rented the whole of a large old house (of which she sub-let the top floor and the basement) in one of the oldest obscurest streets, where the children, deserting their bonfire, came clamoring to open our door, and where the lights and sounds of the party seemed incongruously bright and loud amid the darkness and silence about. There were dark double ogival outer doors and, inside them, another pair of doors, with a design in frosted glass of sphinx-heads and vine-leaf scrolleries.

We pulled a bell, and a Jap let us in. Sue Borglum rushed up boisterously to greet us: she seemed high-keyed and overwrought, and embraced Daisy

with cries of *"Darling!"* In her blatant green
evening gown, with a rhinestone aigrette in her
hair and on her fingers a large scarab and some
diamonds, she seemed to me uglier than ever: her
cheeks were beginning to hang in jowls, her wide
mouth was a grotesque gash of lipstick, and the
pouches under her eyes were as distinctly shaded
off from her cheeks as if they had been drawn by
a caricaturist. Behind her, rose the hubbub of
the party: the hallway and the rooms were full of
people.

We had started up-stairs to put our things away
when Sue Borglum, gesticulating frantically toward a water-cooler in the hall near the staircase,
shouted after us: "Cocktails!—Cocktails!—That
water-cooler's full of cocktails.—Yes! Isn't it a
grand idea?"

Pete and Daisy came down first, and Sue had
already swept them off by the time Larry Mickler
and I had arrived at the foot of the stairs: we
stopped at the water-cooler and drew drinks.
Larry Mickler swallowed his at a gulp. "That
little bastard, Pete Bird!" he complained. "I gave
him ten dollars at my house to get some sandwiches for supper and what do you think he did?
He went out and got liverwurst—the cheapest
kind there is!—and then had the Christ-Almighty
nerve to bring me back four dollars change—six
dollars for six sandwiches!" I asked whether he
thought that Daisy was pretty fond of Pete. "She
hasn't got the capacity for love," he replied, shaking his head with a sneer and turning the spigot
for another cocktail. "But they're two of a kind
—out for what they can do you for! She's a

cold little proposition that calculates every kiss—
and he owes money, or he's passed bad checks, in
every joint below Fourteenth Street. It's wonderful how he's able to get away with it even
where they're cagy! He's got this soft-spoken
wide-eyed way with him.—Well, *he* can have
her!"

We moved on to the door of the front room.
Sue Borglum's front room was spacious and not
without a certain grandeur: I could see, above a
marble fireplace, the wide sheet of a gilt-framed
mirror, which doubled the high white mouldings
and the sombre maroon wall-paper.—Such a house
as I had once imagined for Rita and myself to
live in! Ah, I should have asked nothing better
of life than to have fitted up such a house, to have
passed my days alone with Rita in those high
quiet rooms, hidden away among those crooked
streets, with poetry and love!—But these fancies
now seemed to me naïve, and I was ashamed of
ever having had them. I stoically dismissed them
from my mind, and could still, I found, feel hope
and excitement amid the variety and gaiety of the
Village, so densely intermingling, so vivaciously
chattering about me: the Italian and Russian
painters; the intelligent amateur actors; the mad
baroness who kept a restaurant; the radical journalists and agitators, who, despite the homely
forthright style of their writings, not infrequently
turned out, when one met them, to be engagingly
shy, and sometimes to possess personal charm to
a degree almost cloying; the pretty Jewesses with
thick red lips and glossy black bobbed hair; the
austere and handsome woman managers of theatres and magazines, with their dignity of Mother

Superiors; and the megalomaniac lunatics whom it was the thing rather to like.

Larry Mickler and I, in the doorway, did not at first encounter any one we knew. "Well," said Mickler, lifting his cocktail, "here's to the Seven Deadly Sins! May they never perish from the earth!—Let's drink to the memory of Dostoevsky —the only goddam genius," he added, "who ever understood the human soul!" I drank with him to Dostoevsky. "The Seven Deadly Sins!" said Larry Mickler scornfully. "What chance have they got to-day when everybody wears these horn-rimmed glasses!"

I wondered whether it mightn't be true that a novelist like Dostoevsky was greater than any lyric poet, even so great a one as Rita—but suppose the play on which Rita was working should turn out to reveal wider gifts?—And, stimulated by my cocktail, I asked myself whether, in spite of everything, I shouldn't go to see her again, when she eventually came back from her aunt's: I had behaved so horribly when we had parted, and we had exchanged no letters since she left.

A man who had been leaning over the back of a couch that faced the marble fireplace moved away and let me see the head and neck of a woman who was sitting on the couch and whose bobbed and coppery hair reminded me of Rita's.—What a comfort that it could not be she! Then the wo-man, turning her head with a staccato birdlike movement, in some gay interchange with the man sitting next to her, revealed her profile and I saw that it was Rita. I could see also that the man was Ray Coleman.

My companion recognized him at the same

time: "There's Ray Coleman over there!" he exclaimed. "He's just got a new job on the *Sketch!*"
Larry Mickler made his way across the room. I
followed him, and spoke to Rita over the back of
the couch, taking care to betray no surprise.

"How long have you been back?" I inquired.
"Since last Friday—last Friday night," she replied, as if by frankness and accuracy to fend off
my disapproval.

I asked about her aunt: "She's much better,"
she assured me, smoothing out the creases of her
smile and making her eyes, which looked to me
now like little hard green pebbles of glass, serious
and blank. "The doctor said that she was simply
tired out, that all she needed was to rest. My
mother is still up there with her.—Do come around
and sit down!" I sat down, not beside her on the
couch, but on a stool at one side of the fireplace.

"You know, I was thinking about you," she
said, "just before I left!" "What made you do
that?" I asked. "I went wading in Stony River
one day—in the cold, and everything!—and I
thought about you then—because you liked the
poem, you know!—You know, it was freezing
cold: I almost froze my feet off—but somehow I
wanted to do it!"

I asked how she'd got on with her play. She
dropped her eyes, which had girlishly puckered
over her wading in Stony River: "Well, I haven't
actually *written* very much, but I've thought about
it a lot. I know just what I *want* to write—I've
got it all blocked out, you know!" And sustained
by this triumphant phrase, she lifted earnest eyes
to mine.

I said that she looked awfully well—and it was true: she had already been flushed by the excitement of conversation, and when I spoke to her, she had flushed more deeply, so that she burned like a little furnace, as she had done that first night in Bank Street when she and I had talked about poetry. She had brought back from the country a complexion refreshed from the tarnish of the city, and the contours of her face had filled out again: again she could challenge the world from the tower of her lovely throat, which gave to her little figure a dignity almost extra-human, like the dignity of a great work of art. "And I *feel* so well," she replied. "I went tramping and sleighing and skating!—I did all the things that I hadn't done since I was a little girl! And I tell you, I went *wading!*—you don't seem impressed by that, but I assure you it was no tame experience: the water was so cold that it burned! The snow is still on the ground up there, two feet deep —the river-banks were all crusted with ice—in some places there were little fragile translucent ledges of ice that came out over the water—just like blades of swords made of ice!—You know, I'm going to have a sword that's made of ice in my play—don't you think that's a wonderful idea?" "I should think it would break easily," I replied. "Not if it was sharp enough!" "Perhaps not." "Mine will be!" she held her own, grinning briefly. "Well, anyway, I went wading—and it was so *thrilling!* You haven't any idea how beautiful a river is in winter till you get right out in the middle of it and see the water still alive like quicksilver in the midst of the dead frozen landscape—running away between the wicked jagged edges! It's as if the tighter other things froze, the faster the river ran—like a live vein in a paralyzed body!"

Her feeling for Stony River, which had once so completely enchanted me, now irritated me profoundly. I could see plainly in imagination some tall young country boy, panting with desire and only too happy to accompany her on her uncomfortable escapade: he would have carried her, of course, over the bad spots—would, in fact, probably have carried her most of the time—he had ended no doubt by chafing her feet.

"It must have been wonderful," I replied, and turned away to listen to Ray Coleman. Lina Lemberg, the young Polish girl who had been convicted of murdering her husband, had just been sentenced to death; and Ray was describing with enthusiasm how he had pursued the car which was taking her to Sing Sing, and had succeeded in having her photographed from the taxi. (He had just left the *Telegram-Despatch* for the city desk of the *Daily Sketch,* the most important of the new tabloids.) "I see," said Larry Mickler, showing small white even teeth, "that she says she wishes Nicky were back with her." "She's going to get half her wish," said Ray—"She's going to get it fifty-fifty: she's not going to get Nicky back, but she's going to go to join him!" Larry Mickler laughed with loud appreciation. "Well," he remarked, "the murderer has his fun, and he ought to be willing to pay for it! True, he has to pay dearer than most people—but then he has more fun!"

Ray presented Larry Mickler to Rita: he did
so with obvious pride—with, it seemed to my
jealous eye, something akin to an air of proprietorship. Rita invited Larry Mickler to sit down,
and he took the stool on the other side of the fireplace. Ray Coleman inquired affably how Mickler's own work was going. "It's just the same old
hick-diddling game!" he replied, leaning forward,
his hands clasped between his knees. "We still
manage to land the suckers!" I thought that he
was ashamed of the advertising business, and was
being contemptuous about it for Rita's benefit.
"Our latest masterpiece was putting over Marona
—'Makes the Mouth Safe for Teeth!' was a product of our fly-paper factory." "You don't say!"
Ray Coleman exclaimed, raising his almost con-
tinuous eyebrows, as if this feat commanded respect. "Is that so?" "You know what it's made
of, don't you?" "No," admitted Ray Coleman,
"what?" "Horse-chestnuts! Nothing but horse-
chestnuts! Just nothing in the world but plain old
buckeyes! Can you beat it? A million and a-half
people every morning, sitting down to a breakfast
of buckeyes, with sugar and cream!" "Don't you
do anything to them?" asked Ray. "Not a blessed
thing!—just chop 'em up. We've struck such
terror into the hearts of the boobs by telling them
that ordinary food was soft and ruined their
teeth, and that in a few more generations the human race would be toothless, that now there are a
million and a half people breaking their jaws
every morning over horse-chestnuts! 'Makes the
Mouth Safe for Teeth!'—they find it irresistible!"

"Say," said Coleman, humorously, "isn't it

about time that the Osage orange got a break?"
"You might sell them for their perfume," said
Rita. "They have a marvellous smell, you know!"
"By Jove, that's a good idea!" said Coleman.
"You might have all the women carrying them
around!" I doubted whether on ordinary occasions he would have considered this a particularly
good idea—it seemed to me all too plain that he
had fallen under the spell of Rita and that he
thought only of playing up to her. I remembered
the night when I had first met them and when
Rita had agreed with me that Ray was poisonous.
"They'd be a little heavy, I'm afraid, to carry
around," said Rita. "And they wouldn't be becoming to many people. I might wear one, though
—a very little one—on account of the color of
my eyes!"

She was gay, and seemed to me so pleased with
herself, so sufficient to herself, so remote from
me; and I reflected that, while she had been speaking, I had been aware, for the first time since the
earliest days of our acquaintance, of her acquired
English accent. Not that she always spoke in this
way: she had the accent in which she recited her
poems and the accent of the Village gamine—nor
did she hesitate to bite down on a hard up-country r, when some special situation—a sundae at
the soda-fountain or a hammock on a porch—had
suggested to her versatile spirit the rôle of a girl
in a small town; but, coming in contact with English actresses during the days when she had been
on the stage, her natural disposition toward brit-
tleness and briskness had found their accent a con-
genial modification, and it was this accent which

usually predominated on occasions when she was meeting strangers. Yet how many times since that first night I must have heard her drop into this manner, without ever having been aware of it! And I was sharply forced to take account of the distance between the present and the days when I had first known Rita. Then, I had been in love— and that was what it meant to be in love: so to surround, so to devour, another human being with tenderness, passion, admiration, that their very absurdities and perversities had been fused with the rest in the furnace till there was nothing but a white molten glow—till one resented, not merely the hostility, but even the critical detachment of others, because the point of view of a critic was unimaginable from one's own. But that critical detachment, to-day it was I who exercised it—and at the thought that I could now meet Rita with a mind which had become so cold that I could note her little affectations, I was filled, not with the relief I hoped for and in which I tried to believe, but with horror and fear. She had gone, the creature who had summoned my love— or whom my love itself had created, I hardly now knew which—the being, who had commanded the allegiance of mind, imagination and desire—and could I never now rejoin her again? Was it true that my love had been destroyed? Could I never retrace my way? Could I never get back across that chasm?

"I declare," Larry Mickler was saying, "I don't know where a civilized man can find more hilarious entertainment than in the advertising game. You'd never believe what the boobs will consume

till you actually commence to feed 'em! You can
make 'em do anything, buy anything! All you
need is a gaudy picture and an idiotic phrase and
you can make them do themselves an actual in-
jury! Now, of course, in the case of Marona,
for example, horse-chestnuts are indigestible—
they make the mouth safe for teeth but they ruin
the digestion. But that doesn't discourage the
suckers for a minute. If they get sick, it would
never occur to them to blame it on the Marona,
because Marona, according to the ads, has been
endorsed by eminent dentists. Nothing was said
about stomach specialists.—But then I suppose
it's a desirable thing to provide the peritonitis
surgeons with work—they're usually civilized fellows, the surgeons, and, if they prosper at the expense of the peasantry, that's quite as it ought to
be.—You must have a lot of fun yourself"—he
addressed himself to Ray Coleman—"in the newspaper game."

"Yes," said Ray. "It's amazing really. You
can't lay it on too thick—the more maudlin and
preposterous it is, the better they seem to like it.
Have you been reading Lina Lemberg's confes-
sions in the *Sketch?* They're written by Ted Ma-
hony in the office—you know Ted, a big husky
Irishman who's always half-stewed. You know
that installment where she tells about the birth of
little Annie—well, when he read that aloud in the
office just after he'd written it, the other day, he
almost broke up the shop!"

I asked Rita where she was living. "Well, I'm
not living anywhere exactly," she answered. "I've
just been visiting around." She lifted her eyes

quickly. "I'll let you know when I'm settled."
"You must let me see your play, when it's finished," I said.

"Don't you think it's going to be fine?" Ray
Coleman demanded eagerly. "Have you heard
about the idea?" I assured him that I had. He
turned to Larry Mickler: "She's got the swellest
idea. It's about this old woman who lives in a
tower——"

Larry Mickler leaned forward to listen, with a
polite appreciative leer; and Ray Coleman described Rita's play with an enthusiasm even more
emphatic than he had brought to his previous account of the photographing of Lina Lemberg. And
it seemed to me that Rita herself was gratified by
this enthusiasm.

It had already occurred to me that Coleman
must be in love with Rita: everybody, more or
less, was. But now, with horror, I remembered
that, since Daisy had left him, he must be living
alone in his apartment, and that Rita, when I had
asked her where she was staying, had seemed
evasive about her address. I watched Ray Coleman telling the plot of Rita's play, and Rita herself, following intently and occasionally prompt-
ing or checking up—lifting her eyes briefly to
smile or to put in a quick supplementary word
when Larry Mickler expressed appreciation, and
punctuating the pauses with puffs at her cigarette.

I felt an urgent need to get away, and, looking
up, I saw Hugo Bamman, standing alone like a
heron, just back of Rita's couch, his head thrust
forward, his shoulders hunched up, his long arms
hugged to his sides and his hands in his trousers

pockets, staring out, as I supposed, half-blindly at the people moving about him.

I got up and went around to speak to him: I was glad of a pretext for leaving in the middle of Ray Coleman's recital.

When Hugo turned at my greeting, I was astounded to find his appearance completely transformed. Instead of regarding me at first for a moment with dubious unrecognizing goggles, he fixed upon me a naked gaze of deep-sunken but piercing black eyes. I asked him what had become of his spectacles, and he explained to me that he had been going to a new oculist, who had discovered a revolutionary method of treating myopic vision: this oculist made his patients go without glasses and had them exercise the muscles of their eyes. Hugo's father, to his dying hour, when he had lain sick in his Adirondack camp, had refused to summon a doctor; and Hugo himself was suspicious of doctors, as of all the respectable professions. But in this case, the doctor was himself a heretic and an outlaw: the fact that his methods had been denounced by all the other oculists was enough to convince Hugo of their value. The immediate effects of the treatment were in appearance certainly remarkable: Hugo had unsheathed from behind his mild round blinders a darkly burning and eagle-like glance, beneath a steep and sharp-jutting brow which reminded me for the first time of his father's.

And despite my present scornful point of view toward Hugo's political opinions, despite the fact that it was so many months since I had made any effort to look him up, I had never been so glad to see him. For one thing, without his glasses, he seemed to have become a more interesting person and a person with whom it was easier to communicate: but for another, I found it somehow a relief to be talking again with some one whom I had known before I had come to Greenwich Villiage. As there was no place to sit down where we were, and as the back room, where we found a large table with a punch-bowl and sandwiches, was crowded even more densely, we made our way on through into the kitchen—which, by one of those freaks of old houses renovated and rented out for apartments, had been installed in a former hallway and was thus located between the dining-room and a bathroom (Sue Borglum had sub-let the basement, where the original kitchen had been), so that, in the absence of any other hallway, it had become a thoroughfare for people passing back and forth between the two.

In the kitchen, I was surprised to find Pete Bird, who so short a time before had been displaying so invincible an *élan,* sitting alone, with his elbow on the sink and his hand propping up his head, his visage chopfallen and greenish almost with the mask of death, and his eyelids sealed.

Our entrance did not disturb him, and we perched on the drawers of a china-cupboard on the other side of the long narrow room. I spoke to Hugo of a school-friend of ours who had just produced a successful play; and though Hugo's friendly interest was largely superficial—since he disapproved on principle both of everything connected with his school-days and of everything connected with Broadway success—I found an un-

expected pleasure in returning thus for a moment
to that world of our early years upon which we
had both turned our backs, a world where, for all
its limitations, the ordinary contacts of life had
been easier and more agreeable than one usually
found them in New York: that world had been
conventional, but a common understanding had at
least meant a mutual confidence. In the Village,
I had felt less and less confidence in the people
with whom I came into contact and, what was
worse, since my difficulties with Rita, less confidence in myself. And I found now that—despite
Hugo's stern rejection of everything he had been
taught in his youth—I was aware to-night principally of his good manners, his integrity and his
cultivated intelligence. He had been the first of
the boys I had known at school who had really
interested me, and he had remained almost the
only one.

I remembered now how, on one occasion in our
school-days, Hugo's father had come to see him
and had sat down on the bed and talked. I had
heard something about Mr. Bamman and, although Hugo rarely spoke of him, I had always
been conscious of him, in the background of Hugo's life, as an important and formidable person.
But Mr. Bamman, though his dignity was regal
and his Olympian brow and beard almost those
of the schoolroom Zeus, had turned out unexpectedly agreeable. He had asked me questions about
my studies and my reading quite as if I had been
a grown-up person, and had listened to my opinions with a deference to which I was entirely un-
accustomed. When he had learned that, in our

English course, we had been studying *Julius Cæsar,* he had embarked upon a discussion of Shakespeare very different from any I had heard in my English classes: what especially impressed me was the respectful but urbane familiarity with which he dealt with that great name—as if Shakespeare were a man like himself, as if he were, in some sense, Shakespeare's equal. He spoke of Shakespeare's amazing comprehension of political life, of the eternal universal types of his historical plays; to my surprise, he compared Coriolanus to Benedict Arnold; then in a manner both ironic and serious went on to speak of the Senate and the White House, as he had known them in his time. I had never heard any one talk so before: it was as if the world of Benedict Arnold had for him the same sort of reality as the world of McKinley and Cleveland; and what was more surprising still, as if Shakespeare belonged to the same world as the United States; as if he, Hugo Bamman's father, belonged to the world of history and of literature, and as if he took it for granted that we, since he talked to us as to equals, might hope to belong to it, too; as if, in fact, that world were our world! For the first time, I had had the sense of that reality—soon, at that age, to coagulate from what we see, what we read of or are told, and what we experience within ourselves —which finally supplies so astonishing a connection between the private emotions and thoughts, and the names and legends, of youth.

I reminded Hugo now of this incident, and was going on to tell him of my great admiration for his father, when he broke in: "Yes, Shakespeare and Milton: he used to read them to us every night till I got so I hated them like poison! I never really got to like Shakespeare till I read him during the War—and I can't stand Milton to this day! I dare say it's not Milton's fault: it's probably simply due to the fact that Father and I antagonized each other so."

This frankness on Hugo's part surprised me: I had always found him rather reticent both about his family and himself. Whenever he had happened to mention his father since the days when we had been at school together, it had been always with affection and respect, and even sometimes as if with a sense of failure at having fallen short of his father's standard. Now it was as if Hugo's liberated gaze had been accompanied by some new freedom of expression. But I was sorry, and a little shocked, to hear that his relations with his father had been difficult, and I asked him what had been the matter.

"I don't know exactly," he replied, "but we never got along. He was pretty impossible at home, and I suppose I sided with Mother against him. He was nervous and hypochondriacal, and used to shut himself up for days in his room, and refuse to see anybody. Then, he would suddenly appear in his dressing-gown, and freeze us with wild prophetic looks, and announce that the household was 'hurtling to ruin!' because he'd just gotten a caterer's bill or something. He finally had the whole household so that it was just like some kind of sanitarium—the doors were all muffled with felt, and he couldn't stand to have a light burning or to hear a sound after he'd gone to bed himself. He was never rude or domineering about it, but he used to nag us to go to bed in an insincerely amiable way that used to make me furious. Of course, he could be charming and sympathetic when any emergency or crisis arose, and he was able to embarrass us and disarm us so by having recourse to sympathy and charm, just when we'd been resenting him at our bitterest, that when it actually came to a show-down, we were never able to stand up to him. In any case, he had the effect on me of making me adopt the opposite opinion to whatever his opinion was. We used to have furious arguments about Socrates and Christ: I used to back Socrates.—I must have been an unbearable little kid myself. I never really liked him or appreciated him until after he was dead. The trouble was, I suppose, that he'd identified the household with everything that was stodgy and deadly that he'd been coming to loathe more and more as the years went on.

"He'd had a sort of a crush on Adelina Patti, before he married Mother, and I think that somehow all his life, in spite of the fact that he enjoyed Washington for a while, he was worried by the feeling that he'd really left the great world behind. I remember he got a phonograph record made by Adelina Patti just about the time she was passing out, and when he heard it, he flew into a rage and said it wasn't like her at all, that it was outrageous to allow such a record to be sold—and then he shut himself up in his room and wrote at something or other for days.

"I think that he'd really wanted to be an artist —he had a very fine voice, you know, and loved to sing—but the 1880's got him—and then, when he found himself snowed under by American respectability, he tried to be a saint. Even before Mother died and he went to live in the Adirondacks, he wanted to carry us all away to the wilderness with him—but Mother wouldn't let him."

I had drawn Hugo out about his father with an interest all the more intent because I was trying to keep my mind closed to Rita: but Mr. Bamman and Adelina Patti had opened the fatal abyss, and as Hugo saw me becoming abstracted, he stopped talking and, looking around with eyes which could now see so much farther, he remarked that Pete Bird, who had not moved but was still posed against the sink, looked exactly like a waxwork. "Who is he, anyway?" I inquired. "What does he do?" "Why, I don't think he does anything," said Hugo. "He's just a bum like another.—He writes some wather nice little poems occasionally!"

"Yes," said Pete, not opening his eyes, but speaking with perfect self-possession: "A bum like another—but a poet, nevertheless!" "Have you witten anything lately?" asked Hugo, with one of those veritable hemorrhages of kindliness which, when he feared he had hurt some one's feelings, often followed his bitterest strictures. "I thought that some of your things in *Sedition* were weally awfully nice!" "I'm not a poet!" said Pete Bird, still without opening his eyes. "Ask Giovanni Squarcillupi!—ask Mike Kraus! —ask Miriam Fotherwell Finck!"

"You haven't any manuscripts about you at this moment, have you?" inquired Hugo, who, despite his harsh and contemptuous judgments, had a secret sympathetic instinct for the vanities and aspirations of others. "I feel that I could read a little poetry. These parties seem to be getting less and less stimulating—Sue is getting to be more and more like a wegular Philadelphia hostess!"

Pete fumbled with one hand in his pocket, partially opening his eyes, but still supporting his head on his hand. He finally produced a cough-drop: "Here's a cough-drop," he announced, "if that would do just as well.—Eases irritation, just like a poem. Of course, the cough-drop's a little bit fuzzy, but then the poems are a little bit lousy!" "I know," said Hugo sympathetically, "when you try to find anything in your pocket, you always fish up cough-drops and unpaid bills and things!" "Bills!" said Pete Bird. "They don't even send me bills any more!—I've gotten long past that stage!—Here's a villanelle,"—he said at length—"a little toy of a villanelle!—and here's an experimental poem—an experiment in multiple metaphors—all of my metaphors are multiple—they have an infinite number of facets —like the eye of a fly!"

He handed the verses to Hugo: "You read them yourself," he said—"My eyes are not very good to-night,"—and lapsed back into immobility.

The poems were on creased and dog-eared paper, typed in very small type with rather a wavering touch, but, to my surprise, they had a certain charm, in a rose-petally, snow-flaky way. I could not, to be sure, distinguish very much difference between the sonnets and villanelles, on the one hand, and the "experimental" poems, on the other: Pete Bird's "multiple metaphors" turned out to be quite easy and mild—his description, for example, of his mistress's hands as "little surprising moonbeam violins."

The door into the dining-room opened, and Larry Mickler and Daisy appeared.

"Come on, yuh dope!" said Daisy to Pete Bird. "What d'ye think yuh are, brooding around the kitchen?—a cockroach?" "Get away, yuh dumb cluck!" replied Pete, reluctantly opening his eyes, "and leave me to my meditations!"

"Let's leave him to his slumbers," said Larry Mickler, who was evidently drunker than ever. "The boy-friend's passed out! Too many of those rich liverwurst sandwiches!"

"Come on, Mr. Zilch," said Daisy, still addressing Pete. "The little woman wants to go home!" "Leave me alone for three minutes!" said Pete Bird,—"only three minutes!—and I'll rejoin you in the drawing-room!" Though he talked quietly and sensibly, he was evidently incapable of moving. "Well, all right," she replied, with some bitterness. "But if you don't make it pretty snappy, you'll find me gone!"

"Come on back and let him have his sleep out," Larry Mickler pressed her, pulling at her arm.

But Daisy, ignoring Mickler's importunities as well as Pete's mildly aggrieved remonstrances, turned to me: "Take me in," she demanded, "and get me a drink and dance with me!" She had made up again since I had seen her: her eyebrows had been heavily pencilled to an effect of moth's antennæ and her mouth had been heavily rouged, so that her sallow and waxen complexion merely contributed a morbid paleness to an effect of provocative luridity; and as I found myself responding to her make-up, after my indifference of the earlier evening, I reflected, with dismay rather than cynicism, upon the purely biological basis of the interest which we feel in women, simple animals like ourselves, produced upon a similar model, monotonous and banal, to which only the recurrent brimming over of accumulating spermatazoa imparts a recurrent attraction.

"Very good!" assented Larry Mickler, with a playfulness distinctly malignant. "Then I'll just practise a little marksmanship!" He retreated to the end of the kitchen and, taking up a stand near the bathroom door, he aimed his revolver at a row of plates: "I wonder if I could pick those off in order!"

"Why don't you break them with the butt of the gun?" asked Daisy. "This long-range marksmanship of yours burns me up! You've already won the barbed-wire garters for shooting plaster statues at two yards!"

"Listen, Pete," insisted Larry Mickler, disregarding Daisy, "you go over to the far end of the room and throw up the plates one by one—and we'll see how many I can pot!—like clay pigeons!" "All right!" responded Pete, not moving or opening his eyes. "Oh, don't be *dull!*" cried Daisy with disgust.

Sue Borglum burst in with the Jap butler, who produced, at her direction, from the ice-box, a glass gallon-container of cocktails. She threw her arm around Daisy's shoulder, and exclaimed in a strained excited shriek which she seemed to have become incapable of moderating: "Oh, you *dear* child! You were an angel to come! Everybody's deserted me! Bobby said he'd be here at ten, and it's almost midnight now. I suppose he's gone out with his little cutie. I don't mind his keeping a girl—if he'd only get one that was intelligent, or attractive, or something!—but she's just a dumb little wench out of the chorus—she can't even dance!" "I think all chorus girls are dumb," said Daisy. "I've just lost my job, that's why." "Stand 'em on their heads and they're all alike!" said Pete Bird, without opening his eyes. Sue squawked with delighted laughter.

Larry Mickler, since Sue's arrival had been amusing himself at a distance by drawing his revolver on an imaginary foe: he would whip it out, declaring loudly: "I'll teach those damn goldfish to snap at me!"—then leer humorously in our direction; but as nobody paid any attention to him, he finally came over to the group and poured himself a drink of Scotch from a bottle standing on the table. "No wonder there are so many hold-ups!" he contemptuously remarked to me. "These dubs that we live among are just asking to be knocked on the head and have their pennies taken away from them!" He proposed drinking to Dostoevsky. "We've done that already," I said. "Let's do it again," he insisted, with a suggestion of becoming quarrelsome. "Drinking to Dostoevsky is always in order!" bubbled Hugo, with a tiresome recrudescence of his gushing undergraduate enthusiasm.

"Are you going to take me in to dance or aren't you?" demanded Daisy, turning to me, as Sue Borglum plunged toward the bathroom to greet with effusion another guest who was just emerging from there and whom she seemed not previously to have seen.

Daisy and I left the kitchen together. As we went, Larry Mickler called after me: "So twice is too many times to drink to Dostoevsky, is it?" Pete Bird was still sitting as before, his eyelids dropped in their death-mask and his head propped upon his hand—which, I observed, now that I had read his verses, was finely articulated and long.

"Isn't it wonderful," Daisy observed, as we made our way through the dining-room, "how clean Sue Borglum keeps her kitchen! Most kitchens would have an awful hangover after a party like this—but I bet hers will be neat as a pin!"

I avoided the large front room and led Daisy around by way of the hall, through a door that opened out of the dining-room, to the room on the other side of the house where people were dancing to the phonograph.

Daisy danced well: she was light; and the responsive alacrity of her straight little legs walking backward in the fox-trot had the same prosaic charm as her speech.

"Say, just do me a favor," she said. "Don't leave me with Larry Mickler. If he tries to cut in on you, don't letum—I'll just tellum, no soap!" I asked her what sort of a fellow Larry Mickler was. "Oh, he's just a fool," she replied.

"I'm sorry about to-night," she went on. "I
wanted to have dinner with you, but a whole lot
of things happened. I'm awfully sorry." I told
her that her touzled hoodlum hair-cut went beautifully with her plaid dress, and that the green in
the plaid dress went beautifully with the green of
her eyes. She said, "Yes, and the green of my
eyes goes beautifully with the green of my complexion!"

I held her close: her lips were slightly open, her
eyes partly closed: I wondered whether she were
really lapsing into a voluptuous, languorous
dream or whether she were merely very tired. It
occurred to me, as I looked at Daisy's fingers,
pale, brittle-looking and thin, that her hands,
which I had never considered among her prettiest
features, must be the 'little surprising moonbeam
violins" of Pete Bird's poem.

But now I could stave it off no longer; I could
talk no longer against time: I had to think about
Rita and Ray! My first feeling had been one of
horror that Rita should have been capable of betraying, not another, not me—but herself; then I
had made, in my mind, as I quitted the group, a
movement of repudiation which passed even beyond anger; and, at the time I had been talking
to Hugo and after, this had lifted me to a sudden
elation of lucidity and freedom. But now my
need to love and believe in Rita, even stronger
than my impulse to reject her, reasserted itself.
She must have found, I saw now, in Ray Coleman, with her confounded perverse generosity,
some fineness, some crippled aspiration, which
she had been able to cherish and feed. Was there

not in his persistent desire to meet and entertain
artists the inveterate ungratified longing to think
and to feel like them? Had I not noted in him an
unexpected deference, even in his face something
gentle and abashed, when, after he had advanced
with his usual assurance some opinion on art or
literature, a critic or artist present had expressed
contradictory views? And as I had watched him
just now, in front of the fire, describing Rita's
play, he had seemed to me more nearly amiable
than I had ever known him before. He was
happy because he felt himself on intimate terms
with Rita—because she had told him about her
play, and had allowed him to tell others. That
was his destiny, perhaps—his salvation: to praise
her, to care for her, to soothe her, to guard her
from the pack of suitors who came baying after
her like dogs—and so, at last, he might become
useful and happy—even likable, perhaps! So he
might finally justify his calling: he could buy Rita
security and comfort!

As we danced past the door into the hall, I
glanced across to the couch where I had left Rita,
and the sight of the group which thronged about
it irritated me suddenly in the same way as the
pathetic and exasperating obstinacy of photo-
tropic bugs. "Well," I remarked to Daisy, smiling, "Ray seems to be having himself a time with
Rita Cavanagh!" "Yes," she replied; "I noticed
that! He was trying to tell me last week that he
was all to pieces about my leavingum—but it
doesn't look much like it!"

I remembered how Daisy had complained of
Ray Coleman's making her stay home and listen

to his reading aloud from the *Oxford Book of English Verse;* and I imagined what a sympathetic audience he must now be finding in Rita: I could see how she would take the book from him and begin to read herself, and how she would presently recite her own poems—poems, no doubt, which she had written lately, and which I had never heard. He would flatter her without discrimination: I scorned her for accepting such praise!

"I suppose he's pleased with his new job," I remarked, "but a promotion from the *Dispatch* to the *Sketch* seems almost like a promotion from the morgue to the pound!" "If the boys on the *Sketch,*" replied Daisy, "are any worse than the boys on the *Dispatch,* I'm glad I made my getaway in time!"

"Let's go up-stairs for a minute, shall we?" Daisy suggested, as a record ended. "I want to give the old cuckoo's-nest a comb."

On the stairs, I took her arm and steered her up toward the sombre upper reaches, through the couples who were sitting on the steps: I gripped her firmly in my preoccupation, as if I had been guiding a child. "The trouble about having your hair done this way," she remarked, as if talking for other ears, "is that you have to keep fixing it all the time or people think it's just mussed up!" As we arrived at the top of the stairs, I found that I had gone suddenly hollow, and I remembered that I had eaten no dinner.

Instead of heading, as I expected, for the bedroom where the coats and hats had been left, Daisy went on along the dark up-stairs hallway—

she seemed to know the house well—to a door at the further end.

It was dark inside: by the light that came in through a single window from the house across the scanty back yard, I could see a cot and a simple bureau—the Jap servant's room, no doubt. I clawed the air for the chain of a shadeless electric bulb which was hanging above our heads. "Why don't you try the bathroom?" I suggested. "I don't see any comb on that bureau." "Never mind about the comb!" she replied.

I embraced her and pasted my lips on her half-opened mouth. I thought about the mouth and moth's eyebrows which had aroused me for a moment in the kitchen, but which I could not see now in the dark—and I tried to make up for my stupidity and tardiness by holding Daisy against me very tightly and kissing her again and again—but it was an assault of which I found myself conscious chiefly as a determined physical pressure and a deliberate application of the lips: I felt my arms crushing cartilage and flesh, and my mouth missing its goal against her teeth. It occurred to me that Daisy's lips were really, despite her make-up, not particularly well-adapted to passionate kissing of this kind: I still thought of them as cool-looking and childlike, as they had seemed to me the night of the movies. And I became aware of the succession of my kisses as something tediously mechanical and repetitive. Fearing Daisy might notice this, too, I broke it up by making her sit down on the bed.—I had desired her, and there we were at last! I found myself representing the long stupefied embrace of passion by sheer immobility and weight. I was all too far from being stupefied, I reflected, during the moments when I relaxed my ministrations: some obstinate unconscious loyalty, in spite of all my efforts, kept me cold. And I was distracted by a variety of ideas. I had a vision of the pilloried frog of a behaviorist moving-picture which I had gone to see with Rita: the frog, even with its brain removed, had responded with an automatic kick when an acidulated pad had been applied to one of its legs.—And the consciousness that the little bedroom belonged to the Japanese servant reminded me that the Japs did not kiss, that they did not know what kissing was—and I wondered whether they tried to learn kissing when they set out to become Americanized, and whether it took long.—I murmured, "Daisy darling!" in a low and secret voice.

We became aware that the door was open: I looked around and saw a small spare figure: his face was half in shadow, and I could not see his eyes. I quickly sat up on the cot, and he suddenly withdrew and slammed the door.

"Who was it?" Daisy asked in a whisper. "It was Pete!" I replied.

She got up. "I don't care," she said. "A great help *he* turned out to be!" She pulled on the electric bulb, went over to the mirror on the bureau, and applied her powder and rouge. When she had finished, she said, without looking at me, putting her powder away in the vanity-case, "Take me home, will you?"

We went out and extricated our coats—it was a little like a search in a bad dream—from the avalanche of wraps on the beds; and in silence descended the stairs, looking solemn and matter-of-fact, as we threaded our way among the couples.

So, I told myself, I had not hesitated to wound Pete in his love for Daisy, even after he had shown me his poems, such poems as I had written to Rita, in which his tenderness and his longing had, as it were, been confessed and entrusted to me—to me, another poet! In my glimpse of his face in the doorway, dimly lit by the light from the hall, his pale cheeks and his eyes large with shadow had seemed sensitive and even handsome. Was it Daisy's indifference, I asked myself, was it jealous suspicions like my own, which had given him that gargoyle's mask? Yet one had to be hard about these things: love and poetry, as I myself knew, were paid for with danger and pain!

Sue Borglum protested wildly and loudly against Daisy's leaving so early, and begged me, at any rate, to come back when I had taken Daisy home: she had evidently a morbid fear that her parties were becoming less popular.—I felt the cold taste of winter in the vestibule.

After splashing about in the slush of the dark and deserted streets, I finally brought back a taxi. Hugo Bamman came down the steps with Daisy. He was wearing his old limp felt hat, but no overcoat; and he was carrying over his shoulder the musette-bag he had had in the Army.

We invited him to come with us in the taxi. When I got in after Hugo and Daisy, I found Hugo planted on one of the little turn-down seats, and it was only with considerable difficulty that Daisy persuaded him to sit beside her.

"The tone of Sue Borglum's parties," Hugo began at once to complain, "is certainly getting more and more respectable!—she'll soon be sending out engwaved invitations!" I asked him what he meant. "Why, you just go and meet people now, and talk to them a little, politely—just like a Washington reception. Things used to be so much fwanker and fweer at Sue Borglum's! I remember one night when Leo Shatov got up and did a Cossack dance on the dining-room table—and the Baroness von Samstag-Solferino always used to appear wearing a coal-scuttle on her head!—And she has these little thin sandwiches, now, made of chopped olives and spiced ham and things. There used to be just a great big cheese, and you gouged out what you wanted with your pocket-knife!"

We were about to drop Hugo off at his house, only a block or two from Sue Borglum's, but he announced that he was sailing at midnight and would, therefore, go further uptown. I forbore to show surprise, but asked him where he was bound for. He explained, with his self-conscious giggle, that he was sailing for Smyrna on a fruit steamer: his ultimate goal was Afghanistan.

We asked why he was going to Afghanistan. "Well, I think that it must really be an awfully fine place!" he replied. "You know, it's one of the only places in the world that hasn't been Europeanized—it's all a European can do to get into Cabul at all. Not a trace of a business man or a missionary or a newspaper! The Amir has electric lighting and European plumbing in his palace, but, instead of sending for European plumb-

ers and electricians to put them in for him, he
sends Afghans to Europe to learn how to do
it themselves. When they come back, they're
searched for Bibles.—At the same time, they go
in for witchcraft and all kinds of entertaining
magic!"

He was bubbling now just as he had done at
college over the little pastry-shop in the side-
street where he and his friends had bought cinnamon buns.

"Is that where the afghans come from?" asked
Daisy. "Yes: I suppose so," chortled Hugo. "I
suppose that, even though it's forbidden to bring
in any modern textile machinery, a smart Europeanized Afghan might be able to do a little
profitable sweating in the afghan business!"

I asked Hugo what his literary plans were and
he explained that, when he came back from Afghanistan, he was going out to the American
West to write a novel about one of the big Western cities, either Pittsburgh or Detroit. (He had
already done Boston and New York, though he
refused to pay Philadelphia even the compliment
of exposing it.) "Oh, God!" Daisy exclaimed.
"What do you want to go to Pittsburgh for? I
spent the best years of my life trying to get away
from there!" "Why, I've always wanted to see a
Pittsburgh millionaire," Hugo explained, gaily,
mildly, sweetly. "Wasn't it you who were telling
me about the man from Pittsburgh who bought
ten thousand dollars worth of fireworks and set
them off in the Bois de Boulogne, and then committed suicide?" "Yes," said Daisy, "that was
Phil Meissner's uncle." "I think Detroit must be

awfully fine, too!" Hugo continued. "I've always wanted to see a Ford put together.—I've always thought it must be wather like one of those things in the movies, don't you know, where the man draws a cat, stwoke by stwoke, and then it suddenly comes alive!"

As I listened to Hugo's prattle, it occurred to me to suspect for the first time that he was allowing himself to prattle on purpose. His spectacles had had the effect of making him look owlish and juvenile; but now that he no longer wore them, his intent deep-sunken gaze betrayed the silliness of what he said—betrayed, I mean, that he himself was not silly. I became aware that the undergraduate patter from which, formerly and while still an undergraduate, he had so desperately strained to escape by harsh paradoxes and flat contradictions, was now a habit which he had accepted, partly no doubt because it was difficult to break, but also partly because he found it useful as a screen for his real purposes and ideas. His real purposes and ideas, it seemed to me, as I watched him in the taxi to-night, had by this time completely matured and stood firmly on their own feet; and a certain amount of success, which he had never aimed at or expected, had given him a new assurance. Hugo's novels on the American cities had become almost best-sellers; and he was no longer spurred by the painful necessity of asserting his views in ordinary conversation, but was content to chatter on like a school-boy: it saved tedious contentious explanations.

There was no chatter about what he wrote: Hugo's novels were sober, even morose, and were built with a solidity of cement. They were comprehensive reports on human society, industriously and conscientiously drawn up. And as I thought to-night of Hugo's assiduity, his independence and his sense of responsibility, I seemed to recognize in them those qualities which had for so many years made his father a respected public servant. The son had cut himself off from his family; had even sold, piece by piece, all the furniture and family silver which he had inherited from his mother, and, set by set, his father's library; and he had done this—to the great consternation of his cousins and his aunts, to whom the sale of mahogany and silver was like a massacre of kin—all in order that he might live poorly in Patchin Place, writing appeals for political prisoners, making speeches for striking garment-workers and composing those encyclopædic novels from which he had never hoped to make money. Yet, by the sacrifice of property and family, he had saved the honor of a family tradition which was otherwise largely moribund: he had truly assumed the responsibilities of leadership and shown the disinterestedness of public spirit, in the only fields where, in our generation, he had found it possible for him to work.

I seemed to see that, behind the mask of the outlaw, he had finally gravitated to a position exactly similar to his father's, before his father, in his later erratic years, had withdrawn from public life. For Hugo had applied himself to literature as to one of the old-fashioned professions, Medicine, Law or the Church; and, despite his rôle of eccentric and rebel, had taken on—what

set him off at that time from most of the other
literary men of the Village—the solid and honor-
able character of a first-rate professional man.
Through the late escapades of the father and the
early extravagances of the son, the curve had
come round again.

And I envied Hugo to-night: I could think
only of his established position as a writer, of the
security and the freedom of movement which his
royalties had finally brought him, at the same
time that he had earned the satisfaction of serious
work well done. I myself felt disgusted and
gloomy over the aimlessness and uselessness of
my life. I had seen clearly, at the funeral of my
aunt, that my relations did not think me a success: I was still an underling in a publisher's office, with no great enthusiasm for my work and
with no particular hopes of advancement. And,
on the other hand, I was not a writer: I had not
made Hugo's sacrifice and effort. No wonder
I had never been able to persuade Rita Cavanagh
to marry me! I had offered her merely the
meagre resources and the questionable future of
a young man with vague literary ambitions; and
she had already known many such young men—
had already, on one or two occasions, embarked
on such lives of cramped space and small comfort, without finding them magic carpets. What
wonder that she should now prefer Ray Coleman, with his apartment that overlooked the
Square, his lettuce-green cocktail glasses, his
water-colors of the Russian ballet, and his rye whiskey bottled in bond?

Hugo asked us to let him out at the corner of

Seventh Avenue and one of the upper Twenties.
I asked him where his baggage was. "I've got it
all here!" he replied, indicating the musette-bag
on his shoulder. "Haven't you even got an overcoat?" asked Daisy. "Why, you know, I don't
know why it is," he replied, with the bogus
naïveté with which he masked his stubbornest
manias, "but I can't seem to stand to wear overcoats. They always make me feel so loaded down
and sewed up—and they always make me too
hot! I always feel, when I get into them, that
there isn't a pin to choose between the modern
winter-overcoat and the Iron Maiden at Nurem-
berg." "I should think you'd get your death!"
protested Daisy. "If the people in New York,"
he replied, "didn't wear so many overcoats, they
probably wouldn't catch so many colds! They
bundle themselves up in winter-overcoats and
lower the resistance of their bodies so that the
least little change in temperature brings them
down with the grippe or the 'flu'!"

"Gee," said Daisy, with admiration, rather to
my surprise, "I wish I was going to Afghanistan!
Take me along with you, won't you?" "I'd love
to!" said Hugo. "Come on!"—but he began
looking out anxiously for the street. "Oh, *will*
you?" cried Daisy. "*Take me!* I'm so fed up
with it here! I haven't got any belongings
either! I left most of what I had at Ray's. I
could walk right on the boat now and sacrifice
practically nothing!—You couldn't really take
me, could you?" "Why, yes—come along!" said
Hugo, smiling but, I could see, with some uneasi-
ness: he shrank from the possibility of commit-

ting himself to a woman—even in gallantry, even in jest—and was nervously watching the street numbers—"if you wouldn't mind a few tarantulas and scorpions and things that go with the date and fig trade!" "Well, the fruit's all unloaded here, isn't it?" Daisy determinedly objected, with a strong grasp of commercial realities. "We don't export it over there, do we?" "No: of course—it's all unloaded on us—but the animals may stay behind! I suppose some of them are regular passengers!" "Well," said Daisy, "I've fought fleas and rats and bedbugs in my time—and Greenwich Village bar-flies—so I guess I could cope with a tarantula!"

Hugo stopped the cab. We were all for taking him to his steamer and seeing him off; but he refused to let us. I think that he was honestly afraid that Daisy would insist upon sailing with him—for he leapt out almost before the taxi had stopped, and his leave-taking was abrupt and expeditious. He opened the door again a moment afterwards and tried to give me some money for the fare, but I pulled his hat down over his ears. He waved at us once with a long spasmodic arm, then marched off in the direction of the docks.

"Gee," said Daisy, as we drove away, "I'd like to go to Afghanistan!"

We fell silent: Yes, I reflected, Daisy admired Hugo, just as Rita admired Ray—because he had made himself a place in the world, because he was successful and independent!

I was on the point of taking Daisy's hand when she suddenly snatched the driver's license out of its isinglass frame opposite her and, without a word of explanation, tore it up, photograph and all. "What made you do that?" I demanded. "I can't stand his face!" she said tartly. "I've been looking at it all the way, and if I had to look at it any more, I'd begin to go half-witted myself!"

I was irritated by Daisy's gesture: it jarred upon my mood of enthusiasm for Hugo's sense of social responsibility and I felt against it the same sort of resentment as against Rita's perversities and caprices. But I laughed—with a certain harshness, as if to mock at the respecters of property, and at the poets who succumbed to their bribes—as if Daisy and I alone, now, still stood together against Ray.

Yet, I was thinking the moment after, one couldn't really blame Ray Coleman for becoming infuriated with Daisy: hadn't she squandered all his money and then kept having C. O. D. packages sent home? Hadn't she even complained to me, the night that I had taken her to the movies, of Ray's too conscientious practice of paying all his bills? I thought of Daisy the night of the party, when I had first met her and Rita. Hadn't she behaved like a little fiend?—Hadn't she turned on a phonograph record in the middle of Rita's poems? Hadn't she humiliated Ray by leaving the party with Pete Bird? I found that I forgave Ray more easily for his violent scene with Daisy, which Rita and I had overheard.

But, when I remembered that detestable scene, it was no longer as it had seemed to me that evening. That night I had been a spectator looking on at a melodrama, at a melodramatic tableau of jealousy: Ray pointing at Pete's broken cane;

Daisy abashed among the ruins of the party; and I complacently and gallantly helping Rita on with her wrap. Now I myself had played Ray Coleman's part. I remembered that spiteful scene which I myself had provoked with Rita, in the taxi, and the scenes which for weeks had preceded it. Now it was as if the rôles had been reversed; now it was I who was the jealous blackguard and Ray Coleman who was the solid decent citizen! And now those memories must perhaps always stand as a barrier between Rita and me, as they had done to-night when I had tried to talk to her—a barrier of coldness and resentment which could never be forgotten now and whose shadow must lie, also, behind on all that had been beautiful before. If I could only just now have said the word which would have caused it to fall away!

"I don't want to go home!" said Daisy, as we were crossing Forty-second Street. I suggested that we might go to a night-club. I did not, as I say, at that moment, particularly care about Daisy, but then, there was nobody else that I liked better—least of all did I like myself or want to be alone with myself. "All right. I can't go in this plaid dress, though. I tell you: you go and get something to drink, and I'll go and change my clothes." "I'll go and change, too," I said.

The moment after, she had some sort of qualm: "Give me a piece of paper," she said, "any kind of piece of paper will do." The only paper I had in my pocket was the letter from H. M. Grosbeake, the professor of philosophy at college to whom I had sent Rita's poems and who had invited me to come to see him, but to whose letter I had never replied, though I had been carrying it around ever since: I had torn the blank part off in Daisy's room, the day I had written her the note, and now I gave her what was left, the page with the letter itself. She stuck it into the driver's-license frame behind the isinglass.

I left Daisy at her door.

* * *

Larry Mickler, with his revolver and his passion for Dostoevsky, had made upon me an unpleasant impression. I had come to connect him obscurely with my impulse to smash the peach-brandy bottle, when I had felt myself so helpless with Rita, and I found that I disliked Dostoevsky, because Larry Mickler admired him. I remembered—as I went back in the taxi to my own apartment in Bank Street—Dostoevsky's sadistic manias, his complaisance in self-degradation, his extravagant vanity; I began to feel, after meeting Mickler, that the masterpieces of such a man of genius were a doubtful compensation on paper for the moral bankruptcy of a life. Were not the purity of Dostoevsky's tenderness, the flights of his Christian idealism, to be measured precisely by his perversity, the sub-human depths of his indifference? Were not the Svidrigaïlovs and the Stavrogins—those malignant growths which seemed to sprout and, almost without the author's intention, to swell to such monstrous proportions, in Dostoevsky's novels—were they not the price which one had to pay for the Myshkins and the Alyoshas?

True, it was quite unfair to Dostoevsky to

identify him with Larry Mickler; it was the triumph, at least, of the great artist that, by dint of terrific effort, he had, if only in the world of his novels, succeeded in restoring a moral balance to that universe which he had once felt reeling with the world of his own soul; whereas, in the case of Larry Mickler, who had merely to read Dostoevsky's books, all that desperate idealism, that victory of moral passion, would, it seemed to me at that moment, go principally to give him a good conscience in licking his chops over the cruelties and perversities, and to leave him with the gratified conviction that there was no kind of discreditable behavior which imagination might not redeem.

And Pete Bird, with his charming wistful verses and his swindle of the liverwurst sandwiches! And Rita—without that *mêlée* in which her varying passions had involved her, that possession by all the devils of all the human desires at once, all that panic and anarchy and anguish and deceit of her daily life, would she ever without all this have been compelled to the noble severity, the firm and harmonious form, the bravery of candor, of her verse?

And those poets of whom Rita and I had talked the first night I had known her in Bank Street! To-night, the curses and groans of Catullus only filled me with the same disgust for his abasement at the feet of Lesbia as did my own preoccupation with Rita.—And Verlaine, in his prison cell, with his imbecile alternations between piety and pornography—if he had published his religious poems, as he had originally intended to do, sandwiched in between his poems of lechery, he would have furnished a perfect example, an example forever ludicrous, of the disorder of the poet's mind.

Even Dante, of whom I had once thought, of whom I thought still, as the supreme poet of Europe, who had possessed together the fiercest passion and the most powerful intellect, who had been able to apply to one work all man's highest faculties at once—what stiff-necked, what stupid obstinacy, what fanatic self-confidence, going against all common sense, must have lain back of all that subtlety and feeling! Had not Dante's indignation with his neighbors, as Professor Grosbeake had once suggested, been based upon an utter incapacity for understanding the realities of his time? Yet he had been spurred by such a passion to be *right,* that, balked and exiled in the real world, he had gone to live in the world of his poem, where, passing over both Emperor and Pope, he had sat in the place of God himself!

And even the philosopher and the saint! When I thought now of Professor Grosbeake, it was with a certain sentiment of scorn for the domesticity in which he seemed buried, and with misgivings as to whether his metaphysics were not merely a monstrous hypertrophy, arising, first, from a certain ineptitude at dealing with the affairs of the practical world, and fostered, later, by his practical wife, who had taken possession of him and securely immured him in a life where nothing but contemplation was possible. And had I not just learned that Hugo's father, from whom I had caught for the first time in my boyhood the sense of the unity of life—had I not just heard that he had fed his vision with the dead wood of some area of his nature of which he had never ceased to feel the lack, and that his ringing arraignment of the Congressmen for their failure to search their hearts in a spirit of Christian humility had been purchased at the expense of the tyrannic subjection of his household! And in the case of Hugo himself, it now appeared to me—what I had never understood before—that his ideas had been given their direction by his early revolt against his father, which had made him, not, as his father had been, the prophet of a new moral discipline, but primarily a champion of the oppressed who still resented and feared the oppressor.

But these reflections began to sicken me (I was at once hungry, nervous and weary) : I had succeeded in accounting for all these people, who were precisely the people I most admired, as the victims of deficiencies and derangements; and I now felt that I had been deriving an ignoble satisfaction from knowing the secret of every one's disease. While I was changing my clothes in Bank Street, I began to remember Dostoevsky's miseries : the neurotic family given over to its manias and collapsing after the mother's death; the boy neglected by the drunken father and left without money at his school; the elder Dostoevsky murdered by his peasants; Dostoevsky sentenced to death for plotting against the Czar,—taken out and tied to a stake to be shot, and reprieved only at the last moment; his four years of imprisonment in Siberia, wearing the fetters with murderers and thieves, hauling bricks and pounding alabaster; his later years of servitude as a soldier; his persecution by his brother's creditors; and the epilepsy which had accompanied all from that first day, when, a boy at school, he had heard the news of the murder of his father. Where was there place for ironic patronage in the contemplation of such a life or of the writings which had been its products?

And I remembered how Hugo, too, had suffered in his prison-camp in France. No wonder he hated discipline and authority! It was true that prison had made of Hugo an uncompromising revolutionist, whereas it had made of Dostoevsky an equally uncompromising conservative: Hugo himself was naturally good, and it seemed to him, in consequence, that all the evil which he encountered must be the product of institutions somehow imposed on humanity against their wish; whereas, in Dostoevsky's case, his inescapable sense of his own guilt, of the evil in his own heart, seemed at last to have reduced him to feeling that, though he had been punished for a political offense only, his punishment had been somehow deserved, and that he had actually been expiating crimes of which he had never been accused. He had come to believe in the badness of humanity; and mere political readjustments, in consequence, no longer appeared to him important. Yet the effect of the ordeal in each case—in Hugo's and in Dostoevsky's—had been essentially the same: as Dostoevsky's years in Siberia had caused him so deeply to distrust even the liberalism of educated Russians, so Hugo's weeks in the prison-camp had made it impossible for him to accept,

even in their most genial guise, the complacency
and comfort of America. Both had been forced
to live at close quarters with the basic contentions
and discords, the basic horrifying anomalies, of
our common life. And both were always afterwards to look with the eyes of strangers and ex-
iles upon even the most conscientious, even the
most intelligent, even the most amiable of their
fellows who had never recognized those realities.

Hugo and Dostoevsky alike had attempted to
explain them, to resolve them, those contentions,
anomalies and discords.—And were not these the
prime provokers of literature?—not encountered
in prisons only, but in all treachery, violence, frustration, all the outbreaks of our barbarous nature
and the unlooked-for disasters which befell us at
the mercy of unknown forces. Such disasters and
outbreaks alone could rouse us from our normal
existence of non-thinking and non-feeling, the la-
ziness of bodily processes inertly fulfilling their
functions, of the consciousness inertly drifting
among random and meaningless images—memories and anticipations—with unconscious but cun-
ning instinct steering clear of problems and tasks.
What were literature and art but the by-products
of these collisions with the uncomprehended reality—collisions whose repercussions, when we
had withdrawn into the shelter of ourselves, we
attempted to palliate, to harmonize, to account for,
to subdue to a smoother rhythm in the current of
our thought, now resuming, which for a moment
had been troubled or torn? And was it not true
that the individual artist—the greatest master
even: Dante himself—no matter how detached his

intelligence, how rich his imagination, how comprehensive his range, was never able to escape from the instinct which made him justify his own life? If the poet wrote about himself, or identified himself with his hero, the hero must emerge victorious; or if the hero were allowed to be beaten, he must at least be made to triumph morally; or if the writer confessed to sin or ignominy, the confession itself must be a merit; or if he wrote neither of himself nor of a hero, the historian, the economist or the philosopher, in defending certain values, made them play the hero's rôle. Like the instinct which made us blink our eyes when anything was brought near them, the instinct to produce a work of art (so I somberly reflected to-night in that room where, so short a time before, as I had heard Rita reciting her poems, the language of literature had seemed to me something at once natural and noble)—the instinct to produce a work of art was merely a self-protective reflex like another. Were not imagination and reason like the phagocytes of our physical nature, which, as soon as an infection occurs, rush to mass themselves at the breach, where they ingest the disturbing intruders and put a stop to the progress of the disease?—with this difference, that the work of art, unlike the dead and discharged phagocytes, for some time and under certain conditions, may retain a certain efficacy for others.

For the harmony, the justification, provided by a successful piece of literature was accepted by the reader as valid. Yet the writer had falsified life, because he had pretended to harmonize something of which he was conscious chiefly as chaos, and to explain what he was aware, all too well, he could not fully understand. So, when I had written a sequence of sonnets about the night of my first meeting with Rita, I had not mentioned, as I have not mentioned in my description of that evening, the drunken friend who had kept calling me up and interrupting our conversation; the agonized cries of cats; the howling and sobbing of a baby; the sore throat which, toward the end of the evening, I had begun to find very uncomfortable and which, afterwards, during the days when I had been falling in love with Rita, had developed into a bad cold. So I had also deliberately left out all that uncertain and egoistic side of Rita's character, of which I had already become aware and which was already making me anxious.

A work of art was, then, an imposture. But the reader, himself balked and bewildered, received naïvely the artist's picture as a true diagram of the world. The artist, who had been disconcerted and spurred to compose a work of art by his failure to discover in the universe either harmony or logic, supplied the logic and harmony himself; and the reader, who had also been hungering for harmony or logic, accepted with joyful reassurance what the artist gave him, and assumed that the artist's makeshift was a certified revelation, and the artist an oracle. The reader leaned upon the writer: what for the latter was a vague, a confused, or an approximate form of expression, the former applied literally. All that part of literature which dealt directly with current events—editorial-writing, pamphleteering, history, much novel and play-writing—was but the painting of the thinnest varnish of a comforting reason and art over earthquakes which actually took place, not in the world of art and reason, but in the barbarous animal world, bloody, uncontrollable, ignoble—and all the writer could hope for, at best, was to divert the attention of his fellows, like a bystander at a street accident who, when the rest of the crowd are only gaping, insists upon the removal of the body, or like an actor in a burning theatre who, by eloquence or jest, tries to avert a panic and stampede. Yet the public, remembering the catchwords, the incantations, of their leaders, attempted to enforce them as laws; and a flourish of rhetoric, under pressure of a desperate crisis, would be imposed as a practical programme or developed as a philosophic system.

Or the public got to the point of behaving as if every feature of the artist's work were something premeditated—writing, for example, after the author was dead, "It was about this period that X, in his attempt to understand his own time, decided that it would first be necessary to understand the career of James G. Blaine, and, finding no satisfactory book on the subject, he set out to write one himself," or, "It was in the course of his travels in the tropics that the necessity first appeared to Y of a new and chaster form of expression,"—when the truth was that the life of Blaine had been merely a piece of hackwork for a publisher, suggested by the publisher himself, and that the baldness of Y's prose had been simply the result of enervation caused by the tropical heat. Or some work, which had represented for the writer a furious effort at completeness of understanding, at impersonality of projection—an effort obstructed, to the writer's dismay, by his personal obsessions and mannerisms, his family habits, his organic defects, the limitations of his nation and race, which pursued and exasperated him, like a can tied to a dog's tail—to the public, who knew nothing of his aim, it was precisely the writer's personality which they savored and glorified, descending with gratified complacency those very lines of least resistance against which the artist had struggled to mount, and delighting in those very stigmata which the artist had strained to efface. So posterity would piously cherish a distinguished writer's roughest notes, though these might be merely irrelevant excretions, under the pressure of emotions and interests not commemorated in them at all—productions which derived their only vividness from the acuteness of the writer's need to turn his mind away from his troubles of the body, the heart or the purse, toward something indifferent and remote—or they might be meaningless mechanical notes, the merest rudimentary twitchings of the literary temperament, made in moments of drunkenness or fatigue, but hungrily saved by the writer's admirers for their infinitesimal drops of some peculiar personal color, no more significant or precious in itself than the color of his hair or his eyes. From these notes, the writer's disciples might end by constructing a system which would have filled the writer with horror, but which now carried the credit of his name—just as in the case of ancient poetry, where the text was corrupt or fragmentary, Æschylus seemed to us all the more awful and all the more oracular because, not knowing precisely what he wrote, we did not know precisely what he meant; and Sappho all the more a goddess because there was so little of her left.

Nor were the public readers merely: they were also writers who imitated the author. One had had a vision of movements in literature sweeping over the minds of humanity like the wind that makes waves in the wheat; but would it not, I now reflected, be more accurate to liken such movements simply to the collapse of a row of dominoes, of which only the first has felt the shock, the shock from the unknown reality, and the others have merely toppled over, receiving it at second-hand? Till, at last, the original composer of the symphony, the original inventor of the system, would catch back from the minds of the public themselves (who had merely taken it from him), a new belief in the all-embracing, the all-satisfying character of that pattern, in the finality of those conclusions, which, at the time he had first conceived them, he had never himself regarded as complete.—Some day, like a fool, I should myself read those poems I had written about Rita, and I should be convinced that it had really been like that! Not content with deceiving others, I should finally deceive myself!

But, in the long run, if my sonnets had become famous, the public would have found them out. When the readers had got used to a writer— when our first delight in his peculiar color, his

peculiar music or flavor, had commenced to wear
thin—then the familiar malaise assailed us: we
began fatally to detect once again, beneath the
novel or alluring surface, the presence of all those
grievances, those diseases and insane preoccupa-
tions of the straining, incomplete human being—
all those anomalies, discords, and contentions from
which, in seeking the support of literature, we had
hoped to be set free. And in the end, the public of
readers, when they had found out the weaknesses
and falsities of the system which it had once accepted—when they had perhaps tried to put into
practice some vision, like the morality of Nietzsche
(another favorite of Larry Mickler's), which the
writer had imagined in his bed—they would turn
against the writer and repudiate him.

Yet beyond the work of the individual artist,
there was the concerted general effort, the gigantic
universal imposture, of literature itself!

I remembered the big volumes of Jebb in which,
with the hope of tranquillizing my spirit, I had
lately been reading Sophocles. *There* was perhaps
the supreme achievement of the organized imposture of literature! How many times had one seen
the calmness and the sobriety of Sophocles played
off against the harshness or the cynicism of some
modern tragic writer! These plays had become
the unchallenged example of classic moderation
and wisdom, the touchstone for modern turbulence. Yet in what work of a modern dramatist
had the harshness of Sophocles been surpassed?
I remembered the unruly tempers of the family
of Œdipus: the foolish quarrel of Œdipus with
his father over a casual encounter on the road;

his harshness with Tiresias; the passionate direct-
ness of all his gestures. Did one find even in the
Œdipus of Colonus that spirit of peace and resignation with which Victorian critics sometimes
credited it? Was the exiled and embittered king a
figure of mellow clemency? Surely his final curs-
ing of his sons was one of the most shocking
scenes in literature!—nor did the species of divine
electrocution with which Sophocles finally disposed of him strike precisely a note of tranquillity.
And those sons who quarrel for the kingdom and
who finally slaughter each other! And the passionate obstinacy of Creon, so like the passionate
obstinacy of Œdipus—and the passionate obstinacy of Antigone! The mother and daughter, in
Electra, bandying the most brutal abuse! These
people were, in their way, and even on the occasions when they were animated by some passionate fanatical loyalty, as narrowly egoistic as the
characters of Ibsen, but more quarrelsome and
more virulent!

Was there, indeed, I suddenly asked myself,
from the point of view of barbarous behavior,
very much to choose between Sophocles and Dostoevsky himself? There they were, the old hideous discords—Œdipus killing his father, the old
Karamazov murdered by his sons—that cruel inevitable turning upon the beings who have given
us life! I remembered how Hugo had just told
me that, rebelling against his father, he had come
to hate even those poets whom his father had
loved—and how Rita, in leaving behind her all
that dull and homely life which for so long had
hobbled her youth, had discarded the name of

Aunt Sadie, who had taught her to play Handel
and Bach.—And were not the horrors of Dostoevsky—Myshkin's epilepsy, Zossima's putrefac-
tion and Stavrogin's rape—quite matched by Phi-
loctetes's ulcer, by the unburied corpse of Poly-
neices and by the incest of Œdipus? If even the
form of Sophocles were more chastened than the
form of Dostoevsky, his spirit was more astrin-
gent!

I remembered the story about Sophocles in
Plato—how he had been asked whether old age
had made him impotent, and how he had replied
that growing old was like deliverance from a mad
and cruel master. Was this the saying of a calm
and gentle nature? And what of the tranquillity
of even those later years?—I remembered in the
second *Œdipus,* the terrible description of old age
—"unfriended, feeble, chided, unfit for company,
the crowning ill of all—not to be born is best,
but once we have seen the light it is better to go
soon!" How did Matthew Arnold know that
"from first youth tested up to extreme old age,"
"passion" had never made Sophocles "wild"?

Yet so great was the need of humanity to believe in a human intellect all-self-controlled and
all-wise that there had been superimposed on the
plays of that great master of hatred and horror
a legend which now disguised them—and the
solemn impassive don, laboring day after day at
his desk, explaining, interpreting, translating,
every word of the poet's text—sometimes alter-
ing his words—had pared Sophocles down, had
sapped his power, ironing out to marmoreal
smoothness a style rather nodulous and tough,

congealing angry cataracts of consonants to color-less pediments of prose, and reducing the weighty rhythm, with its urgent pulse of blood, tiding along from one line to another the contractions of swift-spoken speech, to a tongue which could never have been spoken—the British don, after centuries of critics, had supplied us with what men of letters, what all mankind, had desired: a writer superhuman and humanly impossible, a writer who could never have existed—a Master, of impeccable technique and imperturbable moral balance, a writer who could never be supplanted and never be outgrown, a writer unassailable, a classic!

So we had established the myth of the classics: from the written remains of humanity, of beings outraged and wondering like ourselves, we had created the illusion of a fortress of absolute beauty and wisdom, into which educated men might retreat, upon whose invulnerable strength they might rely.

And I thought, also, of those other efforts, those efforts more characteristic of our time, which aimed, also, at an absolute beauty, at an art wholly independent of the appetites and agonies of men—paintings which represented nothing, "pure poetry" devoid of ideas: both, in reality, mere assimilations on the part of litera-ture and painting to the pattern and rhythm of music—which itself had been piously striving—in those composers who named their productions after trigonometrical figures and the integral cal-culus—to assimilate itself to mathematics.

How senseless such attempts seemed to-night!

How could there be anything absolute or pure
about such exercises as the arts, which were but
pleasing arrangements of sensations, and which,
therefore, were inextricably dependent on the senses
we had clumsily evolved to meet our needs and to
find our way through the jungle of nature! And
if the art which derived from our hearing seemed
to us purer than the others, it was merely because we experienced, in the region of sound
divorced from speech, sensations less complex
and complete than through images or words.
These crude games, so much the play of our
bodies, of our primary animal life, that neither
stories, visions, drama, nor music—not argu-
mentation even, not Euclid's geometry itself,
which comes to a climax, like a Greek play, with
the proposition of the square on the hypotenuse
—had been able to liberate themselves from the
type of our reproductive processes—so that one
had always either, as in Greek plays, to work up
to a climax toward the end and then gently and
briefly subside, or, as in our modern ones, to
reach a climax and then abruptly cease. I thought
of the heat of Catullus and Keats, of the mounting excitement of Dante; of the even unimpas-
sioned glow of purely homosexual writers like
Plato and André Gide; of the blank stretches
where the climaxes should be, in the novels of
Henry James.

And I reflected, also, that between the sexes—
Rita's poetry and Catullus's—there was no real
common norm of judgment in matters of literature or art—men and women were each tied to
their stakes: they could only turn in circles about

them. What critic could really pretend to judge the work of men and women side by side?—or, for that matter, the work of different races, or even of different nations—of different periods, generations, each with its own adjustment to make to the world which pursued and pressed it, each with its own particular disasters, its own particular discords and conflicts, which, to be easy, it must resolve? Or even of different individuals!

What a discrepancy—worst of all—what a gulf between the self which experiences and the self which writes! What was the sense, I asked myself, in that room where I had once brought Rita and where we had talked the night through and seen the blue of June on the glass—what was the comfort of "moments of emotion recollected in tranquillity"? As if there could ever be a common denominator, as if there could ever be a fusion or union, between those moments of tranquillity and our moments of pain!

*　*　*

As I went out to buy a bottle of gin at a near-by Italian restaurant, I resolved to disgorge all these ideas in a gigantic destructive essay. But I found now that I was getting a headache: my mind was still going on at a furious fatiguing rate—with slashed and deflated tires, running rackingly on its rims—and I wanted now to make it stop. I had been feeling rather faint with hunger, and, while the waiter was wrapping up the bottle, I ate some bread and drank a highball.

I tried to shift my thoughts to Daisy, as I expected to find her when I should call for her—in her pretty black evening-gown, and much beauti-

fied and refreshed.—After the highball, and a
second highball, I found myself full of enthusiasm
for the night-club.

When I arrived at Forty-fourth Street, however, the door of Daisy's apartment was opened
by Pete Bird, and I saw Daisy sitting on the edge
of the bed, with the same old rowdy plaid dress
and the same demoralized countenance, now unnaturally pale. Pete said, "Oh, hello!" and both
stared at me. I saw that Daisy had been crying:
she had a bandage around her wrist.

I inquired what had happened. "Daisy cut her
wrist," said Pete. "I was trying to open a spaghetti can," said Daisy, without expression.
"Good Heavens!" I exclaimed. "Don't you think
you ought to have a doctor?" "We've had one,"
said Pete. "He's just gone." Daisy continued to
stare up at me, without speaking, with watery,
swollen eyes.

I felt a deep disgust with them both. I protested that she should have waited, that I had
planned to get dinner at the night-club. "Just
didn't want to wait," she replied—then added,
after a moment's pause: "I had some spaghetti
here, and I thought I might as well eat it!"

"I don't suppose you want to do any more looping, then," I said. She answered shortly: "Not
to-night."

Pete Bird had sat down on the bed beside her,
and put one arm around her: he looked like a
faithful dog. She looked like a wounded owlet:
I was astonished to observe that her nose, in the
centre of her pale round face, could appear like a
little beak. She had through suffering and fatigue
reached one of those moments when women

seem completely dispossessed of their sex, and it occurs to us as a surprise that they probably resemble their fathers.

I asked whether she wouldn't like a drink. "You might leave some here," said Daisy. I felt that Pete regarded me with coldness, that he had assumed complete proprietorship of Daisy, so I gave them the bottle and took my leave. "I'm sorry," said Daisy, without feeling, "that I couldn't go out."

I directed the taxi-driver to take me to Sue Borglum's.—I was irritated by Daisy's clumsiness in cutting her wrist on the spaghetti can; and I resented the presence of Pete Bird. I did not particularly want to see any more of Sue Borglum's party—in fact, the thought of returning was repugnant to me. But I had got to the bottom of everything—nothing really mattered to-night. Going back to my apartment alone was the most intolerable prospect of all.

In the cab, I fell to wondering, in my discouragement with art and literature, whether it might not perhaps be possible to find a deeper, more austere satisfaction in scientific writing and research: my mind had been haunted that evening by ideas from my recent scientific reading. In the sciences, at least, one was dealing with ruthless reality itself: *there* one did not pretend to justify; *there* one's work was accomplished in indifference as to whether it solaced men's minds. I regretted now that I had never had the foresight to study physics and biology at college. And in an attempt to exercise, at least, that gift of scientific observation upon which I had rather prided myself, I asked the taxi-driver, as I was paying him, whether he had not been born in Alabama. But he replied that he had been born in New York, and had lived there all his life.

I was struck, when I re-entered Sue Borglum's, by a certain demoralization which seemed to have taken place since I left. In the room where people were dancing, a little baldish man with spectacles was playing on a set of trap-drums: he was apparently under the impression that he was contributing to the pleasure of the dancers; but as his drumming made the phonograph inaudible, they were endeavoring to restrain him. He was complacently smiling to himself, and when any one remonstrated with him, only glanced up and smiled more happily, deafened by his own drums. From time to time, he blew a kazoo.

On the couch in the room across the hall—the couch on which Rita had been sitting—there lay a man (though he might almost have been a woman of the taller more aquiline type) in a green and orange kimono, from which protruded lean bare shanks and feet. He made me pause in horror when I first saw him: his eyes, which had mascara on them, were cadaverously closed, and his unnaturally narrow face had almost the pinched look of the dead.

In the room where the refreshments had been served, there was nothing left now but a sandwich which some one had bitten into, and the purplish dregs of the punch. Bobby McIlvaine was leaning against the mantel: his straight mouth and his narrow eyes seemed to have shut up, at the intimation of danger, like a turtle's shell. Sue Borglum was vehemently haranguing

him, while a girl with lustreless complexion and
lips painted a heavy magenta was expostulating
tearfully with Sue in an endeavor to justify herself for having just thrown a punch glass at another girl, who, in her turn, feminine and frail
in a fashion rather wispy and washy, was half-
hiding, like a frightened chick, behind a species of
woman doctor. This last person, who was broad
and well-tailored, with white cuffs and a black
masculine dress, was herself defying and derid-
ing the first girl—the one who was appealing to
Sue Borglum—with robustious male taunts and
chuckles, which served to convey female malice.

Sue received me with a violent gust of wel-
come, evidently forgetting that she had seen me
before—no doubt my changing my clothes had
misled her—and immediately called me as a witness against Bobby McIlvaine: "Now, tell him—
tell him frankly!" she shouted. "I want him to
know what people really think of his sets! Did
you ever see anything more terrible in your life
than the first act of *April Showers?* I tell him
that as a snug little cottage, it would make a good
annex to the Public Library!" I said that it was a
great pity that the scene hadn't taken place in a
palace, because Bobby was so good at palaces.
"It'll take place in Cain's palace soon!" Sue Borglum breathlessly went on. "Palace! The trouble
with him is that his style has gotten vulgar! It's
vulgar, that's what it is! Palace! It looks like a
movie palace! It looks like some movie man's
idea of a palatial ladies' lavatory!"

I drifted on, after a little, to the kitchen: perhaps I wanted to be sure that Rita had really gone

—perhaps I still hoped to speak to her alone and to break down that constraint between us of which I carried the consciousness everywhere, like an ache at the back of my head.

In the kitchen, I found a little group waiting around the bathroom door. One of the men was remonstrating with the others. In those days, in Greenwich Village, there was always a man in a dinner-jacket who was present on all major social occasions: he was some sort of a bond-salesman or broker who took an interest in the arts. When, as in the case of Sue Borglum's Thursday evenings, these occasions became a little more formal and many people wore dinner-jackets, he began to appear in a dress-suit. Thus costumed, he was now leaning against the sink, with his hands in his trousers pockets—his regular equine face expressionless and almost distinguished— protesting with good-humored gentlemanliness against the vigorous measures proposed by certain other members of the group for inducing the occupants of the bathroom, who, it appeared, had been in there a long time, to give somebody else a chance. It was also suggested that the people inside might actually be ill, that they might even have committed suicide, and that one really ought to find out. "No," said the gentleman in the dress-suit. "I don't think they've bumped themselves off. A little while ago I heard somebody laughing." "Maybe one of them's bumped the other off," suggested somebody in the group, "and it's the one that's alive that's laughing." "I don't think so," replied the arbiter. "I know them both.—I want to get in," he added, "just as badly as you do, but I think we ought to be discreet."

"Well, I'm damned if I do!" declared emphatically a little chunky Hungarian, one of the editors of a communist paper. "Whatever they've been doing in there, they've been doing it long enough!" "Yes," said a furtive-eyed poet, who wore a khaki shirt. "It's time the workers got a break!" The Hungarian's companion, a chunky and pretty young Jewess, smiled a little uneasily, in awe of the communist, but impressed by the man in the dress-suit.

The Hungarian marched to the door and knocked resolutely and clearly. "Look here, old chap!" said the man in the dress-suit, going forward and taking him by the shoulder, though without violence or heat. "Better lay off! Let's be tactful!" "Get away, you animal cracker!" the communist retorted. "Don't try to high-hat me! There are other gentlemen and ladies in the world besides you and your friends in the bathroom!"

The door opened suddenly and widely, and Larry Mickler came out. He was followed by a tall plain blonde, very much flushed and evidently angry. They made their way through the group about the door, looking fixedly straight ahead of them. But when Mickler came up to me—I was the farthest from the bathroom—he stopped and let the girl leave the kitchen alone.

"Well, old-timer!" he greeted me genially—with the exaggerated heartiness of one who has failed to commend himself elsewhere. I asked him whether Rita had gone. "I don't know," he replied, reaching for the bottle of Scotch. "She was in the other room a little while ago.—*There's* a woman who's not afraid to be herself!—These women are all afraid of themselves—they're afraid to say *Yea* to life! Village and college girls, one's just as bad as the other in this goddam country of ours!—Like that rope-haired blonde girl, for instance—she wants it and yet she's afraid of it —when it comes to the point, she's afraid! She pretends to be scandalized, when she's really only sore at herself!—Well, let's drink to Rita Cavanagh, the woman who's not afraid!"

"I'm all for Rita Cavanagh," I said, "but I've drunk enough toasts to-night!" "That's right!" replied Larry Mickler, immediately directing his resentment at me. "Say *Nay,* like all the rest! I'm not surprised you're in the publishing business. The publishers are all *Nay*-sayers! I wouldn't be writing ads, instead of novels, if the publishers said *Yea* to life!—Why, if the whole tribe of publishers—and editors!—and critics!—were combined in one attack, they wouldn't be enough to make a Dostoevsky scratch the bite!" I repressed an impulse to answer, "To hell with Dostoevsky!" —but replied, "I never heard that Dostoevsky had any trouble getting published." I left him glaring, before he had retorted, and went back into the dining-room.

In the dining-room, the girl with the lustreless skin had broken down and was weeping on a chair, while Sue Borglum, her own eyes leaking tears, was making an effort to console her. Sue was saying: "Never mind, Claudette—you can't win! you can't win!" Bobby McIlvaine, who was standing alone, his face locked against the scene which confronted him, produced two theatre-ticket stubs from his pocket and dropped them

into the dregs of the punch. He remarked to me:
"That's a combination that I've always wanted to
try in the theatre—mauve and blue!"

In the front room, to which I immediately returned, I was just in time to witness an arrival
which made upon me a curious impression. I
could hardly at first believe my eyes: there had
appeared suddenly, under the escort of Tony
Scallopino, the proprietor of one of those Greenwich Village restaurants which were beginning, at
that period, to be transformed into small but
increasingly expensive night-clubs, two young
women who, even among that company where
one was not ordinarily surprised at anything, astonished and jarred upon me, like some incongruous image of a dream, remembered after we
wake, some image which owes its strangeness,
its power obscurely to worry us, to the fact that
it has been transferred from its surroundings in
the waking world to surroundings which do not
fit it. They were strangely conspicuous, these girls
—more conspicuous, even, in their way, than the
man in the orange kimono or the woman with the
stiff white cuffs. In the first place, they were
very brightly dressed, one in blue, the other in red
—and I saw, at a second glance, that their dresses,
though gay and even smart, were flimsy and
cheap. Neither was bad-looking; and when they
first came in, I thought they were attractive. The
small one, the one in blue, had blue eyes and
looked a little like a fish; but the other, the one in
red, was quite handsome; she had rich brown hair,
large brown eyes, full cheeks, fleshy lips, rather a
creamy complexion and a nice thick nose. But

their cheeks glowed with a heightening of color, and their eyes were starred with a black radiation, which, among all the varied make-ups of the party, seemed improper and out of place; such faces were not meant for the lighting of ordinary private houses, but for the pink-shaded lights-in-darkness of Tony Scallopino's night-club. And in their eyes I saw that public stare, the stare of the prostitute, which, like the jockey's bowed legs, the tailor's peering eyes, the courtroom intonations of the lawyer, the military officer's curtness, is the universal sign of the profession—that stare which must be always watching, which must meet all the world without winking, without demurring or veiling itself—that stare which sometimes looks amazed, sometimes panic-stricken, sometimes resentful and sullen, and sometimes insane, but which seems always to have robbed the face of some essential element of personality, and therefore of humanity itself.

I gazed at these girls, and, in an instant, the brunette had become aware of my gaze and was welcoming it, with smiling eyes. I approached her, and she began at once, before I had even spoken: "I think this is the most delightful old house! What a lovely old mirror over the mantel!" We discussed the house, the weather, the theatre: she had opinions about the plays that were being given in the little Village theatres: I was surprised to hear her make conversation so cleverly and with such a good manner, but I was shocked to see her ply her trade—she made no pretense of anything else—so brazenly and so promptly.

I was made uneasy, as we talked of other things, to meet nothing in her large fine eyes but a look of sly, humorous complicity. Those eyes, for all their intelligence, had been glazed against the warmth of frankness, the expression of personal feeling, as much as those of any street-walker's who makes off to the streets again the moment her transaction is finished. And this troubled me—I hated and resented it: to-night I had felt myself estranged, first, from Rita, and then, from Daisy—I had felt cut off beyond even communication. And I now exerted myself to make a contact with the brown-eyed girl in red— to force her to meet my friendliness.

But as she saw that I was refusing to do business, she soon passed on to the man in the dress-suit, who happened to be standing near us. Without excuse or explanation, without hesitation or resentment, like some salesman of carpet-sweepers, who, rejected at one door where he has knocked, immediately passes on to the next, she assailed him with her shameless patter.

I wondered how Tony Scallopino had ever dared to bring these women here, and I was aroused to disgusted anger. (I found out afterwards that Sue herself, in her morbid and hysterical fear lest her party should be ill-attended, had telephoned to Tony to bring any one still at his place—meaning, of course, any of his regular patrons.) I remembered how Tony Scallopino, in the days before his advent to the Village, had been an I. W. W. agitator and how, in the course of the long Italian dinners, in his former and cheaper restaurant, he had often sat down at our table and talked about politics with us; I had at that time always rather liked him, but it seemed to me tonight that Tony had become Manhattanized and cynical. It did not occur to me that, from Tony's point of view, the girls were working-people like himself, and that in bringing them to Sue Borglum's party he might be merely endeavoring to make it up to them for a night of bad business at his night-club; I might have guessed, from their technique of hungry wolves, that they were desperately badly off. But I only felt that Tony had somehow become a traitor.

The fish-faced blonde approached me in her turn, hoping to succeed where the other had failed, but I let her see that I was disaffected. She passed on to the creature on the couch, the man in the orange kimono, and by some playful overture, awoke him. But he, nervously starting up, regarded her with surprise and indignation, and exclaimed, in a high peevish voice: "I want to lie down here, please! I've got a perfectly terrible headache!"

Sue Borglum and Bobby McIlvaine had, in the meantime, appeared from the dining-room; and Sue, beholding the girl in red, who had not long been detained by the dress-suit, address herself immediately to Bobby as if she already knew him, had concluded at once that she was some flame of his, whom Bobby had invited without consulting her. And, in a moment, learning that Sue was the hostess, the newcomer had turned to her enthusiastically, exclaiming over the beauty of the old house, the old mirror, the quiet charm of the neighborhood, the delightfulness of the occasion:

"But I'm so sorry to miss seeing Rita Cavanagh:
I admire her poetry so much! I was so excited
when Tony told me she was going to be here to-
night, and then we missed her—she left before we
came!"

I made my way to the hall again, where, in the
manner of Larry Mickler, I drew and drank rapidly several cocktails from the lemon-cloudy lees
of the water-cooler. Then, feeling that these
drinks were weak—they consisted principally of
melted ice—with a vision of a den of drug addicts
gathered together, with gruesome merriment, to
dose themselves with alcohol, I drank what was
left of a bottle of whiskey, which turned out to
be excessively bad, stinging my tongue and con-
stricting my gullet.

Now I began to ask myself whether it were the
revolver Larry Mickler was carrying which had
made me break off with him so quickly and leave
the room without waiting for his reply.

Through a door which led into the dining-room
and which opened behind me from the hall, I
could hear Sue, who had left the sitting-room—
retreating, as was by no means characteristic of
her, at the advance of the outrageous guests,
whom she still believed to be friends of Bobby's—
pouring out, to the equally unfortunate Claudette,
in a shrill, strained, and grating voice, her grievances against Bobby: "It isn't as if I'd ever been
anything to him—I never was! I never wanted
to do anything but help him. Some women would
have tried to get a hold on him!"—etc., etc. At
that moment, it seemed to me that Sue—whom I
found that I now somehow identified with the

woman with the dyed red hair and the slatternly lacy dressing-gown, whom I had seen at the beginning of the evening in the house where Larry Mickler lived—that Sue Borglum was the ugliest and most odious woman whom I had ever known, and that she possessed the most horrible voice. Yet it was not really her voice which made me hate her, but the fact that she was lonely and in pain.

In the room where the phonograph was playing, the dancers had abandoned the floor, driven off by the man with the drums, who, however, still sat trancedly drumming. They sat or lay on the couches and chairs, which had been moved back against the sides of the room—as if washed up, I said to myself, in what I thought was a felicitous fancy, like driftwood, dead fish, and sea-weed left behind by the tide on the shore. Then I remembered Rita's poem, the poem about the beach-fire and the darkness: it seemed to me that my own image had been caught from it, and I felt that I had been travestying it foolishly.

With an impulse of irritation, I broke in upon the imbecile with the drums, interrupting him in a loud clear voice and inquiring whether he knew the time. "I don't know the time," he replied, with his abstracted fatuous smile—"but," he added, after a moment, when he had come to the end of a spasm of drumming, "I've got something else that's just as good!" He produced a pint flask from his back pocket: "And a darn sight better!" he added. He offered me a drink, which I accepted. I sat down on a chair beside him. "This is something," he further observed, after taking

a swig himself, "which makes time unnecessary!"
He had the conviction of quiet humor of a very
stupid person. "If you carry a little flask," he continued, after a brief pause—he had begun softly
drumming again—"you don't need to carry a
watch!"

I asked him whether he knew Larry Mickler,
and when he shook his head, always smiling, I
expressed the extreme distaste I felt for the admirer
of Nietzsche and Dostoevsky. "Why, he's a fellow," I protested, "who smashes the statue of the
Winged Victory that his wife brings home from
college—a perfectly nice little college girl! He
tries to neck other girls in the Jap's room—in the
bathroom!—He threatens them with a gun! He's
the most objectionable man I've ever known!"

And I reflected to the tune of the fox-trot and
to the subdued rat-a-tat of the drum, that what I
had said was literally true: Larry Mickler was,
without any question, the most obnoxious man I
had ever known—and I had failed to put him
properly in his place! I had been afraid of his
damned revolver! Here there had come to me
an opportunity to stand up to Evil itself: it might
be that such a moment as this, such a moment
that tested a man, came but once to a man in his
life! And I had quailed at the thought of a gun!
Yet to stand up to Larry Mickler would be finally
to vindicate one's honor against the horror, the
shame, the despair, of that terrible house! They
themselves, I felt sure, would thank me for it!

I decided to seek him out. I should find him
slinking about the rooms—I remembered his dirty
complexion and his furtive, ill-natured eye, his

cockily waxed mustache. He would ask me to
drink to Dostoevsky, and I should reply: "To hell
with Dostoevsky! What's the good of a Dostoevsky to nourish such worms as you? The world
would be more decent without him!—the world
would be better off if it were rid of all the crip-
ples and defectives who find their only justification in reading and writing books!"

And I was steadied with a deep satisfaction, a
perfect self-assurance: I took on a new authority.
With the most affable friendliness, I compli-
mented the man with the spectacles on his mas-
tery of the traps, and asked him whether he had
taken lessons. He said, no: that he had just
picked it up, and added some quiet pleasantry, at
which I uproariously laughed, but to which I had
paid no attention, as I had been thinking of the
classical statue which Larry Mickler had smashed
on the mantelpiece and which now presented itself to my mind in the guise of a silver-gray
Athena as slender as her spear—and this vision,
in the glimpse of a second, had dragged with it all
the fresh bright beauty of the portfolio of drawings for Homer which Bobby McIlvaine had
shown Rita and me that May night in University
Place.

I arose and thanked the drummer for his drink,
which I extravagantly commended with a conde-
scension almost regal. He offered me another,
which I took.

Walking composedly from room to room, I began scouring the house for Larry Mickler: with a
keen and arrogant glance, I scrutinized the groups
one by one.—I told myself that, once Mickler was

disposed of, I should carry off the pretty brunette, who had come to seem to me very desirable—I should meet her at first on her professional basis, and then I should compel her to be human with me—she should drop that horrible manner and mask, she should share with me her feelings and her thoughts!—She should become my companion —she should love me!

But I could find Larry Mickler nowhere, and when at last I began to inquire, nobody seemed to know what had become of him. In the front room, I was taken aback to discover that the girl with the brown eyes had already reached an understanding with a clownish-looking elderly man, who wore a heavy black ribbon on his eye-glasses. He was pressing her to leave with him at once; and she was explaining that she would have to wait until her "girl-friend" was ready to go. The little fish-faced blonde, for her part, had, in the meantime, been taken in the toils of one of the licensed Greenwich Village lunatics, who, without a penny in his pocket, was exerting the active and ironic intelligence of which his derangement had never deprived him to convince her of the seriousness of his intentions.

I went up to Tony Scallopino, who greeted me with a broad, sunny smile, and asked him whether he had seen Larry Mickler. "I just see him go," he replied.

I stood for a moment without speaking. Then, "What's the idea," I began, "of bringing these girls here to-night?" "They're just two little girls," he explained, "who come to my place to dance. They've had hard luck and they have to

earn a little money. They're two very nice girls."
He had said this with a smiling eye in which I
thought I detected insolence: I found myself
glaring at him. "Well, I think that it was a great
mistake to bring them here to-night!" I declared.

His grin was for a second obscured by a blink,
like the shutter of a camera: he began to say
something more, I don't know what. I only
stared into his face: his eyes were wide open but
shrewd; he still smiled—he had the habitual
tactfulness of the Italian restaurant-proprietor,
but his obsequiousness was gone: he was raising
his heavy black eyebrows, as if in protest and
surprise. I felt that he thought me drunk, that
he considered my objections tactless: was Tony
Scallopino not himself an independent Villager?
had he not been invited to the party? had he not
sometimes loaned money to the lunatic who was
attempting to impose on the blond girl? had he
not talked like a brother to Hugo of the trials and
aspirations of the workers? had he not cashed my
checks?

My lips opened, without my having planned it,
and, despite the gummy tongue of drunkenness,
I heard myself suddenly interrupt him: "You
used to be a Wobbly! You used to talk about
justice to the workers! Well, it seems to me that
now you're betraying the workers! You're trying to give the Greenwich Villagers a taste for
leisure-class luxuries! You've turned your old
Italian restaurant into an expensive up-town
night-club!—and you charge us high prices for
bad liquor! And you have the nerve to bring
these girls—" He tried to slip away, but I seized

him by the arms and pinioned him against the wall: "You used to talk about the social revolution—well, if there's ever a social revolution, you proletarians who run night-clubs will be the first to get the axe!—When I first came down to Greenwich Village——"

He was angry and tried to pull away—I thought I heard him say, "You must be drunk!" and saw him give me a black malign look. With a powerful movement of his arms, he lifted them and pushed me away with such force that I staggered backward and almost fell.—I struck him in the jaw with my fist—and the next moment was looking at the room from a different point of view, and knew that I was lying on the floor.

IV

IN the bright warm room, so alive inside the
bleak November dark, before the fire burning briskly and stoutly, Professor Grosbeake's
three beautiful daughters gave me tea, in their
parents' absence. Among the elegant and slender
spindles of the legs and rungs of the English
furniture, which seemed blacker and stronger-
sinewed, as if they had been brought to a sharper
focus, than American mahogany—which, as in
the case of the Queen Anne secretary, with its
narrow shape, its dark dense grain, its close-laid
shelves above, hooded with a double-loaf top, and
its close-packed drawers below, diminishing in
thickness toward the bottom, its air of having always contained sealed letters and legal papers, all
safely and neatly locked away, seemed designed
for a tighter, compacter, and more downright civilization; among the late pale autumnal flowers, the
roses and the bowl of white cosmos; the white
ruffle-bordered curtains against the black of the
winter panes and the patches of confused pink and
green made by the modest modernist paintings
—Magda, Frieda, and Rosamond, themselves in
fresh light frocks like the flowers, enchanted me
with their loveliness and candor.

They were all very smooth and blond; they
had never bobbed their hair, and Frieda and
Magda wore theirs brushed abundantly down their
backs, like Alice in the Alice books. Rosamond,
who was older than the twins, had hers up: it was
parted in the middle and tightly wound behind in

a blond and young-womanly knot, so that, if one
thought only of her hair, she seemed like a young
German fräulein (Mrs. Grosbeake was German),
whereas, if one thought of her blue eyes, her
straight nose, her long oval face and her long and
graceful neck, she seemed like an English girl.
She served the tea with nice shy manners. Rosamond was dressed in pale blue; and one of the
twins, Magda, wore white, and Frieda, a kind of
lilac, with stockings a kind of lavender, lighter
than the frock. The twins seemed rather German
than English: they had plump round cheeks and
round noses, and were maturely developed for
fourteen.

Frieda had golden-red hair, which gave a singular effect of richness as it came down over her
purple dress; Magda was more heavily built and
slower-moving and slower-thinking than her sister: she was the blondest of all—her hair was the
palest, purest flaxen I had ever seen. And her
blondness made me think of Daisy, whom I expected to see the next day.

(I had lately come back from abroad. My
aunt had left me a small legacy, and very soon
after the night at Sue Borglum's, I had gone to
Europe and had stayed there till fall. When I
had returned, I had been eager to see Grosbeake,
one of whose books I had bought in England and
had been reading on the boat, and in whom I
now felt a new interest. I had also planned to
visit Daisy and Pete Bird, who had left New
York, even before I had, and were now living together in the country, not far out of my way
back to town. Since I had been back, I had writ-

ten to Daisy, and she had invited me to come to see them.)

I liked the English voices of the young Grosbeakes: they had a soft flurried way of speaking, and a maidenly innocence of timbre, quite unlike young American girls (though the twins were beginning already to acquire American slang). "I don't like this kind of crackers," said Magda. "We couldn't get the regular biscuits," Rosamond explained. "The grocer's all out of them.—I'm sorry," she went on seriously to me. "I'm afraid they're not very good!" "You always say 'biscuits,'" said Frieda, "and Magda always says 'crackers.' I think we all ought to say the same thing!" "What do you say?" queried Magda. "Sometimes I say one," said Frieda, "and sometimes I say the other. But I like 'biscuits' best!" "I think these are really crackers," said Rosamond, who did not want my feelings hurt by a discrimination in favor of 'biscuits,' "because they crackle so when you break them." "That's why I think 'biscuits' is better," insisted Frieda, "—because 'crackers' sounds as if they *all* crackled—but *some* biscuits just bend, you know!" "They're not biscuits," said Rosamond. "They're cakes.—Won't you have some more tea?" she urged me. "No," said Frieda, "you know those little soft ones that we had in the country last summer, that you can almost bend in two!" "They were little cakes," said Rosamond.—We heard some one come in at the front door. "There's Father," Magda announced.

I could see Grosbeake taking off his black coat

and his low-crowned black hat and setting his stick
in the stand, before he appeared in the doorway.
He had the rounded back of the scholar, a back,
indeed, almost humped—of which I always used
to feel that the exceptional extent to which it was
bowed was an index to the degree of the difficulty
of his researches. But Grosbeake, beyond this,
had nothing of the physical deficiency—the weak
eyes or the feeble figure—ordinarily attributed
to the scholar. On the contrary, he seemed to
have sprung from some tough ruddy-cheeked English stock which not even a lifetime of universities could enervate or fade. Despite the fineness
of his features, he had something of Mr. Pickwick
and even something of Mr. Punch. And upon an
American who had been living in New York, he
produced a curious and gratifying impression: it
was as if one were surprised and rejoiced, after
seeing a horde of depersonalized masks, at finding some one who possessed a face. With his
fair cheeks flushed rosy by the cold, his salient
nose and chin, his slanting Henry VIII eyes and
his look of having been carved by hand out of
some very sound kind of wood by a wood-carver
of the days before machinery, he gave the impression of being a product, by way of the generations
which had preceded him, of a constant hand-to-
hand encounter with the turbulence of the elements and with the occasions of human life. He
wore black English clothes and his stiff white
cuffs were very white: his collar and his cravat,
and his white locks which came down over his
collar, seemed to me very old-fashioned. He always carried a thickish dark stick, with a brass

top of interlocked apes, which a brother had
brought him from India.

He greeted me with his charming courtesy and
peered up at me with wise and subtle bird-lidded
eyes. "I'm sorry," he explained, "not to have
been able to be here for tea. But there was a
meeting of the examination committee at precisely a quarter to five—something which would
be unthinkable in England, you know." He lifted
sparse old eyebrows in a smile. "Rather than
make the dons miss their tea, they'd allow the
examination to be prepared without adequate
consultation!—I had proposed holding the meeting in a tea-room, but they didn't seem to care
for the suggestion—or to take the hint!" He
spoke slowly and very deliberately, and his voice
had fine up-and-down inflections of sweetness
and irony: his nostrils had inflections, too, and
vibrated while he spoke.

"I'm afraid the tea's cold," said Rosamond.
"I'll have some fresh made." "No: never mind!"
said Grosbeake. He stood before the fire, his
hands clasped just above his stomach. "I think we
shall have snow," he announced. "I think we shall
have snow!—The Dean was very sure we
shouldn't—but I believe that we shall!" I remarked that we had had no frost and that the
afternoon had been warm. "That was what the
Dean pointed out," he replied. "He even insisted
on making a bet with me. He bet me a bottle of
Scotch whiskey against a bottle of my sherry. I
think he'll get the better of the bargain: the
sherry is very good: it was given me by a friend
in the Embassy, who had the privilege of bringing it in!"

He took the cup of tepid tea from Rosamond and sat down in an arm-chair before the fire. He asked me about myself and what I had been writing. I was ashamed to be obliged to tell him that, even while I had been abroad, I had really not written anything—I said that my literary morale had been low, or something equally silly.

"I was just thinking," he replied, "in the Dean's room, in looking at the portraits of the college presidents there—that it may be from certain points of view as much of a misfortune to have too much character, too well-sustained a morale, as to have too little. When I looked at the early presidents, especially the seventeenth-century ones, I said to myself, 'There are men whose character has been overdeveloped!' It's a very special combination of qualities, you know, that's required for a mind capable of original work. A man mustn't have his character too vigorously developed, because he must be able to experiment with ideas. It's like going to buy a hat, you know—first you try one on and wear it for a bit to see how it goes, and then you try on another. But a man with a strongly developed character is unable to do that.—But, on the other hand, of course, he must still have character enough not simply to drift about without preferring one idea to another."

Grosbeake had a curious irony, which was always at the same time benign. It was the irony —one sees it seldom—of a mind which is at once innocent and subtle, and which has, in consequence, something divine about it: an irony without malice. He had a touch perhaps of the

vanity, or rather, of the dandyism, of the modern
mathematical philosopher, who finds himself provided with paradoxes at once so surprising, so
attractive and so sound. I have heard him comment with his calm amusement on the mistakes
of unmathematical philosophers when they attempted to invoke mathematics: "It's curious,"
he would say, "how peculiarly unfortunate they
are in their choice of mathematical examples!
They always seem to hit upon something which
isn't necessarily true at all—which might quite
as well be the other way, you know! Bradley,
for example, in his *Logic,* when he wants to give
an illustration of a particularly indisputable truth
—something we must accept as self-evident—that,
if B is to the left of C, and if A is to the left
of B, then A must be to the left of C, also—
when, of course, that's not true at all!—if you
prolong a straight line indefinitely, you come back
on the other side!" Though, when Bradley's
Logic was written, non-Euclidean geometry could
hardly have been widely known. (There may have
entered, also, into Grosbeake's attitude, in this particular instance, some traditional opposition between the points of view of Cambridge and Oxford.)

But no one could have been farther than Grosbeake from the essential triviality of mind which
academic arrogance or complacency so often tries
to disguise. For if Hugo Bamman and his father were the modern type cf saints, Grosbeake
was a modern type of sage, who taught wisdom in
casual conversation and virtue only by example.
I had felt his influence even in college, at a time

when I as yet knew nothing of his philosophical
ideas. For Grosbeake had the most comprehensive mind, at home in the most varied fields, with
which I had ever come into contact. For him,
philosophy was an attempt to take account of all
the aspects of the universe, and to find in them
coherence and a meaning; so that Grosbeake's
comment on any subject had a special significance and value, and, despite the fact that he
never made an effort to expostulate or convert,
was likely to present itself long afterwards as
something to be seriously considered in making
up one's own mind on the subject. And though
he detested every sort of preaching (Mr. Bamman had been a born preacher), and though even
the study of Ethics was inconceivable to him, he
had the effect, more than any one else I had
known, of making moral distinction attractive. I
remember his saying once of some student, a student of whose abilities he thought well, but who,
as punishment for some escapade, had had his
chapel cuts taken away from him, so that he
couldn't go out of town over Sundays, that it
would "do him good," because he would now
work during the week-ends. "So you do believe
in doing people good!" some one present had
caught him up. "I thought you didn't believe in
that!" "That's an object," Grosbeake had replied, a little taken aback, "which I believe is
best promoted indirectly."

Mrs. Grosbeake came in before dinner: she
was a broad, handsome, placid German woman,
very thoroughly educated and very practical. One
always felt that she was a kind of base upon

which Grosbeake's metaphysics rested; for he was more sensitive and nervous than he appeared, and, although intellectually imperturbable, was in other ways easily disorganized.

We had dinner in the white-walled dining-room—it was a solid and attractive Colonial house. The Grosbeakes had brought over their own silver, as well as their own furniture, and the pieces had always seemed to me to possess plainly discernible personalities, even physiognomies: there was a squarish silver tea-pot which squatted flat upon the table and had a very sharp emphatic spout that jutted straight out from the base and was balanced on the other side by a long straight high-cocked handle. And the cream-pitcher, the sauce-boat, and even the little salt-cellars straddled sturdily on three tiny legs, like some sort of blunt-beaked beetles, or rather, it occurred to me to-night, like the snouted and pot-bellied demons of Bruegel or Callot. Even the color and substance of the food seemed to have a special richness and density, as if they had been painted in a still-life: the bread and the boiled potatoes looked particularly white and firm, the mound of currant jelly particularly lucent and red, and the beefsteak particularly vivid in its contrasts of red and brown. The Ambassador's sherry was delicious. In spite, however, of the satisfaction which Grosbeake had seemed to feel in it, his epicurean tastes were really indulged almost exclusively in the things of the intellect, so that I have heard him relish a page of Hume as if it had been a wine, whereas food and drink themselves, as well as other material comforts, he usually disregarded. Now he dominated the table, talking tranquilly and blandly; and in the presence of their father and mother, the three lovely Grosbeake girls—unlike young American girls, who usually dominate their parents—were entirely in abeyance, with only an occasional low rapid interchange between the twins, who were sitting together.

"I've been reading Sinclair Lewis's *Babbitt*," Grosbeake remarked. I asked him what he thought of it. "Oh, very good," he replied. "Though a little unfair to Babbitt, I think. Of course, I know very little about the American cities of the Middle West—I can't pretend to speak. But from the students from the West whom I've had in my courses, I get rather a different impression. They're very alert, you know—very eager to learn. And they do well: they grasp things very quickly. So I don't think that the families they come from can be quite so uniformly benighted as Lewis represents them in *Babbitt*.—And I feel, in reading your friend Hugo Bamman, that he paints a little too sombre a picture of the business men and their families in much the same way.

"It seems to me rather a mistake, you know, to hold the business men up to ridicule for their Rotary Clubs and their fraternal organizations. Under conditions of that kind, where the city is quite new and the people have no institutions, they have to create some sort of institutions in order to hold the community together. Rotary Clubs and societies of that sort, imperfect as they may be, fulfil a very necessary function.

"It seems to me that, from some points of view, the most unfortunate feature of American business is its failure to provide real leaders. Professor Pittinger, who has been making a study of the subject, tells me that it has become impossible, for example, for the president or one of the directors of a large corporation to leave a controlling interest to his son. He can only leave him an investment, and the son can spend the money as he pleases; but he inherits no responsibility and no power, and the surviving officers of the company don't recognize his right to any. That seems to me unfortunate, because where the father has to make his own way, largely without advantages, to a position of importance, the son, who has had the advantages, finds himself with no power. You often find in England that the squire who has lived in the country, and has had to deal at first-hand with his tenants, and with his animals and land, has a far stronger sense of realities than the more enlightened Londoner."

"But he sometimes mistreats his tenants and mismanages his estate abominably," Mrs. Grosbeake interjected.

"If he does," continued Grosbeake, "he knows better what he's doing, nevertheless, than the average Liberal member of Parliament, say, who has the best intentions in the world, but who lives between his club, and certain houses to which he goes, and the House of Commons—always seeing the same people, who are all people of precisely his way of thinking, who are living in precisely the same way—so that he never at any

point really comes into contact with realities—
and so never really knows what he is talking
about. Even Morley was a little like that.

"I wonder whether it mightn't be an advantage, both to the sons of business men and to the
businesses themselves, if the second generation
could take over some responsibility in connection
with their fathers' work. They seem to me very
intelligent—so far as I've been able to judge
from those I meet in my classes—and the effect
on trade and industry of even one generation of
such men might, I should think, be enormous.
In that event, the Rotary Clubs might become
very important institutions—they might provide
the moral leadership for business."

I had so long been taking it for granted that no
good could come out of business, that this idea of
Grosbeake's seemed to me a very queer and for-
eign one; but I reflected on what he had said.

I always listened with interest and respect to
Grosbeake's opinions on American matters. He
had studied American affairs with the attention,
at once sympathetic and detached, which he applied to everything, and he often succeeded in
illumining them with that uncanny divination
which he displayed in all sorts of fields quite outside his special province. At that time, it had become the custom for Englishmen who visited
America—we encouraged it, of course, ourselves
—to edify us with generalizations about American life and institutions—generalizations often
based on a round of cocktail parties in New York,
or, at most, on a lecture tour. So many of the
prizes in America always went to the third and

second-rate, that we had become, especially since
the War, a paradise for British mediocrities—
poets, novelists, and universal critics, who had
often great success as lecturers. They went about
patronizing the Americans with a gusto and a
giddy elation which suggested that they might
themselves have been patronized at home; and they
would sometimes tour the country from coast to
coast and return again and again. It was, therefore, peculiarly gratifying for an American to
discover in Grosbeake those qualities of tough-
ness, richness, eccentricity, and independence
which one had admired in English literature and
history, but of which one had so often been
disappointed in the English celebrities who
visited us.

After dinner, we sat before the fire. Mrs.
Grosbeake seemed to contribute a ground-tone of
infinite repose: she made one feel that the body
of humanity was invulnerably solid and sound,
and that it was deep and contained many trea-
sures which had never been brought to birth.
She sat with her feet side by side, resting square-
ly on the floor, and she wore some sort of leather
sandals, with very wide blunt toes. These sandals, like the modernist paintings (which Grosbeake had bought from a former student, in
financial difficulties), were one of the odd notes
of unconventionality in the tranquil conventional
household; and they surprised me in the same un-
warranted way as when one found Grosbeake, in
certain of his writings, carrying his philosophical
principles through morals into the field of political criticism and bringing in an indictment
against nationalism or capitalism.

I had never, as an undergraduate, read anything which Grosbeake had written, and I had never taken any of his courses. I had, however, in my senior year, sometimes gone to his house. After meeting him once or twice at teas, I had run into him one day in the hallway of one of the recitation buildings: he had recognized me and had talked to me about an article which I had just written for the college magazine, and which had aroused a certain amount of controversy. I had attacked wholesale, as a sinister conspiracy against freedom of action and thought, the policy of the English Department, the administration of the Dean's office, football massmeetings, compulsory chapel, and the custom of compelling freshmen to wear little black caps; and I was surprised and rather embarrassed by Grosbeake's expression of friendly interest. I replied almost apologetically—I had been dismayed by the rumpus I had roused—that I seemed to have laid myself open to a good deal of adverse criticism. "Ah, well," Grosbeake had reassured me, "one can't take up any position, can one? without doing that." My complaints had been made in resentment, and they had been answered with resentment by the faculty, the alumni, the editors of the college daily, the officers of the athletic association, and some of the more ardent and articulate freshmen, who insisted that they asked nothing better than to pay homage to the college tradition by continuing to wear their little black caps: it had never occurred to me, at the time, that I was engaged in doing anything so dignified as taking up a position, and

I had felt that I must be careful, in the future, to conduct the controversy with more scrupulousness and sobriety, that I must remember my intellectual responsibilities. And half my bitterness and indignation against the college authorities was gone at finding an elderly and important professor willing to consider without heat what I had said.

He had invited me then to his house, and I used to go there on Sunday evenings, when the Grosbeakes received faculty and students. I rarely heard him talk about his subject, and did not understand him when he did: I had only the vaguest notion what it was. I figured him as eternally occupied with solving the same sort of problems with which I had struggled in Trigonometry and Permutations and Combinations. I did not know that those strings of puzzles were not the whole of mathematics, but merely multiplied illustrations of general mathematical laws, in which no one had attempted to interest us. And still less did I realize that Grosbeake had passed beyond Mathematics proper to Symbolic Logic (it was principally the fact that we had in our faculty another of the small but infatuated band of the students of Symbolic Logic—a man with whom he wished to collaborate—which had brought him to the United States and which had kept him there so long). I did not know that Symbolic Logic was an attempt to provide a universal language for all the branches of science, and that this attempt to formulate relations common to different departments of thought was itself a deeper expression of the same genius which had given rise to Grosbeake's interest in such varied fields of human activity, and of his extraordinary instinct for tracing their inter-relations. Aside from his personal distinction and charm, it was this gift which had fascinated me: he had usually talked to me about literature, but, aside from his appreciation of poetry, plays, and novels as such—which was in itself remarkable—he had also a brilliant faculty for reading into them social and moral history and revealing their philosophic implications. He was the first person, since Hugo's father, who had helped me toward the kind of education which I had begun when Mr. Bamman had talked to me at school about Shakespeare.

I had, however, never guessed at Grosbeake's real importance—and indeed his importance outside his special field had never really appeared until a year or two before the War, when he had turned from mathematics to philosophy. When I came to read his books, I was astonished. First of all, Grosbeake's tone and style, in his philosophical writings, were not at all what I should have expected. His manner in conversation was rather urbane, dispassionate, and dry: he seemed, as I have said, to approach ideas with a certain epicureanism of the intellect. But his writing had a close tough grain: it was crystalline, in the sense that it gave an effect of the hardness and clarity of crystals rather than of the limpidity of crystal; it had a peculiar earnestness and intensity, and a kind of incandescence. But what had surprised me most—I had already had some idea of the universal scope of his mind—were the power of his imagination and the boldness and stoutness of his spirit.

Grosbeake was one of the first modern philosophers, really competent to understand the new
physics of relativity and quantum theory, who
had made an attempt, on the full scale, to trace
the consequences of these discoveries for the
concepts of general philosophy, and to construct
a system which should admit them. This had
brought him to a drastic rejection of the philosophical assumptions of old-fashioned mechanis-
tic science.

Since my recent encounters with the world
in New York, which had made me feel my
own weakness and baseness, I had myself been
haunted and oppressed, as on the night of Sue
Borglum's party, by the thought that humanity,
after all, was merely another race of animals,
whose behavior was fixed by their environment,
and by the cells which they had had from their
parents, and that the earth and all its creatures
was only a complicated interaction of hard little
particles like bullets. I now learned that it had
lately become possible, in the light of scientific
research—that it had even become inevitable
(though I was far from being able to follow all
Grosbeake's arguments) to regard the universe,
not as a machine, which had once been wound up
and was still running, but as an organism in
course of development. The unit was no longer a
bullet, but something called an event; and the
world was a flux of events. The relativity of time
and space and the anomalous behavior of elec-
trons, in undermining the "iron laws" of nature,
had opened flood-gates of speculation which the
ordinary reasonable mind, the kind of mind

which respected science without examining its assumptions or attempting to force them to their consequences, had long tended to regard as closed. And despite the surprise and disapproval of other mathematicians who, capable of practising only one trade, prided themselves on sticking to their lasts, Professor Grosbeake had late in his career emerged as a metaphysician.

I wanted to make him talk on this subject, and I inquired vaguely about the congress of a scientific association which he had attended the summer before. He told me briefly of some of its proceedings, then added, after a pause, with his bland and serious irony: "If you want to see the sort of men that the mediæval church must have been made up of, you should study an assemblage of modern scientists. I thought about them last summer that they must be very like the mediæval doctors. They're all more or less internationally minded, you know, and they're men of strong character and conviction—and they're all authoritarians: they subscribe to a body of dogma and they won't countenance any heresy. If a scientist has evolved an hypothesis which runs counter to the established hypothesis, they won't give it a serious hearing—if he's performed an experiment, you know, which conflicts with accepted experiments, they refuse to look at it!"——

At this point in the conversation, Magda and Frieda, who had to go to bed, came in to say goodnight. They kissed their mother, who spoke to them in a low voice, but they hesitated about kissing their father—in the midst of solemn discourse and with a visitor present. Magda hung back by her mother's couch, but Frieda cut the knot by dashing forward, diving for his bald brow—I saw her own beautiful hair over her shoulders, like some spilling of gold by the gods—and running abruptly out of the room. "Oh, good-night, my dear!" said Grosbeake.—"They have never executed any one," he continued—Magda kissed him on the cheek, more diffidently: "Good-night, my dear!—But there are other methods of suppression even more expedient and effective; for burning calls attention to the victim."

His criticism of contemporary science soon led him into metaphysics.—The entrance of those gold and white girls—the offspring, so late in life, of that old bald round-shouldered man who had spent long years in the obstinate plumbing (by means of formulas so difficult and abstract that they excluded even ideas of number, so far beyond the ordinary reaches of even scientific minds that they dismayed even mathematicians) of that mysterious reality which is at once what we find outside us and what we think about it—the entrance of Grosbeake's lovely daughters had had the effect on me of a revelation of the human vitality, the creative force of flesh and blood, which is embodied in abstract thought. It was as if my imagination had fully conceived for the first time that the logician's chain of propositions, no less than the astronomer's systems and the physicist's analysis of the invisible, was as much the ripened fruit of rich natures as the poetry of Shakespeare and Dante, or as those beautiful long-limbed children, the breed of the Kentish seas and of the forests of the Rhineland, who had brusquely embraced their father.

He talked to me about the book he was writing. All that I had ever learned at college of philosophy had been a conception of the external world as a colorless and soundless wilderness whose true nature one could never know, which one could not even imagine—but which I did, none the less, imagine as a vast landscape of polar spaces in whose eternal twilight one wandered, preoccupied and deluded by a flicker of magic-lantern pictures which danced inside one's mind and forever remained private to oneself. I had now learned, however, from Grosbeake that since, for example, the high flush of Rita's cheeks and the sound of her voice reciting poetry had so radically affected my behavior, they must belong as much to reality, to that Nature which was no longer outside one, as the blood corpuscles and the light-waves, the sound-waves and the vocal organs which were assumed to have produced them. And it now appeared that Grosbeake admitted as belonging, also, to reality those æsthetic values which, for example, had made Rita, when she wrote her poems, feel that the pavements of the Village were harsh and the sound of the river musical. And so, finally, he told me, moral values, which he identified with æsthetic values, must be equally a part of that reality which he found it impossible to split into two divisions of mind and matter, body and soul. Those moral judgments, then, I reflected, which had given rise to my disgust and despair the night of Sue Borghum's party had been, after all, as real, as much to be taken seriously, as the biological and neurological processes to which I had tended to reduce them.

What astonished me most, however, was that Grosbeake now crowned his system with a new conception of God: he brought God back into the universe of science, under what appeared to me at first an unfamiliar form. For Grosbeake's God was as different as possible from the tolerant and moderate Great Spirit, the enlightened parliamentary monarch, of the modern liberal theologian. God, for Grosbeake, was the ultimate harmony implied by the æsthetic and moral values of which men were aware in the universe; and our moments of divine revelation were simply those when we realized most indubitably the necessity of this harmony and order, when we became most acutely conscious of this creative purpose of God. And it was, then, this creative purpose which, in the interest of the ultimate harmony, determined which possibilities, among the infinite possibilities of the constant flux of events—the development of the universal organism—should make themselves actual.

I listened to Grosbeake with excitement. He seemed to me at that moment to justify to me those instincts and those beliefs which—suspicious of all the world and uncertain of myself most of all—I had lately come to doubt. And I was moved by what seemed to me the greatness of his mind and the boldness of his spirit amidst the modesty and mildness of his home.—I mustn't keep him up, then, and tire him: Mrs. Grosbeake had already gone to bed.

I said that I must go, and he got up and brought a bowl of nuts, which we cracked in front of the fire. He told me some Victorian anecdote about

Gladstone and Disraeli, whom he always called "Dizzy."

As I finally came out of the warm house into the white-framed glass-sided porch which enclosed the front door, I felt a tinge of crispness in the air, as when the first ice-splinters web a pond, and I caught the chilly fragrance of the roses and the white and daisylike cosmos, which had been set out in vases for the night—and as I took leave of Grosbeake—gazing out through the glass at the pavement lightly dappled with leaves and the dark grass glittering with wet—my mind bemused with a vision of God as a vast crystal fixing its symmetry from a liquefied universe—I felt a delicious delicacy of iciness, glossy fall-leaf slivers and black rain-glinting glass.

"It's beginning to snow," said Grosbeake. It was true: it was not raining, but snowing. A great flake alighted on my sleeve. "So I win my bet with the Dean," he said. "I shall have his Scotch whiskey and not he my sherry!—You know, the weather's the only subject on which I really regard myself as infallible. It comes from being bred on the Kentish coast—learning about one's weather from the narrow seas! What does Dean Mosely know of the weather?—coming from an inland city like Indianapolis!"

Grosbeake stood in the outside door and regarded the large flakes with satisfaction. "Dean Mosely kept insisting," he continued, "that there were none of the signs of snow—and when he came to enumerate them, I saw that it was true: there were none of the signs. But I knew it was going to snow!"

* * *

It was a heavy snowstorm for November. It had snowed, and then rained, and then frozen: on the train, the next afternoon, when I scraped a peep-hole in the frost-glazed window, I disclosed a vignette of fences, strung with wires of ice, and tree-branches decked with crystals, like glittering chandeliers.

But it was late when I arrived at my station: the falling darkness and the cold lay heavy on the little town. I finally succeeded in getting a taxi, which had no cushions on the seat and which bucked over the frozen ruts. There were nice white houses on the road and all the people seemed to be inside them: the windows were orange against the snow, which was bluing and graying with the night.

To the east, when we had left behind the town, an army of corn-stacks in the grayness were frozen to their posts; and to the west, the skies were split across with the tragic gold and black of a late November sunset. The grandeur of the winter landscape—since Grosbeake had predicted the snowfall—had associated itself in my mind with the grandeur of the philosophic mind; and as I gazed at those last gigantic cracks of a light beyond human skies, I remembered the fiery walls of the world of which Lucretius had said that the thinker, in sending his intellect beyond them, had broken Nature's locks and won the freedom of the universe: they seemed to speak to me of bold and lonely thought.

The house, when we finally pulled in to it, was so low that it seemed sunk in the snow—deep-embedded in the winter ground, which held it fast: there was a single yellow square of light.

Pete Bird hurried cordially out—I could see Daisy standing in the doorway. Pete insisted on my not paying for the taxi: "Just put it on my bill!" he told the man.

Inside, I found Daisy transformed: she greeted me with her frank American smile, but it was this time unmistakably the smile of the young American girls of my boyhood, who had never used lipstick or rouge. I was surprised to see her wholly without make-up: her lips were a pale coral-pink and her hair, which at Sue Borglum's party had been mongrel, muddy and dull, was now an even flaxen yellow. She was wearing a neat white apron over a pretty blue dress, and looked exactly like some model little housewife in a bright-colored American advertisement, smiling sunnily over the lightness of a new kind of pancake-flour or the flavor of a can of baked beans.

She apologized for the apron—she was just getting dinner, she said—and I thought that she knew she looked well in it. I told her how healthy and lovely she looked. "Just feel this!" she invited me, hooking up her little short-sleeved elbow: I found it studded with solid bulging muscles. "Good Heavens!" I exclaimed. "How did you ever get like that?" "Just working!" Daisy explained. "We fixed the place all up ourselves. When we came, it was just a dump!"

Pete himself, to my surprise, with his slight erect figure, seemed wiry, effective and hardy. He wore a khaki shirt with a smartly tied navy-blue tie, which gave to his old gray trousers and his old Norfolk jacket which did not match them, a gentlemanly air of roughing it.

Daisy amiably excused herself and went to attend to the dinner on the stove. Pete Bird—a casual and cordial host—invited me in before the fire.

The hall had been a little nondescript, a cross between a work-shed and a hall-closet; but the living-room was orderly and cheerful. There was a bright rag-rug on the floor, and there were bright prints and maps on the walls—Pete was a great hand at making maps—and lamps with warmly glowing lampshades, also the work of Pete. And there was a large old-fashioned fireplace, where big logs were roaring and snapping on tall black old-fashioned andirons, still stiff-necked, though lame and leaning crooked.

I expressed my enthusiasm for the fire, and admired the fireplace and the room. Pete received my compliments with the easy nod and brief word of the owner of an Adirondack camp: he made one feel that the spacious fireplace was something he had had specially built, and evoked a vision of moose-horns and bear-heads under heavy darkling rafters.

"That black log's not burning well," he announced. "Either it's frozen in the cracks or it's cranky!" He hooked it and wrenched it with a poker and an old rickety pair of tongs which did not come together: he had a master's way with the logs. "Get over there, you old alligator!" he commanded. "You *will* be hard-boiled, *will* you!"

"I'm sorry," he remarked, as he stood up in front of the mantelpiece, which was almost as high as his head, and invited me to sit down before the fire—"I'm sorry that I can't offer you a drink—but the only things you can get around

here are apple and alcohol, and both of them are
vile. We've finally come to the conclusion that it's
really more considerate to the guests not to offer
them anything at all!"—"We hoped you might
bring something with you," said Daisy, looking
up with her sweet candid smile: she was dealing
out white plates around a table in the middle of
the room. I apologized for not having thought
of it. "We never think of it ourselves—if you
can believe me," Pete insisted. "It's almost impossible now to get any kind of decent liquor, in
New York or anywhere else—and the kind of
drinks that you *can* get just don't interest me!"
I agreed with him heartily, and added that the
trouble with New York was that everybody there
drank far too much bad liquor. "That's why we
came to the country," said Daisy. "We decided
that it was that or the drunkard's home!"

"Now, good people!" Daisy invited us, mim-
icking the kind of women who say, "Now good
people!"—"The dinner is all ready!—if you'll
just sit down and fly at it!"

The dinner was an admirable pot-roast, with
onions, potatoes and carrots. We all ate a great
deal and did very little talking while we ate.

The table was thick-legged and long: it seemed
that Pete had made it himself—and that he had
also made or made over most of the other pieces
of furniture. When they had moved in, the place
had been desolate—full of rubbish, mould and
rats. It had taken them all summer to make it
habitable: Pete had rummaged in old barns and
houses and unearthed many mutilated antiques,
which he had then, with great patience, repaired.

He seemed to know a great deal about antiques. The principal prize was a comb-backed rocking-chair, for which Pete had himself supplied new rockers; but they warned me not to try to sit in it, because it always went over backwards. I told Pete about the Grosbeakes' furniture, and he remembered that there was a Queen Anne secretary something like the one I was describing, in the Metropolitan Museum.

For dessert, we ate golden canned peaches, and we drank a great deal of black coffee. "Now, don't worry about the dishes," said Pete to Daisy. "Just stack them in the kitchen, and I'll do them later myself!" "If that doesn't mean," replied Daisy, "that *I'll* have to do them in the morning, when they're all greasy and cold." "Don't be silly!" said Pete, indignantly.

After dinner, we sat around the fire. I asked them what they did in the evenings. "We just do this!" said Pete. "We read aloud," supplemented Daisy. "We've read Bulwer-Lytton's novels almost entirely through." "Is he any good?" I inquired. "Fine," said Daisy. "Besides, he's the only novelist that they've got in the village library." I was amazed at the idea of Daisy spending long winter evenings over Bulwer-Lytton; but as I had talked to her, I soon discovered that she had always been addicted to novel-reading and had excellent sense and taste—it had apparently been only Ray Coleman's reading aloud to her out of the *Oxford Book of English Verse* that she hadn't been able to stand.

I saw now that her ordinary vocabulary was partly literary, and that it was the combination of

literary words with slang which gave her speech
its peculiar charm—as when she had said, at the
time I had first talked to her, that the horse she
had seen in her delirium had been "leering" at
her, or when she had told me that Ray Coleman
in Paris had seemed "pretty affluent."

I asked her what writers she liked best.
"Well," she said, "when I was a girl at school, I
used to think that Compton Mackenzie was the
swellest thing in the world—I thought that that
was what life ought to be like—that was what I
thought Phil and I were like, when we ran away
from Pittsburgh. But I soon found out that the
old racket was more like a Russian novel!"

Russian novels reminded me of Larry Mickler,
and I asked Pete and Daisy about him. I had
never seen him before or since the night of Sue
Borglum's party, and I had never been able to explain him: he had come to seem to me—like the
elephantine creature whom I had encountered in
the doorway on Thirty-fourth Street—a sort of
demon who had fleetingly materialized out of the
infernal fumes of the evening. "Oh," said Daisy,
"he's perfectly harmless—he's just a fool, that's
all. He's usually controlled by Alice, his wife.
He was just acting up that night because Alice
wasn't along. He's always threatening to do
something desperate, but he usually ends up with
Alice administering triple-bromides." I asked
what Alice was like. "She's just a clean stalwart
college girl," said Daisy. "She doesn't know
quite what a genius is," Pete Bird contributed,
"but she thinks that Larry is a genius. He wrote
a novel once which he was never able to get pub-

lished, and he's always threatening to write another. In the meantime, he's in the advertising business, which he says he can never respect."

"I don't like Larry Mickler," Pete added, after a pause. "He cheats at limericks!" I asked him what he meant. "Why, he gets you to play this game where you both have to take the same first line and make up a limerick to fit it. But he's got the limericks all made up beforehand. When I finally got wise and supplied the first line myself, he couldn't do a thing—he got sullen and wouldn't play. Our relations have never been cordial since. —That's why he tried to make out that I gypped him on those liverwurst sandwiches."

I had been watching Daisy follow the talk with a childlike seriousness and candor. Though it was cold, she wore no stockings—for reasons of economy, she said—and she shifted her slim and pretty legs, with their straw-colored sharp-toed slippers, in the movements of a good little girl listening restlessly but attentively to the conversation of her elders. As we spoke humorously or gravely, told limericks or deplored the demoralizing effects of the city, she would respond with gravity or humor, turning her eyes from one speaker to the other. She seemed sober-minded, shy and nice: I felt that some of the limericks embarrassed her: I came to think of her almost as a *jeune fille* and vaguely confused her in my mind with Grosbeake's golden-haired daughters.

Like all people who live in the country, they commenced about ten to yawn: when I suggested that they must be tired they confessed it with little protestation.

"Now," said Pete, "we have a guest-room which is always at the disposal of the guests—but it's as cold as a fiddler's bitch to-night, and if you really want to keep warm, you'd better sleep here on the couch." "But what about you?" I asked. "If you can stand the cold, I can." "Oh, we sleep in here!" replied Pete—and opening the door into the next room, which had the aspect of a store-room—barren as an attic and littered with all kinds of junk—he produced a gigantic set of bed-springs, which he manœuvred through the door with nonchalance and set out on a pair of trestles.

I explored the regions beyond: there was a bedroom behind the living-room, like a plunge into a cold black lake. Through the little low square-paned window, I saw the moon, cut in brightest coldest silver over the lonely and frozen fields. There had been something almost miraculous about Grosbeake's predicting the snowfall—as if Nature had admitted him to her secrets!

I returned to the smell of wood-smoke and the yellow-shaded lamps of the living-room, and announced that I would sleep on the couch.

How jolly it was, I reflected, back amid the warmth again, to go to bed in front of a fire, in the country, in the winter-time, in the house of friends! And as I undressed in the dark and grisly store-room, which evidently represented the house as they had originally found it—before they had taken it in hand—I was moved by admiration for what seemed to me their pioneering heroism. They had established, with no help and little money, in the midst of that hard rural wilderness —if but in a single room—these amenities and decencies—this core of civilization!

And they were right! Who should know it by this time—all the more since my visit to Grosbeake!—better than I? All that dignified mankind, all that kept them from the brawling and the squalor which, the night of Sue Borglum's party, had seemed to me the universal fate, had been built up through endurance and patience, through steadiness of purpose and good faith, through property well administered, through families standing together, through lovers true to their pledges! How had I ever been taken in by that foolish and shallow philosophy of living only for the moment?—that philosophy I had learned from a woman, which was possible only for a woman, given up, by her woman's nature, to her impulses, passions and moods! I remembered how I had once used to wonder at Rita's constant preoccupation with death, both in her poetry and in conversation, and I could see now how such a life as Rita's, looking always upon the image of itself, must be ridden by the terror of death, because death meant for it the end of the world.

When Daisy was in bed, Pete Bird summoned me back into the living-room, and I wrapped myself up in blankets and lay down before the fire on the couch. But the coffee had made us wakeful and we went on talking in bed. At first, we told funny stories, till we had obviously exhausted our best and had begun to fall back on second-rate ones. Then Pete regaled me with reminiscences of eccentric Greenwich Village characters who had flourished before my day—there had been one uncompromising prophet, who had made a practice of robbing fur-stores: he would hide himself among the furs at the back, till the shop had been closed for the night, then climb out with his booty, through a window: he had, however, never profited by these activities, but had given everything he stole to the poor, and had lived himself in the direst privation.

We agreed that the great days were passing. I tried to remember some of the songs which Bobby Edwards had used to sing in the restaurants. Pete, it turned out, knew them all by heart and could sing them from beginning to end. We agreed that there had been something remarkable about Bobby Edwards. I said it was the curious prestige which very clever people sometimes acquire by pretending to be stupid. Pete said that this was not quite it, because Bobby Edwards did not look stupid: the thing was that he never changed his face and consequently had everybody buffaloed.

These songs led to other songs: Pete and I finally got to the point of singing *My Bonnie Lies Over the Ocean* and *There Is a Tavern in the Town*. "I suppose this burns you up," I said to Daisy, who had for some time been lying silent. "I suppose you want to go to sleep." "Oh, I guess I can bear it!" she answered—then added, after a pause: *"My Bonnie Lies Over the Ocean* always reminds me of when I was a girl in Yarmouth— in Canada. My uncle used to sing it.—And he used to sing *The Girl I Left Behind Me,* too. I used to love to hearum sing that!" Her voice, as she lay in the darkness, divested of the emphasis of day, had almost the timbre of a child's—and it moved me with the charming pathos of young girls' voices, the pathos of frailness and freshness. "Did you come from Canada?" I asked. "I thought you came from Pittsburgh!" "My mother came from there," she explained. "My aunt still lives up there. I used to be up there a lot when I was a kid.—Yes, I'm really just a country girl!" she said, burlesquing herself. "That's why I take so easily to living out here. My other aunt," she went on, after a moment's recollection, "married some kind of a nobleman.—I always thought there must have been something wrong withum—he must have had syphilis or something. But he was a real nobleman, it seemed!"

When we were tired of singing ballads, we experimented with hymns: I rendered, with what I felt at the time was an impressive solemnity and resonance, *Oh God, Our Help in Ages Past,* and *The Starry Firmament on High.*—But the second of these was met by silence—I received no response from the bed. And when Pete and Daisy replied to my good-night, it was plain they had been asleep.

Those magnificent hymns! I went on thinking. What a first-rate poet Watts had been! And that grandeur of the universe, of the moral principle it implied—did one not feel it, also, even, in the calm complacent firmament of Addison?

Perhaps the effect on my imagination of Grosbeake's religious ideas had been, in recreating my conception of God, to revive for me a vision of the Devil; but at any rate, my recent image of Larry Mickler as a species of hobgoblin combined itself with my assimilation of the gravy-boat and cream-pitcher at the Grosbeakes' to the demons of Bruegel and Callot, to inspire me with the idea of a satire in which I should ascribe to a race of demons all those anti-social views and habits which had come lately to seem to me so sinister.

My mind, laying hold upon this, worked for a time with great clarity and speed: I even framed sentences and paragraphs: "The attitude of the demons toward each other is entirely devoid of the amenity and dignity characteristic of human behavior. In their amorous relations, they are neither romantic nor faithful. Many of the demons do not function sexually, but among those that do—notably the succubæ and incubi—their matings are wholly physical and transient, and involve neither responsibility nor affection. A human being who has seen the demons at close range is not perhaps disposed to consider this unnatural. The more hideous and monstrous types have died out, like the larger and more powerful: the bat's ears, pig's snout and ape's mug appear only in modified forms; and such a bestial and complex mask as that worn, for example, by Dürer's Satan would probably be impossible to-day. Yet the devils which have endured to our own time are still sufficiently unsightly and grotesque, and in a sufficient variety of ways, to appear repulsive to human taste as objects of amorous desire, and impracticable even for each other. We do not wonder when a female demon, coming straight from the embraces of a male, makes no scruple of spitting and jeering at him in the presence of other female demons, or in the presence of another male; or when a male, who has been mating with a female, makes her the victim of one of those

practical jokes to which the devils are so inveter-
ately addicted—impaling her in a public place or
hacking off her arms and legs and leaving her on
a crowded thoroughfare. We should, however,
be quite wrong in supposing that the devils resent each other's ugliness: being entirely without
ideas of beauty, they are, in consequence, impervious to ugliness, and do not even, as has sometimes been supposed, esteem it for its own sake.
The demons exchange, in their amorous intercourse, in a manner not unlike ours, pledges of
lasting affection and epithets of tender endear-
ment; but these expressions are simple reflexes
involved in the physical process itself and as in-
voluntary as it; they attach no significance to
them and we should wrong them in supposing they
do. The devils are sterile, and unable, or unwilling, to reproduce their kind.

"The fiends have a highly developed literature,
which reflects their habits and ideas. It is mostly
printed on crude loose sheets which are passed
around from hand to hand; and it consists chiefly
of obscene anecdotes and stories of atrocious
crime. We must, however, bear in mind, in connection with this literature, that to the demons,
whose point of view is so incomprehensible from
our own, a scandal is not a scandal, nor a crime,
a crime: the former they enjoy as a farce, and the
latter as a practical joke. They have an interesting school of poetry, of which the leader is Blashtalatshk. I have met Blashtalatshk and found
him a devil of high intelligence. His horns are
rudimentary and his lower jaw is lacking: but his
enormous dark eyes are among the most sensitive

and glowing that I have ever seen. His poetry and that of his fellows is, of course, devoid of the moral ideas and of the ennobling emotions which distinguish human poetry to-day: it is exclusively occupied with the mere representation of sights, sounds, smells and other sensations, which the demons have a genius for recreating with vividness and precision, though occasionally with so much complexity as to produce an effect of incoherence." . . .

At this point, however, I dropped it: I found that my satire was boring me, and that it also went against my conscience. My portrait of the demon poet had been a caricature of Pete Bird, and I had no desire to caricature Pete: on the contrary, I liked him. I found that I did not want to write a satire: to satirize humanity was to slander it, and I no longer thought so ill of humanity. Pete and Daisy and the rest, after all—even Larry Mickler himself—were not really base: they had disliked their lives as much as I had. If I had disliked them and found them base, it was because I myself had been tarred with the same stick. Moral problems, I now saw, were too complicated, and human nature too delicate a matter, to be hacked by the axe of satire. So, regretting the emphatic prose style with which a simple moral conviction may supply us and which I now found myself obliged to sacrifice, I decided to be scrupulous of the truth.

Still I could not sleep: I sat up against the arm of the couch, and saw the round cold winter moon, of which I had before had a glimpse on the other side of the house, now studding with its

white blinding pearl the pane of the room where I
lay. When had I seen it before, setting so, but
the moon of summer then, embedded in the morning glass? I thought of Rita, in Paris now. I
had been wrong about her and Ray Coleman:
Rita had merely, at the time when I had seen her
and she had seemed to me evasive about her address, gone to stay at Duff Burdan's studio—all
the rest had been a gruesome fantasy of my jealous imagination and my shaken self-confidence.
She had gone abroad for the first time, by herself, at just about the time I was returning, and
I had had a letter from her the day before: it had
come just as I was leaving town for the country.
She was staying, she wrote me, in a little Left
Bank hotel, and had as yet seen nobody. But the
early morning market-trucks, she said, which
rumbled through the Rue du Four and made the
walls of her bedroom vibrate, though they kept
her awake after midnight, made her feel that she
was "really a part of Paris." I seemed to divine
behind her letter an aching loneliness—the loneliness of all Americans when they first try to live
in Europe; and I imagined about her, as she
wrote, the dark brownish walls of the room, the
dispiriting wash-basin and slop-jar, the stuffy and
musty French bed. It was partly the fact that I
could pity Rita, and that at last she had written to
me, as well as the spectacle of Grosbeake's equanimity, which made it possible for me to think
well of humanity.

Not that her letter was plaintive or effusive: it
was, on the contrary, dry and brief; but the fact
that she had written me at all—she very rarely

wrote letters—seemed to me to imply, on her part, an unusual degree of desolation; and the two poems which she enclosed in her letter—she told me she had composed them at night when she could not sleep on account of the trucks—were the palest things of hers I had seen. The first was meagre, terse and wistful: it ticked off, in three brief stanzas, three images from that countryside of her youth—a lone elm, a gray stone fence, a pond athrob with frogs at nightfall—and I recognized in their phantom faintness—so unlike the stinging actuality which she usually gave to such things—that dim aspect which, to the traveller abroad, even the best loved and known sights of home come to wear in alien places, as if they had perhaps never existed, but were the receding images of a dream.

The other poem was a sonnet; and when I first saw it, I did not know what to make of it. It seemed very unlike Rita: in the first place, she never wrote sonnets; and my first thought, when I commenced to read it, was one of solicitude: I felt distressed that her isolation should so disastrously have affected her poetry. Then it dawned on me, after I had finished it, that it was supposed to be addressed to myself. I reread it with attention: it was the first time she had ever written me a poem. Then I became aware of the true situation: the trouble here with Rita's style was simply that, for the moment, she had become infected with mine. It was I who was addicted to sonnets; and I could recognize in this one of Rita's, my own forcible-feeble rhetoric and my adjectives in monotonous pairs—all those un-

availing devices with which I had muffed the kind
of effects that she would clinch with a single short
verb or a commonplace idiom. I had never
thought myself much of a poet, but now that Rita
seemed to be talking my jargon, seemed to be
trying to reply to me in the language in which I
had been apostrophizing her, I found that I was
sickened by it. And I was horrified to observe
that even the banal imagery with which Rita
could usually perform miracles remained, in this
ill-inspired sonnet, irredeemably banal.

My first feeling had been one of depression, the
result partly of wounded *amour-propre*—because
Rita, having written me a poem, should have
written me such an indifferent one—and partly of
pained concern that she should have sacrificed a
poem for my sake. I had been embarrassed as to
what I should write her: I wanted to urge her to
suppress the poem, but, as it had been written in
an effort to be nice to me, it was impossible to be
so ungracious.

Now, as I lay staring into the fire, I thought of
the sonnet again, and ran over it in my mind. It
had been a memory of our first days together,
when we had talked about poetry; and now suddenly, for the first time, I was touched that she
should have remembered those days and should
have tried to let me know it. I had thought only
of the artistic sincerity which she had sacrificed
for her subject! Now I was able to take account
of the sincerity of some personal sort which must,
after all, have come into play to induce her to
sacrifice it. In her dismal Paris hotel—so cold
and dark in November—had she been trying to

recall, to reaffirm, in spite of all our quarrels and
failures (and she had known then, as I had not
known, how life undoes the soundest of our reasons and depreciates the dearest of our hopes),
those moments of common understanding and
common enthusiasm of the days when we had
first talked freely together—when we had both,
for that moment, found a language for those
deepest unspoken convictions, for those deepest
realities, of such different lives!—And I began
even to wonder at last—a possibility I had never
admitted—whether, that night at Sue Borglum's
house, when I had met Rita with my freezing,
blank looks and my tiresome disapproval and
when, reminding me of the poem which I had so
loved when I had been in love with her, she
had tried to describe to me the river all lined with
sword-blades of ice,—and when I had listened
only with contempt—I wondered now whether,
after all, she had not herself been glad to think of
the hours—how rare in the world they must be!
—when poetry had burned with love. Had not
the river itself been the symbol of the breaking
and fraying of passion, of the dispersal of the
torrents of the heart?—and had she not, when she
had told me, at Sue Borglum's, of the river alive
in winter, for all the frozen countryside about it
and though cramped by the ice of its banks—had
she not tried to tell me something more, to speak
again to the old comrade and admirer, over the
head of the angry lover—to establish again that
contact—which I now chose to make impossible
—but which had brought once, if only for those
moments, that common light into a world which,

for her as well as for me—it occurred to me now for the first time—must be chiefly a world of darkness?

The last log had a comforting beauty—all woody, rosy luminosity—but I saw that it must soon crumble. I put on another log, trying not to wake Pete and Daisy. I glanced over toward their bed—they had turned to each other in sleep. The log smoked, and then caught fire: it sent up little tongues of flame. What a pity that I couldn't write a satire, making use of my wide knowledge of demonology, for lack of misanthropic conviction! The log began to crackle and blaze.

I looked for the moon, but it was gone: I craned around the side of the couch and saw it low, vaporish and gray, as if dissolving in the ichor of dawn. So I had watched it set so many times, on guard at night, in France—in that terrible, dull, dead hour when night is over and day not begun, when one must either make verses or be dull, be dead, as the earth and sky, as the soldiers in their deepest sleep—I had run into Hugo in Toul—I had not seen him since the beginning of the War and we had only had a chance for half an hour's talk in a café—he had been so funny about his unit, so funny and so good-natured, that unit which was soon to condemn him to the horrors of the prison-camp—what a great fellow he really was, in spite of the fact that, as Grosbeake said, he did caricature American business men too grimly—how few there were like him! —that France where Rita had never been till she arrived in that dreary hotel, where the market-

trucks kept her awake!—I rolled over and went to
sleep.

But I had scarcely closed my eyes, it seemed,
when persistent coughs, steps, and bumpings compelled me to open them again: it was Pete, in the
gray, early light, getting into his pants and khaki
shirt; he was rolling up his sleeves before the
window.

I tore myself out of my blanket-cocoon and—
though he begged me not to get up—I blinkingly
pulled on my clothes, and followed him out into
the cold undersea of the early morning ocean.
He had gone into the shed to chop some wood: I
had used up the last log during the night, and he
wanted to make the room warm for Daisy. He
begged me again not to bother; but with eager, if
incompetent, helpfulness, I hacked up a large
crooked limb, as well as several of the planks of
the floor.

After this, we went in and had some coffee—
Daisy was still asleep. We talked about literature
and drinks: Pete had volumes of Shelley and
Keats, and a treatise on French wines, which he
said were the only books he had not sold when he
had come away to the country. Sitting close
against the stove, I examined the wine book with
interest. "Never buy 1916 Burgundy," Pete admonished me, with an air of independent knowledge. "From 1910 to 1914 are all good years—
and 1915 is fair. But you have to go back to
1904 to get really A-1 Burgundy!"

I had to leave before noon—it was a long way
into the town and a long way back to New York.
We talked a little about a taxi; but as it was al-

ready growing late and as the nearest telephone was at a farm some distance away, I decided that I would undertake to walk, and Daisy offered to go with me. Pete had promised to call on a farmer and examine his grandfather's clock— putting clocks in order, it appeared, was one of his curious useless aptitudes—in return for which service, he explained to us, he hoped to be able to induce the farmer to make him a present of a crippled lowboy which was being used as a kitchen-table.

"I can supply the handles," he assured us. "Nothing easier in the world! Just take them off that old bureau in the store-room. But I *don't* see how I can supply that missing leg without a lathe.—But, after all, why not have a lathe?" he went on, with the liberal enthusiasm of a thoroughly practical man. "Think of all we could do with one! We could make regular tables and chairs!—Why, I'd be turning out table-legs so voluptuous that all the local oafs would be trampling over one another to buy them!" "I suppose," said Daisy, "that you're going to buy the lathe with the money we owe the grocer." "My dear child," Pete retorted, like a millionaire who takes pleasure in explaining that he always saves money on his clothes by having them made when he is in London, "you can get a lathe from Sears Roebuck for ten dollars! You simply say that you want to buy it on instalments, and they send you the lathe. Then you don't pay them anything more—and by the time they've sent a man for the money and he's gotten way out here, you've had time to turn out a whole dining-room set, enough legs and rungs for several dining-room sets, and you've sold the sets and ordered another lathe from another mail-order company, paying the first instalment out of what you get for the sets—so that by the time the first lathe is taken away, another one is just arriving, and the work goes merrily on!"

We set out—Daisy and I—on a hard crust of frozen snow, which broke through at every step and let us down into powdered depths. Daisy was dressed in high laced leather boots, a white sweater under a tan leather jacket and a round knitted white cap. I had never liked her so much: a certain strength and independence of character, which I had felt in her even at the period when she had seemed most demoralized, had now fully come into its own. Her frankness and her common-sense jokes, which I had once thought the typical products of Pittsburgh and New York, now seemed to me the wisdom of the country, which the false values of the city couldn't fool.— I began to think—it had already occurred to me —how delightful it would be to live with Daisy in a solitary farmhouse in the country, to chop wood to keep her warm, to sit with her at night before the fire, to read Bulwer-Lytton's novels aloud. I thought wistfully of Bulwer Lytton, whom it seemed to me I should like to read.

I congratulated her on leaving New York: "I began to feel before I left," I said, "as if the Village were a cage of wild animals—I began to feel that it might be just as well to make good your escape in time." "I certainly felt that way," said Daisy, "but I didn't know anybody else did.

—I thought everybody ate it up but me.—I got so I felt that I couldn't trust anybody!"

We strode, plodding, through the snow. "You know, Pete and I," she went on, "just after that last time I saw you—we got on a train with our last money"—(the money, no doubt, from Pete's books)—"and got off at the first town that looked good to us out of the train-window. We went to the real-estate office and asked for the cheapest thing there was—and we finally got this old hell-hole. The owner said that, if we'd fix it up, they'd give it to us free." The idea of this exploit enchanted me, and I envied Pete more than ever.

I told Daisy how much I liked Pete—what a relief I thought she must find him after living with Ray Coleman. "To tell the truth," she replied, "I don't notice much difference. The only thing is that I get along much better with Pete. We can sit around and wisecrack for hours.— The time that we had that party—the first time that I ever met you—I'd only seenum a few times, but I said to-um, 'I get along with you better than with anybody else I know.' " "What did he say?" I inquired. "He just grinned," said Daisy. I remembered how I had felt myself when it had first burst upon me that Rita, instead of scorning my apartment, enjoyed it. "So," Daisy continued, "we went out and went to Julius's bar together—and here we are now!"

I told her how wise I thought them to have left New York for the country—how glad I had been to go abroad—what a fool I had made of myself the night of Sue Borglum's party. "As far as I'm concerned," she replied, "that night was about the worst I remember—about the worst sunk I've ever been."

"You know," she added, after a pause, "I cut my wrist that night—you knew that, didn't you?" "Good Heavens!" I exclaimed, "Why did you do that?" "Why, because I'd lost my job, I suppose," she said, "—and because I got tired of the traffic going in and out of Gus Dunbar's rooms—and I'd been drinking so much that I didn't know what I was doing anyway.—I felt like such a tramp—that I'd been so inconsiderate of other people, and just gotten myself into a worse mess than before.—I cut my wrist," she went on, "with Gus Dunbar's razor-blade. I never saw anything spurt the way the blood did —it seemed as if all the blood in my body must be just in my wrist—it spurted clear across the bathroom. I just stood there and looked at it— the only thing I could think of was the leak in the hose, in that movie that you and I went to—don't you remember?—a little while before. If Pete hadn't come in just then, I'd probably have bled to death. But he arrived and called a doctor and put a tourniquet on my wrist: he certainly stopped it in short order—it seems he knows all about tourniquets."

"Oh, my dear," I said, "did you do that?—Is it really all right now?" "Yes," she said. "The doctor said that I really ought to have an operation, but I'm almost all right again now without one."

I made her take off her gauntlet: I saw that she could hardly move the fingers of that hand which

Pete had once described as a "little surprising moonbeam violin"—they were as stiff as the fingers of a doll which a child tries to make hold a broom.—"Why don't you get them operated on?" I asked. "It probably isn't a very serious operation." "Can't afford to," she replied.

"What had happened, anyway," I asked, "before I came to get you that night?" "Oh, it was horrible!" said Daisy. "I'd gone around to Larry Mickler's to see Larry about getting Pete a job—he was a friend of Gus Dunbar's.—When I'd called him up on the telephone and suggested sending Pete around, he'd said for me to come—but I told Pete to drop in after I'd been there a while. I could see what Larry wanted, but I thought that I'd jolly him along a little if Pete could get anything out of it. I thought that I could fix it all up and get back in time to have dinner with you. Well, when I got there, he made me drink and then he tried to grab me. And then before Pete arrived, his wife came in. It was awful: that was really one reason that I cut my wrist, I guess—I was so disgusted with everybody!"

I thought with pitying superiority of Larry Mickler. I felt to-day that I myself was so very far from being capable of behaving in such a way as to make a young girl lose faith in life!

We marched on—we were in wagon-ruts now: there was a long, rising road before us, with a straight row of trees on each side. We climbed the hill—there was a farmhouse at the top—we started down the slope of snow.

"Our favorite yokels live in there," she said.

"You ought to see me giving parties for the yokels—I have the time of my life—and so do they: they think I'm swell—they never saw anything like me before!" "It must be nice to live in the country," I said—I felt envious of the yokels. "It must be nice to know your neighbors—which you never do in New York." "Yes," said Daisy, "I get to take positive pride in competing with the other housewives to see who can have the best-looking kitchen. You know how sloppy Gus Dunbar's looked?—I think it was that as much as anything that discouraged me with life that time—well, when I came down here to the country, the first farmhouse kitchen that I saw brought out a suppressed housewife's complex,"—I remembered her remark, at Sue Borglum's, on the neatness of Sue Borglum's kitchen —"and I used to feel ashamed unless our kitchen was just shining!"

There was still a stretch at the bottom of the hill. What a marvellous walker she was!—And she had felt as I had done, that life without honor was horrible! But where Rita could save her self-respect with a poem, where even I could imagine a satire, Daisy could only cut her wrist!

We walked on for a time in silence. I could be so happy with Daisy, I thought—taking long walks in the snow in silence!

"I was in a pretty bad way myself," I presently remarked. "That night that we went to the movies, you really saved my life! You don't know how sweet you were!" "Well," she replied with amiability, "you weren't so sour yourself!"

We were coming now into the town: we had

reached the first white houses. I was cheered by a sudden inspiration: "Look," I said, "we couldn't get a drink, could we?—Isn't there some kind of a bootlegger in town?—I've got plenty of time before the train." "We might go to Ned Lovejoy's," she said thoughtfully.

It was just a room in a private house: there was an oil-cloth-covered table; a stove—which was pleasant after the cold; some "cabinet-size" photographs of members of the family, paralyzed in family groups; and an old-fashioned tinted picture of a little beribboned girl, smiling innocently and sweetly upon a sweet-natured cat and dog who ate amicably out of the same bowl. I don't know which was worse—the gin or the ginger-ale. Ned Lovejoy was inclined to converse, but we discouraged him and he left.

"You don't think that Pete and I are getting to look alike, do you?" asked Daisy: I assured her that they weren't in the least. "That's what Gus Dunbar said when he was out here a couple of weeks ago: he said we were getting alike. They say that people who live together do get to look alike."

I began to tell her again how much I approved of her course; how I had come to detest New York. I explained that I was going away, and intended to stay away as long as I possibly could. When I had returned in the fall from abroad, I hadn't been able to get back my job; and I had decided that, before looking for another, I might as well go on squandering my legacy, to the extent of a trip to New Orleans: I wanted to be there for the Mardi Gras.

Against the cold, sunny light of the window, her sharp nose, pale eyes, and blond hair looked almost Scandinavian. I told her how much I had enjoyed myself—how fine it was to have seen her again—how much I wished I were living in the country. "Why do you go to New Orleans, then?" she asked. I replied, not without a touch of wistfulness, that I had nowhere in the country to go. I tried to summon another drink; but Ned Lovejoy was absorbed by his radio, of which we could hear the sepulchral buzzing—and there was a long, rather stupid silence. I went and found him, and got him to bring us some more ginger-ale and gin, of which I had almost ceased to notice the taste.

I told her how splendid she looked with her outdoor complexion and clothes; and how much I liked and admired her.—She said suddenly: "Take me to New Orleans!" "Come along!" I replied. "I'm sailing just after Christmas." "Take me away from all this!" she went on, burlesquing a woman in a play saying "Take me away from all this!"—but it seemed to me, and shocked me a little, that she was partly in earnest. "Pete can't go on like this!" she said. "He'll have to go back to the city and get some kind of a job. We owe everybody in town! I get panicky about it sometimes. Living with Pete like this is just like living with another woman—you just live on your wits from day to day—you don't dare to think ahead.—You know: you can keep yourself on the go and keep using your vitality up, just so you won't mind things so much—but every now and then I begin to think about the situation and then I don't know what to do!—I never thought I'd be living like this—I never thought I'd be with anybody the way I've been with Pete and Ray!" . . .

I remembered how, suddenly one night, she had left Ray Coleman for Pete, and had never come back—and I remembered how she had begged Hugo to take her to Afghanistan. What if I could really get her away from Pete! I wanted a mistress now, and I liked Daisy so much—I desired her so much. But I couldn't flatter myself that she cared about me, she merely wanted to get away—and all that treachery, that promiscuity, that stealing of other men's girls, had come by this time to seem to me detestable: I had known Pete Bird through his poems, and had stayed in his house and read his books, drunk his coffee and eaten his food—and I remembered how bitter *I* had been when Rita had not scrupled to betray me, poetry, devotion and all, for that fellow from Columbus (or whoever it had been: I never knew; if it was not merely some image of herself, that self which could not mate with others, because it had already, in one body, made a union of female with male).—Pete Bird had, as it were, built his house with his own hands, and he possessed no legacy.—I did not even doubt now that he had, as he said, been slandered by Larry Mickler in the matter of the liverwurst sandwiches.

The cold light on the cold road where I was looking, early as it was in the day, was already beginning to darken; and I had a consciousness of stoic fortitude at the thought that, if the sun was short, I could endure the closing-down of night.

—I spoke to Daisy of the sad imperfection inherent in all human relations, and of the necessity for loyalty and faith in a world where love was sure to fail us. "But," I warmly and earnestly broke off, "you know all about that better than anybody! You know all about everything better than anybody! You're one of the most intelligent girls I know!" And I told her again how much I liked her and how well she deserved of life.—It was time for me to go.

At the station, I tried to get some gum for her out of a solitary slot-machine, but it was apparently frozen up. There were some country people standing about, and I was a little shy of kissing her good-by; but we kissed, as I was getting on the train: I touched her coral lips for an instant. It was deliciously cold, moist and light, like that moment of ice and winter flowers inside the glass of Grosbeake's porch.

V

IN that asphalt sky of August, the summer sun burnt a blunt point of light, like the blinding violet-livid torch with which a worker on city mains gashes through a tough piece of pipe. A gray haze blurred the vistas of Fifth Avenue and dulled the too full-blown bushes and trees which one saw beyond Washington Arch, as if the buildings and pavements themselves, under the action of the terrible heat, were vaporizing and fogging the air.

Down a side-street, an old white truck-horse stood sleeping and stupefied, its head lowered like a lizard's and its eyelids closed, while the driver, sluggish and sweating, piled a mountain of boxes on the dray. And farther over, on Seventh Avenue, I saw a barefoot ragged boy, who had flung himself down on his stomach above the grating that ventilates the subway, and whose coat was blown up violently behind him, like the streamers of an electric fan, by the warm, sudden gust from the trains.

My handkerchief was sopped with sweat, and I was refreshed by an unexpected breeze which washed over the butt of the island the hot, bilgy river-smell, as if, now that the people of the Village had abandoned the Village for the summer, the waterside were invading the town. I saw nobody anywhere that I knew. On the corner of Twelfth Street, where Rita had lived, the obsolete beer-saloon still bore its discolored blue Pilsener sign.

It occurred to me to examine, as I passed them, those landmarks of Abingdon Square which, the

261

morning of my first meeting with Rita, when I
had been drunk with peach-brandy and poetry,
had seemed to me impressive and romantic, but
which I had afterward passed so many times
without ever observing them closely. I now
found that what I had taken for a statue of some
interesting celebrity of the quarter was merely a
monument to the soldiers of the ward who had
died in the European War; and that the object
which had figured to my fancy as a temple or a
tomb was simply a disused band-stand.

Daisy and Pete had come recently to town.
Gus Dunbar, who was now in Boston, had, at
Daisy's instigation, taken steps toward getting
Pete a job there; and Pete had gone on to see
about it, leaving Daisy for a few days in New
York. She had called me up the day before, and,
with the idea of getting away from the heat, I
had suggested our going to Coney Island.

She was to meet me at the pier. I had not been
to Coney Island since my childhood, and for
some reason, I supposed that the boat left from
the foot of Christopher Street. At the docks, I
learned otherwise, and took a taxi down to the
Battery, along the wide cobbled avenue that runs
along beside the wharves.

There was the funny high yellow façade, built
of wood but with an aspect of pasteboard: it had
precisely, I remembered, the quality of the amuse-
ment-places of my boyhood, and it looked faded
and flimsy now.

Daisy was waiting in the cavernous anteroom.
In a corner of the high, darkish space, she
showed charmingly neat, small and clear. In

spite of the roundness of her hips and the smartness of her clothes—her white dress and her tight *cloche* hat—she might almost have been mistaken for a child. How cute and how chic she looked in those short, tight skirts that cut off her slim legs just above the knees! "Well," she greeted me with her unblinking smile, "the first twenty years of my life I spent waiting for the Coney Island boat!" I apologized and explained. "But why didn't you find out first?" she protested. "It's a good thing you didn't think it left from the foot of Forty-second Street!"

"Well, how do you feel?" I inquired, as we climbed the flight of steps. "I feel pretty sassy!" she said.

I had of course missed the four-o'clock boat, and now we should have to wait for the five-o'clock one. But up-stairs, the gray-timbered shadow of the low-roofed leaving-place was tranquillizing and cool: through a low narrow opening that ran along the side, one had a glimpse of the crude, unshadowed blocks of the enormous down-town buildings, where only one sheer green roof and a steep crane, on a float that was green, broke the cliffs of colorlessness.

I had brought some gin, and I bought some ginger-ale at the refreshment stand. "I must tell you my joke," she said, as we drank that impossible concoction—at once too bitter and too sickeningly sweet—for which I had acquired a certain affection, because I had come to associate it with Daisy. "I've made up an idea for a joke. There'll be a caption that says 'Striking a Happy Medium'—and then there'll be a picture of a

medium—you know, a spiritualistic medium—
with a big piece of bogus ectoplasm coming out
of her mouth and a grin of satisfaction on her
face, and a man with his arm all raised, just
ready to smack her down.—Don't you think
that's pretty good?" I told her that I thought it
was terrible.

There was a large, old, slot-machine phonograph standing against the wall: it was lyre-
shaped and had a mirror in its belly, and seemed
stationed as an outpost and siren for the frivoli-
ties and gaieties beyond. We put a nickel in and
started it playing an antiquated xylophone record of the *American Patrol:* its patriotic gallop,
half-stifled behind the glass and losing itself in
the wide, gray waiting-room, woke in my heart a
happy response as if to Fourth-of-July bands of
my boyhood.

Then the boat was in; the doors were opened;
we went down and stepped over the side. Assailed by the sunlight, we were dazed: in the
brightness, we seemed merely to enter a smell
of white boat-paint and to ascend to a brisk and
merry tinkling of some pretty antique tune.

I pulled camp-stools beside a rail on an upper
deck.—Sea and shore were rawest gray and the
sky a raw, pale blue—it was not that the blue
was pale, but rather that blue was lacking. The
sun streaked the water to the west with a bright
glaze of zinc.—I got some more ginger-ale and a
couple of paper cups from the little soft-drink
bar below.

On one side, as we left the dock, we looked out
at the Statue of Liberty, a solid, dull slug of gray

against a colorless, burning sky; and on the other, at the old red fort, round and full of holes like a mouse-trap, with its rusty and abandoned barracks.

The thin strains of linkéd sweetness, with now and then a note frailly sour, of the harp and violin—some old musical-comedy tune I remembered from my college days—seemed to me even in this false and elfin echo to keep more that was human and charming than the pace of the newer dance-music had ever allowed it to possess; and as I glanced at Daisy, gazing out like a charming, good-natured child, at the sights of the passing shore, I was touched with sentimental revery.

Then the music was blotted out by the vehement snoring of a steamer and the pert sput-sputtering of a tug.

She seemed unusually carefree to-day, and I saw that her lips were rouged an unusually pretty mauve. I told her how pretty she looked, and she replied by complimenting me on the harmony of my clothes: "With most people," she said, "their socks, for instance, haven't anything to do with the rest of their clothes—but your socks match your suit." My socks, which were a grayish blue, had been given me as a Christmas present and I had worn them only by accident on the same day as a gray summer suit. "But you have the worst-looking nails I ever saw!" she went on. "They look just like mechanics' nails, except that mechanics' nails are dirty." I explained that I always cut them with a pair of library shears, implying that I regarded any other method as effeminate.

I now decided to speak to Daisy of a matter which had been worrying me since I had met her at the pier. I said, "I think you've got some egg or something on this cheek." She took out her little mirror: "That's just a streak of cold-cream," she replied. "It always does that when I leave some on and the powder sticks." She rubbed it off. In the stunning sun of that windless, unshaded day, we were dumb for a time.

Governor's Island, the harbor in summer, the old patriotic tune, the statue of the soldier in the park, had brought back to me another vision which for some moments loomed bright in my mind.

Once—it seemed to me long ago—on a morning in early July, I had come back to Governor's Island when it had been green with trees and grass, and when the barracks had been low, white houses: there had been soldiers in khaki grooming horses or standing at the water's edge, in white shirts.

I remembered how, the afternoon before, though we had not yet been in sight of land, the empty horizons of those waters had held already the presence of home. The hours had seemed to run more smoothly with the homing ship—and in that calm summer evening, the sea had scarcely breathed. The silver sun had dipped, had sent its silver path along the blue, and had sunk at the end of its path—spreading yellows and reds, which the night took.

Then at last the yellow star of a lighthouse had been winking in the black—it did not seem like the play of a machine, but a deliberate human signal; and then a lightship spangled with stars. A quarantine tug had presently come out to us from the still invisible shore, and sent out some men in a boat: they transacted their business quickly, rowed quickly back to the launch and were pulled up in their boat with such promptness that it seemed to leap over the side. One had heard American voices: that was the American way of doing things!

Then a bed of lights on the water: after nearly two years of France, Coney Island had seemed incredible!

Then land on either side: there had been trees and lawns on the shore, and large, white American houses, with here and there a lighted window, set along on a little hill that sloped down to the water—and each of the houses had its boathouse and its little pier. Now soon one was to walk in such houses!—to play one's part again in that life hidden there behind those lighted windows, in that life grown now so strange and yet the life of home!

There had come to us a sudden sweet smell through the quiet summer night: trees and flowers; the summer grass; the luxuriance and rankness of America. And then, as the ship passed on, a smell even more unmistakable, a smell even more of home, surrounded and saturated us: it was the rotten smell of the river, which, when to-day I had smelt it again in the Greenwich Village streets, had made me think of the salt bilge-water of the harbor, but which had breathed then the grease, the sour heat and the smoke of the factories, of the city. Dark chimneys were disturbing the darkness with their noiseless eruptions of red. That evening, on Riverside Drive, the benches would be full of couples, and all would be soaked from the Jersey bank by the glue-factories' hot, heavy fumes.

Then suddenly I had almost caught my breath —I had been curiously moved by the sight of a single, solitary street-lamp on the Staten Island shore. It had merely shed a loose and whitish radiance over a few feet of the baldish road of some dark, thinly settled suburb. Above it, there had loomed an abundant and disorderly tree. But there was America, I had felt with emotion—there under that lonely suburban street-lamp, there in that raw and livid light!

Then, from somewhere behind those shadowy lawns, one heard the moan of an American train, and then its faint bell, and the swift, shuffling sounds of its progress. It was speeding away with eagerness and sureness to American cities at night—far, perhaps—to the farthest reaches of a continent without frontiers! There had been a petulance and a sadness in the piping of the French locomotives—they had spoken always of the dead hours of dawn and the carloads of wounded men. But these trains were bringing soldiers home—and far away from Europe—at night!

In the morning, off South Brooklyn, at anchor, we had seen the smoky rose of dawn come up over the black roofs of the city, and we had listened to the river-traffic waking with soft puffs and toots. The colors had begun to come out on the vermilion smoke-stacks of steamers. The gray sides of a battle-ship were clear: it was soon trimmed with live figures in white suits. We had put down a motor-boat, which sprang away, when it touched the water, as if the water had given it life: a blue sailor, standing at the tiller, and negligently and gracefully leaning to balance the tilt of the boat, was guiding it in bold easy curves.

Now the varied craft of the harbor were coughing and sneezing all about us, fully waked-up for the day: squat shouldering ferry-boats and tugs; a tiny motor-boat darting like a waterbug; railroad barges, floating freight-cars—Delaware and Lackawanna; New York, New Haven and Hartford—all those dear, square names of home!

Then the shore was moving: to the left, the docks had begun to bristle with the first thickets of the forest of masts. In a moment, the sky would be crowded, and one would behold, above the docks and the shipping, the tremendous towers of the town!

At that moment, on our way to Coney Island, the freshness of that other summer day, when I had come back to the United States with what seemed infinite freedom before me, was recreated in my mind so vividly that I tried to describe it to Daisy. But for Daisy, the things which had delighted me—the boat leaping into the tug, the sound of the train in the dark, the sailor guiding the boat, had no special significance or point, because they were things which she took for granted, and which seemed perfectly commonplace. I felt that she kept waiting for these incidents to develop into anecdotes, in which something entertaining should happen.

When I had finally given it up, she put her hand over the middle of my face and regarded me

attentively. "You'd be very good-looking," she
said, "if it wasn't for your nose." I said, "I
know I've got a terrible nose!" "No," she reassured me. "It's cute. But it interferes with any
Adonis-like beauty that you might otherwise have
had."

In the harbor, the harbor of the August day
which was actually about us, the lowering of the
zinc-bright colorless sun had made of the water to
the west a gleaming sheet of zinc; and to the
east, it had begun to blue. A bell-buoy clanged
and bathed. Before us, we could see the steamers
moving out toward the open sea, their smoke
trailing back from seaward. A fresh, easier,
breezy sea-smell reached us—it was a lightening
of the load of life.

"Doesn't that feel nice, though!" said Daisy.
"I think I'm going to enjoy this trip!"

I asked her about Pete and his job. "I'm so
glad we're going to Boston," she said. "I'm tired
of the country, but I don't want to live in New
York! I think New York is terrible!"

Sea Gate—and beaches rank with bathers; little
brummagen summer bungalows with green or red
roofs.

Then a monumental buff hotel with a blunt
obelisk tower rose alone from a level shore—
where, however, we could presently make out the
skeletons of roller-coasters and the squirrel-cages
of ferris-wheels.

Now, more quickly than in our bemusement
we had expected, the boat was pulling in toward
the boardwalk: we could see a row of improbable
objects—the sails of a bright-red Dutch wind-

mill; the teeth of a gigantic grinning mask; a rocking full-size Noah's Ark, with animals sticking their heads out the windows and with curious half-clownlike figures, which made the spasmodic movements of automata and which seemed the true unearthly inhabitants of that city of enormous toys.

When the boat stopped, as we stood on deck, waiting to get off, we suddenly again felt the heat. "The sun makes me reel!" said Daisy. We walked, dazed, up a little gang-plank and down a very long white pier. The hotel, which rose now to our left, against the dazzling zinc of the sky, was a dull and solid slug, as the Statue of Liberty had been. The sea was now quite blue.

I was enchanted by the Noah's Ark: there were an ostrich, a giraffe, and an elephant, wagging their heads out the portholes; a Noah, who, at regular intervals, threw back his Uncle Josh beard and took a swig from a bottle of whiskey; and a fisherman who, at similar intervals, jerked up an old shoe on his hook. There was also a mysterious monster, labelled "Hank," half human and half brute, who in paroxysms shook his window-bars. An urgent and ominous fog-horn sounded at the same short intervals. I was all for going inside.

"Let's go in swimming first," said Daisy, "while we've still got the sun—then we'll feel fine—then we'll have another drink. Then we can go and do things, huh?" She squeezed my arm: she seemed happy.

We floated, on our way, through warm currents: the balm of hot buttered pop-corn; the fragrance of burnt molasses; the sweet-acrid odor of orange-peels.

And then, after the close, musky smell, human and marine, of the damp-and-dry gray boards of the bath-house, I met Daisy in my hired bathing-suit, and we walked out under the boardwalk to the beach.

She had brought an old bathing-suit of Pete's which had enormous brown and white stripes and which was in places much too tight for her. With her fair skin among the tanned bathers and her hair tucked behind her ears, she looked like one of the Mack Sennett bathing girls, in the old-fashioned movie comedies. "I know it looks awful," she said, when I kidded her about this, "but I thought it didn't matter at Coney Island—and I couldn't afford to get a new one."

There were tiny children playing in the surf, in tiny slips of bathing-suits of yellow, pale green, and red, like the variously flavored fruit-drops— orange, raspberry, and lime—in the glass jars we had passed on a candy counter; or like the bottles of colored soft-drinks—cherry, orange, and lemon soda—which we had seen at a soft-drink stand —they were splashing in wild delight or fleeing from the sea with squeals.

Daisy worked, for a few minutes, squinting, in an ineffective under-water side-stroke. I, still partly bemused by my drinks, flung myself with abandon to the waves, and swam around a small stone breakwater in what—although I unexpectedly ran into the breakwater—I thought was pretty good order.

"That was a marvellous wallow of yours!" said

Daisy. "I thought you were trying to push the breakwater over! I was just going to yell out and tell you to stop, it was built there on purpose!"

She had brought out of the surf, about her shoulders, a great strip of glossy gold-brown seaweed, and she wore it as a boa: it went beautifully with her hair and with the taffy-colored stripes of Pete's bathing-suit, both darkened by the wet. Her slim legs below her full hips looked almost like the legs of a bird.

We lay on the sand for awhile. "Your hair seems a different color," I said. "In fact—I don't know whether it's just my imagination or not—but it always seems a different color every time that I see you." "It is, I guess," she replied. "They put white henna on it when they bleached it for the *Gambols*—and I always used to put peroxide and lemon-juice on it every so often, but I haven't been able to lately. That's why it's pink, I guess." I asked what color it had originally been. "Oh, Gee: I don't know," she said. "It's so long ago!—Mouse-color, I guess!"

I inquired about a system of vivid blue veins on her thigh. "That's my charley-horse," she explained; "I got it in the first *Gambols*." I asked her why she didn't go back on the stage. "I'm too short," she replied, "and my feet are too small for me to dance well—and I don't like it, anyway: I always get independent and cut too many rehearsals. That was why I got fired the last time."

Beside us, a brown young man had his arm about the shoulders of a young woman in an old-rose bathing-suit, with large carpet-like flower-patterns, which richly harmonized with the purple tan of her skin: she presently slipped a hand beneath the top of her companion's bathing-suit and affectionately rubbed his back. A handsome blond girl in blue, who seemed to have two men in attendance, was pawing the sand with one foot. Another girl, in a turquoise costume, had stretched out on her back on the sand, with her shoulders between a man's knees: he was passionately stroking her arm.

I watched one really beautiful woman, very blond and rather Germanic: she wore a pair of red bathing-trunks with an orange stripe down the side, belted and athletically faded, and a plain white bathing-shirt. She lay voluptuously, one knee elevated and her head on the knees of a barrel-shaped man, who wore horn-rimmed spectacles. Her skin was extremely white, only toasted a little about the shoulders; and she had smiling darkish brown eyes. I watched her as, presently, she got up and walked over to the water, and—while her companion bobbed in the surf—with an easy and graceful crawl, lay voluptuously along the swell.

"This is all artificial sand, you know," said Daisy,—"Oh, yes: they spent half a million dollars fixing up this beach. There didn't used to be any beach at all. That was the same time they put up the hotel. I wonder if they're making money."

Gray steamers were passing quite close along the gray line of the water—they made me think of summers in Europe, of coming back from abroad in the fall—at the age when I had been last to Coney Island, there had always been uncles and aunts sailing to or from France—there had been an uncle who brought home from Paris silk stockings for my cousins and aunts—he had had a bluff and ironical way of retorting, "You don't say!" which was precisely the way Daisy said things—it was the American way.—The Americans went to Paris, and then they came back again with silk stockings and things they had bought, and that frank American smile, and that straightforward way of speaking.—The people who interested me most were, almost all, I reflected, now abroad: Grosbeake was in England for the summer; Hugo, in spite of his enthusiasm for the American Middle Western cities, was still in Afghanistan; and Rita was still in Paris—yet I did not at the moment seem to miss them and did not want to go abroad myself. What fun we had had together after all—Rita and I—though we had never been easy and friendly together, as Daisy and I were to-day: there had been one evening— we had been drinking raw gin—Rita would never have drunk the gin and ginger-ale to which Daisy was addicted—when we had told each other things about ourselves which had seemed at the time to mean a great deal—I couldn't quite remember what they were—she had told me something about her girlhood, it was that night she had sung me the song about *the foggy, foggy dew*—and I had told her how my father had died of tuberculosis —and what a rotten time I had had at boardingschool, and how I intended to write a novel about it. Those nocturnal drunken conversations which seemed to mean so much!—which did, no doubt, mean so much. All literature, perhaps—and not poetry alone, but even the systematized facts of

Hugo's documented novels, even the formulas of
Grosbeake's logic—was in the nature of a drunken
language, expressing, by certain symbols, sensations and emotions merely—the readjustments,
that would be, of our little corner of nature to the
universe of which we were part—which was forever passing into new phases and where each
phase meant a new adjustment for every part—
where, then, a new art or idea was something
more than the mere compensation for an individual weakness or disaster, it was a necessity of universal development—I would think it all out some
time—the sun was hot on the sand.

"Well," said Daisy, "now that we've earned
that other drink, how about going in?"

Hot dogs were being roasted twenty at a time, on
wide polished iron slabs: they were crisp, with a
delicious stink. At an oilcloth-covered table, Daisy
and I ate one apiece, dabbing them gamboge with
a little long-handled wooden spoon from the common mustard pot.

"I'm ravenous!" said Daisy, biting into the
pulp of her roll.

Dim and languid from the swim, I was watching the reflections of girls, in wide hats and bright
summer colors, shine briefly in the silver high
myriad-paned mirror, in the sun that bleached
whites whiter and blues and yellows white.

"Do you want another?" I asked, when she had
bolted the last morsel. "Not now; maybe later,"
she replied.

We did the shooting-galleries after this, and
the ring-throwing and ball-rolling games. We
were both quite good: we knocked over any num-

ber of moving ducks, which was what we had decided to concentrate on; and we won a baby-doll
in a chemise, a miniature roulette-wheel, an harmonica, an atomizer and a trick pistol which shot
off a snake. Daisy was so delighted with the
snake that she kept shooting it down the ball-
rolling table, so that the Jap had to find it and
bring it back. Every time, with oriental patience,
he would stuff it into the pistol, hand it back to
Daisy, and caution her politely with a smile, as he
indicated the trigger: "Now don't put your finger
on that!"—whereupon Daisy would shoot it off
again. I was somehow obscurely reminded of that
horrible night at Sue Borglum's, and I took a
dislike to the Jap and made Daisy move on.

"Let's send some goofy post-cards," said Daisy,
in front of a post-card store. We went inside and
selected several with fastidious care. I sent cards
to Hugo and Rita; and Daisy sent cards to Gus
Dunbar and Sue Borglum. "I'm going to be
dirty," she said, putting a cross on a bathing beauty, and writing, "X marks my room."

I asked her if she would care for a pin-cushion
heavily encrusted with sea-shells and inscribed,
"Souvenir of Coney Island," or if there were
anything else she would like. "I'd like some
moccasins," she said. "Very well," I replied.
"Will you really buy me some?" she asked eagerly. "You great big munificent old thing!—I
haven't got any slippers now, and I used to keep
getting my feet full of splinters and thumb-tacks
in the country."

It turned out that her feet were so small that
the man had to get a special size out of the stock-

room at the back. The woman in the shop, fat
and sharp-eyed, became very friendly with Daisy
and, while the man was looking for the moccasins,
tried to engage her in conversation. "Do you
mind my asking what kind of lipstick that is?"
the woman inquired with interest. Rather to my
surprise, this seemed to embarrass Daisy: she explained that it was called "carnation," but when
the woman asked her how much it cost, Daisy said
that she had forgotten, and became markedly unresponsive. "If they can't find the right size," she
presently remarked to me pointedly, "we might as
well go!" The moccasins, however, were forth-
coming: they were moccasins for a child and I
did not suppose they could fit her; but they did.
She looked down at her little blunt-toed foot with
its border, at the throat, of gray fur: "That's all
right," she said shortly.

"That woman certainly took a friendly interest," I remarked, when we were out on the boardwalk. "Yes," said Daisy. "I never know what to
do when people like that get chummy."

I had been surprised at Daisy's shrinking from
the familiarity of the woman in the shop, and I
was now to be surprised again. I had lingered in
front of a side-show, where there were posters of
a Hula-Hula Dancer, a Dog-faced Boy, a Mer-
maid, an Hermaphrodite and a Magician, and I
suggested going in. But Daisy evidently did not
care to. "My mother would never let me see any
freaks," she said. "They're all fakes, aren't they?"
she asked, a little timidly.

As we walked on, she shot the snake off again,
and I had to go and get it out of an umbrella-
stand bristling with pennants and canes.

Then I discovered the Eden Musée—I had forgotten that it had moved to Coney Island and had thought of it as having perished. I had not visited it since my childhood, when, coming up to New York with my father, he had used to take me to see it in the days when it had still been on Twenty-third Street: there I had seen for the first time moving-pictures, along with the automatic chess-player and the manipulator of liquid air. And now here was the same old policeman in his high obsolete helmet; the same refined widow in black, with the tight waist of the early nineteen-hundreds; the same old hayseed with his spectacles, his flopping wide-brimmed straw hat and his flaccid carpet-bag—but now no longer posed inside, where they could no longer be mistaken for real people, but set out in front as a guarantee of the authentic antiquity of the show.

I induced Daisy to go in.—There they were, that awful group of my youth, though it seemed to me their number was diminished: Jenny Lind, Mary Queen of Scots, Anna Held, Oliver Cromwell, Beethoven, Brigham Young, General Grant, Napoleon and Booker T. Washington: I was sorry to see that Marshall P. Wilder no longer had a place among them.

I did not examine them closely, however, for Daisy, who seemed never to have seen wax-works before, hurried on to the more dramatic tableaux set back in compartments along the side. She passed before them, gazing in silence. The groups were not particularly interesting, but they presently led us to the "Crypt." We entered a darkened curving passage. I was delighted: it was the

old "Chamber of Horrors," which in the Twenty-
third Street days had used to be down-stairs in
the basement. We gazed at the Opium Den; the
Execution of a Burmese Criminal (it seemed to
me now that the elephant who steps on the criminal's head had shrunk since I was a boy) ; the
Cannibal Feast; the Whipping Post, "still in use
in the State of Deleware"; and, the electrocution
of poor Lina Lemberg, who had finally, a few
weeks before, been executed for the murder of
her husband. The witnesses, in the Death Chamber, were regarding the proceedings with simpers,
and I wondered whether they had not been bor-
rowed from an old tableau of a lobster-and-cham-
pagne supper, with Mephistopheles in the background, of which the personnel of revellers seemed
to me, like the Burmese elephant, to have dwindled
since the Twenty-third Street days. I suggested
this to Daisy. "I don't think this is very exciting," she replied. She seemed to look at everything so perfunctorily that I was afraid she was
being bored: as she had never seen the Musée in
her childhood, I could not expect her to share my
interest in it.

Several tableaux farther on, I found that I had
turned a corner and left Daisy behind—still staring, no doubt, at Lina Lemberg. I was before a
group of the Spanish Inquisition, and I had a
sudden happy inspiration for enlivening the entertainment for Daisy. I climbed quickly over
the railing, put my straw hat on the head of the
presiding inquisitor—he had a lean and sallow
face, and the hat came down over his eyes—and,
with my back to the railing, struck an energetic

pose among the torturers with red-hot irons, my-self applying to the victim's blood-streaked shoul-der the cork-screw I had brought for the gin. In a moment, I heard distinct light steps, which stopped—then, after an instant's pause: "Come on out of there, you old cut-up!" I climbed back over the railing. "I thought you were real at first," she said, as we reached the exit. "You gave me quite a turn!"

On our way out, I caught a glimpse of Roose-velt, the Teddy Roosevelt of San Juan Hill, who, with his handkerchief knotted about his neck, his Rough-Rider puttees, his felt hat, his mustache, his glaring teeth and his eye-glasses, made me think of that younger America which I had as-sumed we had forever left behind, but which to-day seemed quite close to me again. It had been a boy's America—and not merely because it had been the America of my boyhood. Roosevelt, who had been so charming with his children, had become the idol of the Americans of that time for very much the same reasons—he had been every-thing that a boy could imagine: Dan Beard, Old and Young King Brady, Frank Merriwell, and Stanley in Africa, all rolled into one. I asked Daisy whether she remembered the time when Roosevelt had been a great hero. She said, "No," —and showed so little interest that for a time I relapsed into silence. Then she let me see what she had been thinking about: "I've never seen a dead person," she said, "except an aunt of mine that died."

"By the way," I asked, after a moment, "what became of that thief that Ray Coleman caught—

the one that didn't steal anything of yours, but
stole the bathrobe of the man next door, or something?" She was silent. "Don't you remember?"
"Yes, I remember," she replied. "But I don't
know what became of him. I was thinking too
much about myself at that time to pay much attention to anything else."

"Would you mind taking me to dinner?" she
said presently. "I'm absolutely starved!" I asked
her where she wanted to go. "I'd like to go to the
old Seaview, if you don't mind. I don't know
how the food there is now—but I'd just like to
see the place.—I went there with Phil Meissner,"
she added, "when we first came on from Pittsburgh."

The Seaview was quite remote—beyond a kind
of grassy common, criss-crossed with bald paths.
It was an old-fashioned summer hotel, of the cu-
polaed and pillared design of the days before concrete and brick: like all wooden hotels by the
shore, it had a flimsy discolored look, and seemed
peculiarly desolate and dry. The dining-room was
entirely empty: only a few of the tables were set.
One side was all high narrow windows, separated
by thin wooden frames, which looked out on the
boardwalk and the sea; and on the other, an old
closed piano stood against the wall, and space had
been left for a dance-floor; slim pillars from floor
to roof at intervals threaded the room. We waited, but no one came. I finally hallo'd; and a
waiter appeared from the pantry. He came forward without inspiration, as if he expected to be
asked for cigarettes or to be asked to direct us to
Luna Park. When he learned that we wanted
dinner, his eagerness to serve us was extreme.

"Well," said Daisy, as we sat down, "the table linen's nice and clean, anyway." It was true: very white large napkins had been folded into angles and stuck into large clear goblets.

"I'm going to have clams," said Daisy. "They used to have the most wonderful clam-cocktails here." I ordered a melon for myself, and bluefish for both of us afterwards. I also ordered some ginger-ale and poured out what was left of the gin. "I don't think I'll have any," said Daisy, "until after I've had something to eat." She looked a little pale and was silent for some time, and I hoped that the Chamber of Horrors hadn't upset her. She smiled broadly, however, at last, and proclaimed: "Look out, Food: I'm coming!"

I asked her how she and Phil had ever happened to come to the Seaview. "Phil knew the manager," she explained. "The manager gave a party in my honor—just some of his men friends. We had champagne, and I'd never had anything to drink before—I was awfully young—I was only seventeen. I thought it was swell, and I got lit. They kept filling up my glass with champagne. You know how men are when they've got a girl that's young and kind of cute, and they're trying to get her tight. I had on a little black dress like they wore then, that buttoned up the back, and the bottom buttons got unbuttoned—and then every man that danced with me would unbutton another button—so that pretty soon it was unbuttoned all the way up to the waist. I didn't know anything about it and just went on smiling and dancing, and thinking I was cutting quite a figure, with my legs hanging out all the time!"

I laughed about this.

"I certainly enjoyed those clams!" she said, when all the little hollows in her plate were empty around the red-splashed glass of sauce. She smiled: "After all," she declared, "say what you please—there's nothing like a good plate of food!" I asked her if she would like some more clams. "Yes," she answered, after a moment's thought, "I believe that I would." I ordered another clam-cocktail.

I asked if it weren't true, as I had heard from Hugo Bamman, the night of Ray Coleman's party, that she and her husband, on their honeymoon, had ridden on a motorcycle all the way from Pittsburgh to Atlantic City: this had seemed to me tremendously romantic. "It wasn't Atlantic City," Daisy explained. "It was here."

"What was Phil Meissner like?" I inquired. "He had a lot of charm," said Daisy, "and a lot of brains, too—but he never did anything with them except perfectly foolish things. For instance, he'd spend days inventing something that worked by electricity to make the blinds open in the morning—he could lie in bed and press a button and make the water-basin fill, and when it was full, the faucet would turn itself off, and everything!"

"Were you very much in love with him?" I asked. She shook her head, as if in scorn. "I didn't know anything about anything then. He was the first regular beau I'd ever had: my father wouldn't let me go with the boys. I was all excited aboutum at first.—I was so much impressed withum when I first marriedum that it was just ridiculous! I couldn't even go to the drug-store to get a tube of tooth-paste without askingum what kind to

buy. But I wasn't really in love withum—I didn't
know what it was all about—and then, by the time
I might have been in love, everything was pretty
well wrecked.—My father followed us here and
burst in on us with a detective at four o'clock in
the morning. He made us get up and get married then and there—we hadn't gotten married
before we left because Phil didn't want to attract
attention. Dad said I'd either have to marry Phil
or go back to Pittsburgh. So we got up and got
married at four o'clock in the morning—it was
the night after the champagne party and we both
felt like nobody's business. Phil was sore as a
crab, because Dad had a Catholic priest marry us,
and Phil wasn't a Catholic—but Dad threatened
to havum arrested for abducting a minor, and he
had the detective right there.

"Things were never quite the same after that.
I don't blame Phil for being sore: nobody likes to
be forced into a thing like that—especially with a
hangover, at four o'clock in the morning!"

I had been thinking: her father from Pittsburgh—why had they named her Daisy?—I remembered that old song of my boyhood,

> "Daisy! Daisy!
> Give me your answer true—
> I'm half-crazy!
> All for the love of you!
> It won't be a stylish marriage—
> I can't afford a carriage!
> But you'll look sweet, upon the seat
> Of a bicycle built for two!"

—that old song of an earlier time to which
Daisy's name seemed to relate her—and her large

hips, too—I had never been aware how round they were till I had seen her in her bathing-suit— they were the kind that had been admired at the time when the song had been new—they went in for slender hips to-day—but I liked Daisy's none the less—how bicycles had gone out, too—but she and Phil, appropriately enough, had spent their honeymoon on a motor-cycle.

"Are you happy now with Pete?" I asked. She shook her head: "I don't know if I've really ever been happy—but I've sworn to go through with this with Pete: I'm tired of leaving people." "Are you and Pete married now?" She shook her head again and grunted negatively, "uh-uh!"

"I know I'm not happy now," she went on, "because I keep having these dreams where some kind of a great piece of good fortune is just about to befall me—and they're the goofiest dreams!—When Prince Charming comes along, he's always just a great, big, strong, clean-limbed American who gathers me up in his arms. It's so silly! I feel ashamed of myself after I wake up.—And I'm always dressed in the costume that I wore in the first *Gambols,* when I came out in a white old-fashioned dress, with curls and panta-lettes and everything. I loved it—Gus Dunbar used to say that I looked so sweet and dewy that he wanted to smack me down. But you know one night the boys from Notre Dame came and stole my picture in that costume that was on show in front of the theatre—and they published it in the college paper. They sent me a copy of the pa-per: I was tickled to death. That was the only one they stole!"

I had been watching, through the tall, open windows, the double, white, pearly globes of the boardwalk lamps, so pale, so chaste and so bright, hanging gracefully, like lilies-of-the-valley, from their straight, slender stalks, against the background of the paler blue, now the cooler blue, of the sea, where a buoy shone ruby-red.

When we came down the steps of the hotel, all was in deep blue dusk, with the lamps a double rope of moons. "Have you noticed this?" I asked, waving my hand toward the lamps.—"I suppose the last time I was happy," she said, "was back there in the old Seaview dining-room!"

We were confronted, when we turned back toward the amusements, by a large and very garish electric sign in the form of a gigantic human foot, on which a red Mephistopheles was standing: by means of alternate systems of bulbs, the arm of the Mephistopheles was made to jerk back and forth, prodding energetically with a spear an illuminated corn on the big toe, which at each jab changed the color of its light, first blue, then purple, then green. The legend, which flashed on and off, proclaimed, in contorted, striking letters: "Take a Walk with Clancy's Corn Fix. Knocks the Devil Out of Sore Feet."

"Oh, do you see that sign?" said Daisy. "That was Larry Mickler's idea. He's making a lot of money out of it: they've got them all over the country." I was glad to know that Larry Mickler, through a truly Dostoevskian device, had constrained his sadistic instincts to serve this beneficent end.

"I hope we get somewhere soon!" said Daisy

presently. "I've got to go to about eighteen ladies'-rooms!" We had been walking along the
boardwalk and were only just reaching the shops
again. Daisy presently disappeared in a small
and rather sordid-looking restaurant.

There was a penny-in-the-slot place next door,
and as I walked back and forth in front of the
restaurant, I stopped and looked in. I saw, standing before me in the doorway, a tall, young man
with a stoop, who had a darkish tooth-brush mustache, which I considered a little silly, and rather
large brown eyes of the kind usually described as
spaniel-like: he was wearing, like everybody else,
a straw hat with a black band, which, it seemed
to me, he had pulled too far down on his forehead. I had a feeling of mild irritation that he
should be standing and staring so innocently, so
well-meaningly, and so lackadaisically, square in
the middle of the doorway, where he made it
difficult for people to pass. He was laden down,
I saw, with packages: no doubt some woman had
made him carry them.—Then sharply I pulled
myself up from that vague and absent moment:
the man was my own reflection in a mirror opposite the door. On either side were other mir-
rors which distorted people's shapes.

I continued to gaze at myself: how had I ever
failed to recognize—especially after Daisy had
remarked on it—my ridiculous bulbous nose? My
eyes, which I had hoped were intelligent, had only
appeared to me canine—and my mustache was
unsuccessful. My pockets were bulging with the
atomizer, the mouth-organ, the baby-doll, and the
pistol with the snake; and I was carrying the rou-

lette-wheel and the moccasins, which had been wrapped up in pasteboard boxes. I seemed to myself a figure from the funny-papers: Mr. Suburban American, at the sea-side, with packages and a straw hat.

I went back to the door of the restaurant: Daisy had not yet emerged. There was a radio playing outside, and for some reason the programme included some vaudeville or night-club woman soloist singing *Mamie Rose,* that popular song of several years ago which Daisy had started on the phonograph when Rita had been reading her poems and which had desolated me so on the day when I had seen Rita off at the station and had been waiting for Daisy in her rooms. Now I listened idly for the words, parts of which, on that horrible record, I had never been able to catch. The contralto, whose voice was rich and deep, delivered them with a masterly casual emphasis, in that nondescript dialect—perhaps the result of Irish actors learning from Jewish comedians how to sing Negro songs—which has become the language of American jazz:

> *"There she goes,*
> *Mamie Rose*
> *She—loves—me!*
> *Don't seem to show it!*
> *How do I know it?*
> *It's A B C!*
> *She's smart as Satan—*
> *She's aggravatin'—*
> *But when I want a little lovin',*
> *She don't keep me waitin'—*
> *She's proud and snooty,*

> *But she's my cutie—*
> *She tells me, Fireman, do your duty!"*

That was the line that I'd never been able to hear!
—That song, but a few years old, seemed already
to belong to the past, like *Daisy* and the *American Patrol,* and the old musical-comedy tune which
the musicians had played on the boat, and I found
that I had at last come to feel for it a certain familiar affection. Furthermore, I now thought it
quite good: there was something rather unexpected, something even quite original about the
manipulation of the tune: what was original and
unexpected was the repetition, in some sort of
minor, of the pattern which had just gone before
—recommencing, with *She's proud and snooty,*
what one had thought was entirely finished—and
recommencing it agreeably and queerly, so that
for a moment one always paused to listen. I wondered how the composer had arrived at it. He
was a man named Harry Hirsch, I remembered:
I imagined him: a small, young Jew with very
large, intense, black eyes, like motor headlights;
after the success of the musical comedy in which
Mamie Rose had been sung, he had probably taken
to wearing spats. He was no doubt the son of
a Rabbi or of the Cantor in a Synagogue: the
base of his music was German, and I imagined
some dark room of a stifling apartment on the
East Side, in which his youth had been fed on
Schubert and on the light opera of Vienna and
Berlin, cities which his eyes had never seen. But
what had he done to this music?—what had made
him repeat those bars of the sweet German mel-

ody with which he had begun, but transforming them abruptly, by daring what any hack worker in the field would have told him *a priori* was impossible, what would have lasted in commonplace hands impossibly too long? By carrying us beyond expectation, by breaking into that new accent, half agonized and half thrilling, he had enchanted the public so completely that not merely had *Mamie Rose* turned out to be one of the principal factors in the success of the musical comedy in which it had first appeared (and where, as a matter of fact, the director had been afraid to feature it), but it had been heard on every radio and phonograph; at every college prom, at every Greenwich Village ball; from the most perfunctory chirpings of the orchestras of restaurants to the jazz-bands de luxe of roof-gardens; on the vaudeville circuits of small towns and in the scores of feature moving-pictures; worked up for the Elks summer fair; struck up, with the words thrown on a screen, during the intermissions of burlesque shows; ground out at "dancing academies" where, from New York to Los Angeles, clumsy and inarticulate young men pushed wary and inarticulate girls about a crowded, monotonous floor—and as I had heard it once, late at night, sung strangely from a summer street by a child's voice, nasal and shrill, following subtly and with marvellous accuracy the deviating minor strain, and repeating it again and again!

Where had he got it?—from the sounds of the streets? the taxis creaking to a stop? the interrogatory squeak of a street-car? some distant and obscure city-sound in which a plaintive high note,

bitten sharp, follows a lower note, strongly
clanged and solidly based? Or had he got it from
Schoenberg or Stravinsky?—or simply from his
own nostalgia, among the dark cells and the raspings of New York, for those orchestras and open
squares which his parents had left behind?—or
for the cadence, half-chanted and despairing, of
the tongue which the father had known, but
which the child had forgotten and was never to
know again?

But the relations between Schoenberg, the
taxi-brakes, and the Synagogue, baffled further
speculation.—And, in any case, what charmed
and surprised one, in this as in all works of art,
was no mere combination of elements, however
picturesque or novel, but some distinctive individual quality which the artist himself supplied.
Of all the young Jews in New York who had
listened to the service in the Synagogue or who
had been kept awake at night by taxis, how many
had written good music, even good popular music? I thought of that personal color or rhythm
which, the night when I had been dressing in
Bank Street to take Daisy out to a night-club, had
seemed to me, in the work of an artist, as little
important or interesting as the color of his hair
or eyes, or his way of mispronouncing certain
words; but I could recognize now that it was
precious. And as I recalled my gloomy meditations of the night of Sue Borglum's party, I remembered how the Greeks had given Sophocles
the name of "the Attic Bee."

Yes: I saw it: there it was: it was acrid, but
still honey; and it was something more than

beauty of verse. The Greeks' idea of sweetness
had been as different as possible from Stevenson
and the "honey-dripping style." I saw it now,
not merely in the nightingales and the ivy of that
chorus at Colunus for which the jury had applauded Sophocles, when his competence to dis-
pose of his property had been called in question
by his son; but in the passionate frankness of
Antigone, even in the asperity of Oedipus, even
in the guile of Odysseus. I thought now of the
exquisite proportion, of the style with its unique
combination of modulation and pith, of the
strong and sensitive hand placing with so firm
and light an emphasis those culminating scenes
where the nobler instincts of humanity reassert or
declare themselves: Electra when she speaks to
the urn which she believes contains her brother's
ashes, Neoptolemus confessing at last that he can-
not act against his nature to deceive even an out-
cast who has trusted him—as, in the case of
Dostoevsky, I remembered, no longer the con-
tention and the horror, but the brightness of the
high comic sense which interpenetrates all that
is turbid, which flowers constantly in such charming passages as that in *The Idiot,* for example,
where the young girl buys the hedgehog from
the boys and sends it to the Prince for a peace-
offering, and which makes even of *Crime and
Punishment* a comedy rather than a tragedy. It
was not that the Athenian jury had merely dem-
onstrated their gratitude for—that the crowds at
Dostoevsky's funeral had merely regretted being
deprived of—a sedative to which they had become addicted; but that both had been ravished

by the taste—and by it had been partly repaid for
the harshness of the common life—of that miraculous secretion of the mind which there was only
one man to supply. And so every sort of good literature, so every sort of good art, provided an ali-
ment, a stimulant, as natural and necessary as
food and drink themselves! Even the tannic tinc-
ture of Poe, which seemed to turn the throat to
leather and to petrify the taste, had its own peculiar tonic value, and even from the coarse, used
mash of Byron it was possible to extract a strong
brandy—even the writer of popular music—The
radio was hawking and halting; I had already
been waiting a long time—much too long, I began
to think. And I suddenly remembered how Daisy
had slit her wrist on the night when I had left
her at Gus Dunbar's apartment.

I was on the point of going in to look for her
when she finally appeared: I was so much relieved
to see her that I did not at first notice how pale
she was. She said that she was sorry to have
kept me waiting, and we walked on for a moment
in silence: then I asked her whether she had been
ill. "No: I'm all right," she replied. "You were
such a long time in there," I said.—"Are you sure
that you're all right?" "Yes, I'm all right,"
she said again. "You were sick in there," I
challenged her, stopping. "Did you throw up?"
"I'm all right!" she repeated. "It was just the
smell of that place, I guess!"

I made her sit down on a bench: she wouldn't
let me get her anything, and neither of us spoke
for a time. A fresh, fishy breeze was blowing in:
I hoped that it would make her feel better. A

lighthouse was winking punctually; the ocean was grayest blue, and the low waves were pale as porcelain on the sands of palest buff: the late bathers were coral limbs. Some children, still playing on the beach, were holding out into the ocean and the night the brass-bristling frost-crystals of sparklers.

I asked Daisy presently how she felt. "All right: fine!" she replied.—I tried to find out whether there were anything seriously wrong with her. "No," she said. "To tell the truth, we haven't had very much to eat out in the country lately: the grocer and the butcher in the village wouldn't give us any more credit, and we had to live on the things that we already had in the house—which were mostly corn-flakes—corn-flakes without cream or anything—that was about all we'd had for a week before we came in. I guess I overdid it with those clams."

I said I thought that the gin had been rotten and that the ginger-ale had been inferior. I began to produce the toys from my pockets. She took a sudden interest in the harmonica and amused herself by working out tunes on it: her most conspicuous success, from which she seemed to derive a good deal of satisfaction, was *Nearer My God to Thee*. After a while, she said: "Well, let's go on!" I asked her whether she wanted to go home. "No," she declared, "not yet: I want to do some more things!—don't you?"

We explored Luna Park—all bright minarets and festoons of white imitation pearls. I offered to take her on the "Thunderbolt"; the "Shoot-the-Chutes"; the "Dragon's Gorge"; but she did

not seem very eager. "Why don't we try that
Noah's Ark thing?" she suggested, as we were
wandering a little aimlessly, "that thing that you
wanted to go into when we first came."

We went back to the steamboat pier and found
the Noah's Ark still rocking and sounding its
sombre fog-horn; it was lighted up now with
green ship's lanterns, which revealed the elephant,
the ostrich, and the giraffe, the fisherman pulling
up the shoe, the old patriarch hitting his bottle,
and the monster shaking his bars. "Do you
think you can stand it?" I asked. "Oh, yes," insisted Daisy, smiling. "I want to go in, don't
you?"

We bought tickets and mounted the gang-
plank. Inside, the Ark was rather a sell, as there
was nothing amusing to see—the animals and the
monster turned out to have been constructed so as
to be visible merely from the outside. We found
that we had been let in for an assortment of banal
and disconcerting sensations. We had to walk on
a shifting platform—pass along a wobbly corridor—climb a flight of quaking stairs. Our hats
were almost blown off by a violent blast of air
and when we tried to catch hold of the railing, we
received an electric shock. I was afraid that it
might make Daisy sick again, and asked her
whether she wanted to go back: "No, I'm all
right," she replied. We went through with it to
the end, in silence and rather solemnly. I felt
protective and tender toward Daisy, and contrite
at having brought her in: I was only just beginning fully to realize that she had probably, when
we first started out, been faint for lack of food;

that she had been drinking on an empty stomach; that she had been sickened by the Eden Musée and upset by my stupid joke; and that revisiting the Seaview Hotel, which had brought back her first days with Phil Meissner, had finally overcome her. I became acutely aware, too late, that if she had insisted on going in for the Noah's Ark, it had been entirely because she thought I wanted to.— The last stunt was a spiral slide which landed us on a whirling platform: in my efforts to rescue Daisy, I fell on the roulette-wheel and broke it.

It was now time to go home, we decided—but as it turned out that the last boat had left, we were obliged to go back by the bus.

On our way to the place where the buses stopped, we passed the poster of a spiritualist fortune-teller. "Did I tell you my joke?" asked Daisy. "About 'Striking a Happy Medium'?" "Yes," I said. "I think it's fine!"

As the bus left Coney Island behind, a cluster of bright, pearly globes among the vivid red pumps of a filling-station repeated the pearls of Luna Park and the drooping white lamps of the boardwalk.

Along the boulevard to New York, were aligned little sections of shops, bright-windowed and built in new concrete: drug-stores; grocery-stores; automobile show-rooms; a bank.

There were girls in summer dresses, hatless, with bobbed heads and pink or tan stockings, strolling out, alone or in couples. Down side-streets, I could see little houses with compact and screened porches giving way to the wastes of building-lots, where a lonely and random street-

lamp would light untidy bushes and trees. That
was the America to which I had returned when,
coming back after the War from France, I had
been greeted by that other suburban street-lamp
on the Staten Island shore! That was the America to which to-night I felt myself returning again
—those neat and new little shops, those girls wandering out in the evening between the drug-store
and the building-lots—hardly knowing what they
expected but half hoping for some new turn to
their lives! Had not Daisy been once such a girl,
walking out in the streets of Pittsburgh—had not
Rita, in her up-state town?

I asked Daisy about her father, of whom she
had told me at dinner that he had not let her go
out with boys. "He was Irish," she explained.
"He lost all his money when we were just kids.
But he was determined that the fact that he'd
lost his money shouldn't make any difference
about our being well brought up—I guess it did
all right, though." She smiled her candid smile.
"That's one reason they used to send me to my
aunt's in Nova Scotia so much." I remembered
her timidity about the freaks, her "independence"
about rehearsals, and her coldness with the woman in the store. "That was one trouble about
Phil and me," she went on. "Phil's father and
my father had known each other very well when
they first came to Pittsburgh. We used to live
next door to the Meissners, before they made
money and moved. And in those days, Dad had
a much more important position than Mr. Meissner: he was one of the principal men in the Bil-
lings Company and Mr. Meissner was just a clerk

in a bank. Then when the Meissners made money
and Dad was down and out, they got snooty
about us—and Dad didn't want me to go with
Phil—Phil had the reputation of being the wild-
est boy in Pittsburgh. Dad was fit to be tied
when I ran away withum!"

I marked another filling-station: a crowd of
great white stars, which seemed uttered by a
rocket's detonation.

Now we were passing a row of small houses
with tapestry-brick façades and, in front of them,
little green lawns enclosed by little hedges.

"Dad was really a bright man, though," Daisy
presently went on. "He was one of the first
people in the country to design certain kinds of
trucks.—He invented all kinds of things—he invented a kind of siren."

A filling-station where the lights were dimmer
and the pumps a duller red was outshone by the
lunar beauty of the radiant white pergola which
followed it.

"Did you ever hear them talk about auto-horns
—in a store or anywhere, I mean?" she asked.
"It's a shout. There's a *toot-toot,* and a *beep-beep*
—and an *oorah*—and a *blah-blah,* and a *blurp-
blurp.*—Dad's was a kind of a *oorah*—and it was a
humdinger, too!—it had an authoritative sound
and it wasn't ugly like most sirens."

In the show-rooms on either side appeared the
present-day glories of the motor industry: the
Lancerd was celebrating its "Silver Anniversary"
with a new model in "distinctive" apple-green,
posed with dignity behind its plate-glass pane, in
a white-balconied Colonial salon.

"It was getting indicted for manslaughter," Daisy went on, "that really ruined Dad: he and another man ran into each other as Dad was coming out of a garage. It was really both's fault—but the man was killed and they indicted Dad—though he'd been a month in the hospital himself. They made him pay a big fine and he lost his job—and he never could get back after that.—He used to come home drunk and sit down on the edge of my bed and hold directors' meetings all by himself—I used to think it was funny, but my mother used to be so worried!"

I had been brooding on the name of Meissner, which seemed to raise for me vague associations. "Did they ever call Phil Meissner, 'Junior'?" I finally asked. "The family always calledum that," she answered. "Why?—did you ever knowum?" "Did they live in a great big house with green and blue stained-glass windows?" "Yes," said Daisy. "Why? Did you ever knowum? They lived on Aylesworth Avenue. That was where they moved to after they lived next door to us."

Phil and his family were the people, then, whom I had visited as a child, when I had gone to Pittsburgh with my mother, and who had come back into my mind, when Hugo, at Ray Coleman's party, had said that Daisy came from Pittsburgh! I told Daisy how much I had envied Phil Meissner's elaborate toy railroad and his device for making dinner-plates jump, but how obnoxious, on the whole, I had thought him. "He was spoiled to death," said Daisy. "That was what was the trouble withum, I guess."

And this discovery that Daisy had married a

boy I had myself known in my childhood had an
effect out of all proportion to its apparent importance or interest. Hitherto, I now fully took
account, I had regarded Daisy as an alien—first,
as a denizen of Broadway, and afterwards, as a
product of the Village. But she seemed now to
have taken her place in the world which I had
always known. She was no longer of a different race—of an exotic glamor or guile: she was
simply an American girl, who had grown up in an
American town like other American towns, lived
in a house like other houses, gone to a school like
other schools. I seemed to have been given a new
vision of the fluidity of manners in America, the
plasticity of social position—of the swiftness and
adventitiousness of the way in which such things
changed. If Daisy's family had gone down in
the world, the Meissners had obviously come up.
But the human material was the same; and in the
face of its constant fluctuations, attempts to fix
social differences became ludicrous and futile.
Americans might turn into anything!

What, for example, might not be made of
Daisy? On each of the occasions when I had met
her, I had seen in her something different, as my
own mind had been differently disposed by my
personal situation at the time and by the influ-
ences by which I had been affected—by Hugo,
first; then, by Rita; then, by my disgust and dis-
illusion the night of Sue Borglum's party; then,
by my evening with the Grosbeakes. And I
could see how she herself had taken the color
of each of the men with whom she had lived
since she left Pittsburgh: Phil Meissner's ex-

travagant tastes; Ray Coleman's constrained cor-
rectitude; and Pete Bird's engaging humor. She
had even, I noted, begun lately to talk exactly like
Pete. She had been eager to accept whatever they
gave, and how little they had had to give her!
Phil with his inherited money, his egoism, and
his silly jokes; Ray with his substantial salary,
his ignoble employment and his meanness; and
Pete with his pennilessness and uselessness, his
gentlemanly hobbies and his charm—they seemed
now to me like figures of comedy for familiar
American types.—But what hope was there for
Daisy with any of them?

"I declare," I said finally aloud, "I don't see
why you haven't been able to do better than Pete
and Ray! Haven't you ever found anybody in
the Village that really amounted to something
and that you liked at the same time?" She shook
her head, not turning from the window. Then,
after a moment, she turned: "You know the only
person," she said, "that I ever thought I could get
a real crush on was your friend Hugo Bamman.
I actually got all hopped up, that night he was
sailing for Egypt, or wherever it was, about the
idea of going away withum. I think he's good-
looking, too—especially since he's stopped wearing spectacles. Some people think that scar spoils
his face, but I think it's smart-looking.—But he's
certainly cagy about women—Myra Busch was
crazy aboutum, you know.—Either that or he's
afraid of them.—He's so sure of himself, too—
he knows what he wants to do.—None of the
men I've ever lived with were sure of themselves.
—You know what you told me out in the country,

about my knowing about everything better than anybody—well, I wanted to say at the time that that isn't true at all. That's just the trouble: I don't know what it's all about. I want somebody to tell me!"

Daisy's mentioning Hugo reminded me of the world as I had seen it through his eyes when I had first come down to Greenwich Village: then, like him, I had thought myself a rebel against the standards of a bourgeoisie—that is, in a country like America, where there was really only one class, or rather, as I had just been reflecting, no classes, properly speaking, at all, against an abstraction of all the worst qualities attributable to respectable Americans; then later, when I had been in love with Rita, all the interests and occupations of the common life had seemed to me on so low a plane and of so lax an impulse, that I could feel for them nothing but contempt. Now my trip to Europe since the War had had the effect of making me more content with America, even at her worst; and my conversation with Grosbeake *à propos* of Lewis's *Babbitt,* though Grosbeake's opinions had surprised me at the time, had in the long run had the effect of helping me to approach America from a different point of view than the point of view which, at the time when I had thought like Hugo, had allowed me to take account only of American mediocrity and timidity. To-day I seemed to have reentered that world and to find myself perfectly at home there: now I found that it no longer inspired either hatred, apprehension, or scorn.

"By the way," I presently asked, "where did

you get that line about 'the downfall of western civilization'?—You know, that night I took you to the movies, you said that you probably looked like the downfall of western civilization." "Oh," she said, "that was just something I picked up at the Ritz Bar in Paris!"

The little tapestry-brick houses had been supplanted by apartment-buildings, also in tapestry-brick, and with attractive green or brown awnings at the doorways and windows; but now the awnings came closer together and the crowded house-fronts were laced by zigzagging fire-escapes: they got dingier, balder, denser. We were in Brooklyn, and now Brooklyn Bridge repeated the fire-escape zigzags.

Delancey Street, with its car-tracks and hooded subway entrances; the Bowery, with its El.

We got out at Astor Place. I asked Daisy what she wanted to do. "I think I'd like a drink," she said. "It's so long since I've been absolutely free, without any housework or anything, that I feel like making the most of it!" "Have you gotten over your sinking-spell?" I asked. "Sure," she replied with conviction. "I feel fine!"

The oppression of summer, again, hung over and hushed the city-streets: the very taxi horns seemed muted. The greenery in Washington Square, behind the arc-lights, looked heavy and dark; and the benches overflowed with Italians, dirty and sweaty, swarming to the air, giving out the sounds of life, but heavy-footed, slowed down and subdued.

My rooms in Bank Street were stuffy and messy: the colored woman who took care of them had abandoned me without warning and they had not been cleaned for a week. I threw open all the windows. In the house across the court, the people were sitting on the fire-escape in their undershirts. A baby was howling and sobbing.

I had brought in some ice from a drug-store, and this time we had Scotch instead of gin. It was pretty good Scotch, as it went, and we had highballs with mineral water. It was pleasant to relax on the couch, with the cold misted glasses in our hands, alone, with nowhere to go, with no buses or boats to catch.

"Who did you say you were staying with?" I asked.

"Sue Borglum," Daisy replied—and added: "I think she's going nuts. Have you seen her lately? She's turned green!—She's turned absolutely green!—But I can't worry about her!— I've got all the worrying I can do with Pete and myself!"

"Did you ever know Peter Kester?" I asked. "No," said Daisy, "Who is he?" "He's a great friend of Rita Cavanagh's—she always used to be telling me about him. I met him yesterday for the first time—he's just come back from New Mexico.—He's just a nice old bozo, who paints rather mediocre landscapes. He's just like all the American painters of that generation that you meet at the Washington Irving Club.—He wears tortoise-shell-rimmed eyeglasses with a big black ribbon—and he thinks that Picasso is a clown!"

The electric lights were hot, and I got up to turn one out. "Why don't you turn them all out," said Daisy, "and just turn on that lamp in the alcove? It would be a lot cooler." I turned on the table-lamp in my study and put the others out. I was glad that the things in the room were obscured by the shadow now: I had been feeling that that Leonardo was not a particularly suitable picture for New York in the summer time.

When I came back, she had stretched out along the couch, with her head propped up on a pillow against the arm and her highball clasped in her hand. "I hope you don't mind my lying down," she said. I sat down on the edge of the couch beside her.

The voice of a radio, dimly muttering or hoarsely warbling, came in to us from across the back yard. I was reminded of my recent meditations while I had been waiting for Daisy in front of the restaurant, and I told her now about looking in the mirror and mistaking myself for some one else.

"You're not so bad!" said Daisy. "I think your mustache is all right. In fact, I've always liked the way you look." I replied, "Well, I've often told you how much I like the way *you* look!"

Encouraged, I began to describe to her my consoling æsthetic revelations in connection with the popular song.—I had always thought of her, I told her, also, ever since that first night I had met her, whenever I had heard *Mamie Rose*.—I talked on, and even got as far as the Attic Bee.

But all the time that I was talking, she was looking at me, serious and flushed, as if I had been making love to her. At last I stopped and said, "You're such a darling!" and kissed her. We said little after that. . . .

When, from the profuse delight of that love, hot, moist, mucilaginous and melting, I found my thoughts springing up again, they seemed unfolding like fresh new leaves in an atmosphere of gentleness and peace.

I thought of Daisy under her different aspects, as she had seemed to me at different times—and I remembered the literary productions which at one time or another she had inspired—all so different from my present vision of her, from our present reality: first, the night that I had met her at Ray Coleman's, the cool Gallic short story I had imagined, with its humanitarian irony—then, the night that we had gone to the movies, the romantic apostrophe of the sonnet—then, the night that I was to take her to a night-club, when my alienation from Rita had had the effect of thrusting away from me all the rest of the world as well— Daisy along with the others—the desperate exposure of literature itself, on which my mind had run so furiously and interminably—then, when I had visited Pete and Daisy in the country, the savage moralistic satire which the letter I had received from Rita and the spectacle of Grosbeake's equanimity had prevented me from writing. I had, in fact, rejected all these projects—as I had outgrown those phases of myself of which my successive conceptions of Daisy had been merely the reflections in another.

And now I felt that I should be content if I could only make some sketches of Daisy, as I remembered her at different times and places—if I could only hit off, in prose, her attitudes, her gestures, her expressions, the intonations of her voice—preserve them so they should not vanish, as Degas had done for his dancers—as Toulouse-Lautrec had done for the women of cabarets. . . . I dreamed a whole series of Daisy. . . .

So I should perhaps save myself at last from that dreadful isolation of the artist which had appalled me in Hugo and Rita—both forever, it seemed to me now, occupying impregnable solitudes with the creation of impossible worlds—so, by the way of literature itself, I should break through into the real world—as to-night I had seemed at last, with Daisy, as if by a simple mutual transfusion, to come so naturally into contact with life. . . . Such pictures as I imagined of Daisy would grow directly and freshly from life. And it seemed to me to-night that literature was as amiable as writing ballads, as necessary as making tables—and indeed that, when one came right down to it, there was really no difference in kind between carpentry and literature.

I bent over Daisy—her head on the pillow had that look—the little soft round chin and the soft bare throat—of women in those moments when they have dropped off, along with their garments, all the ruses and resolutions with which they meet the world—when we see them just awakened or lying thinking at night, with wide eyes and anxious mouth, and we realize how gentle they are, how much they wonder, and how tender toward them we must be. . . . I wondered whether she would leave Pete for me. . . .

"Let's run away together!" I suggested.

"Oh, I couldn't—now," she replied. "I told Pete that if he got a job, I'd stay withum."

It seemed to me now that I wanted above everything to go away somewhere with Daisy.

"I'll take you on a motor-cycle!" I proposed.

"No, you won't!" she promptly replied. "I've done my last motor-cycle elopement!"

"Still you must have had a lot of fun!"

"I didn't know whether I was ever going to get there alive. We had about six accidents. . . . The real reason for the motor-cycle, I found out afterwards, was that I was afraid I was pregnant and Phil wanted to bring me around. He thought that a motor-cycle trip would be just the thing. . . . There! I'd told you that we weren't married! Oh, well—never mind!" She was silent a moment, then went on: "That's something that nobody but Phil would think of—taking a girl on a motor-cycle trip to bring her around! . . . He wouldn't even let me ride in a side-car—he carried me all the way on the handle-bars!"

I made her turn and embraced her anew, kissing her with pleasure and compassion. When she told me of the rejection and death of her love, I recognized the fate of my own. And it was so sweet to include in my arms that warmth, that solidity, that slenderness—and to feel that she followed me! . . .

In the peace and silence again, I could hear that poor child still crying, and I remembered how once, as a child, I myself had lain awake with the heat, and suffered and complained.—Then, in a moment, I remembered, also, how those same children of the Village had figured in the poem which Rita had recited the night of Ray Coleman's party and which she told us she had written that

day. On that very day when she had filled my
imagination with the splendor of her genius and
her beauty, when she had seemed to me a goddess
or a muse—on that day, her own mind had been
haunted by visions of imbecility and deformity—
she had seen only, among those children of the
streets, the most wretched and the most afflicted,
and she had seen in them only the crippling of the
spirit and the clouding of the mind by love. . . .

What relief and what a rebirth, our only real
birth into this world, when from the fears and
snobberies of youth, from all our preconceived
ideas, from all those foolish abstractions we
learn, all those things that we think we think,
we find at last in these beings who have crowded,
offended, disgusted or fought us, that interest
and that value which we have found only in a few
or in one—when, youth's passion and anguish
spent, we see rising about us that reality of those
we have looked on as strangers, and know that it
is our reality—that what is strange to us is
strange to them, that what hurts them hurts us,
that what is good for them is good for us—when
we no longer dread the fool nor hate the one who
wounds us, but can sleep in our beds in peace and in
peace face the waking world! . . .

I kept telling Daisy how smooth her skin was,
and she was finally moved to retort: "Are you
used to women with scales?"

"I suppose I ought to go," she said presently.
"I don't want Sue Borglum to have it on me that
I stayed out all night."

"I've been so happy with you to-day," I said,
"and I'm afraid that you haven't been happy."